Where I Belong

Single Dads of Meadowbrook, Volume 1

Rose Fresquez

Published by Rose Fresquez, 2024.

Where I Belong is a work of fiction. Names, characters, places, and incidents are either the product of the author's imagination or are used fictitiously, and any resemblance to actual persons, living or dead, business establishments, events or locales is entirely coincidental.

Paperback ISBN: 978-1-961159-21-1

Give Thanks to the Lord, for He is good! His Faithful love endures forever.
Psalm 107:1

ACKNOWLEDGEMENTS

I want to thank the Lord, my Savior. Without you, Father, there's no point in trying to do anything at all. It's my prayer that I can honor you with my words. I thank you for connecting me with an amazing group of people who helped support me in accomplishing this novel.

To my husband Joel, who works so hard to provide for our family, so that I can stay home and take care of the kids. I'm so blessed that we get to journey through life together.

To my children Isaiah, Caleb, Abigail and Micah, you fill my heart with joy. Thanks for the giggles, laughter and encouragement.

To my editor, Deirdre Lockhart. You're a true blessing from God. Your insights and wisdom have helped shape this story. To my friend Mary Mintz, Thanks for re-reading the manuscript to clear out any slip throughs. To my Beta Team, Thanks for willing to answer any questions I have during the early stages of my manuscript.

To my insider team, thanks for always suggesting the coolest ideas.

And to my Street Team. Thank you from the bottom of my heart.

CHAPTER 1

Jason

Being a good father is more than providing shelter, food, and education. It's more than cheering from the sidelines at soccer games or applauding at dance recitals. As I navigate my Honda Pilot through Manhattan, the lingering question of true fatherhood shadows every turn of the wheel through the hustle and bustle.

"I had it first."

"Did not!"

"Did!" My eight-year-old twin boys squabble, undoubtedly over something trivial. I savor their bickering and my daughter's outspoken complaints, a better soundtrack than the radio for a little over an hour-long journey from Meadowbrook.

"Why can't we just go to the neighborhood school?" Frustrated, eleven-year-old Eden voices a question she's posed one too many times.

"Daddy wants us to go to good schools." Felix sounds older than his years. "If I'm going to be a gamer, a small school will not do it."

"And I get to fly airplanes." Atticus's fist pump flashes in the rearview mirror. "Oh, and the city has the best soccer teams!"

A smile tugs at my mouth, though the truth is more complex than good education or sports programs. When we needed a new start four years ago, moving to Meadowbrook seemed like the right decision despite the commute.

"I'm sure there's a soccer team in Meadowbrook if we ever stayed home longer than an hour." Eden huffs. Poor girl, longing for something simpler, something closer to the childhood she must envision.

"I work here," I explain again. "It's nice to have you guys close in case of emergencies, and... it's easier for Grandma to pick you up from school."

3

I inch forward through slow traffic. A siren wails, horns honk, and the city thrums. Contentment relaxes me as I take in New York—the city rife with possibilities for business owners like me and jobs for anyone pursuing their dreams.

When I stop at the red light, I check the kids. They're the reason surrender isn't in my vocabulary.

Atticus leans closer to the window and tips his face up, probably hoping to sight airplanes, and Felix, in the middle seat, talks about including his brother's airplanes in the video game he intends to design someday. Although they are identical with similar facial structure and brown hair and blue eyes like me, I can tell them apart. Atticus has an athletic build, while Felix is leaner.

Eden has folded her arms, her defiance as tangible as her pout. She gazes out her window. Her blonde locks she inherited from her mother, but like her brothers, she has my blue eyes.

Lately, her spirit has been more akin to that of a moody teen. Good thing she's bound by the school's uniform policy. Otherwise, each morning would present a new battleground over her attire.

The boys squabble again. The rearview mirror frames their small hands grappling over a squishy ball.

"Boys, drop the toy." They need to get into school mode. "And I don't want to get any reports about you two attempting to change passwords on the teacher's computer."

"We only changed the screen background to airplanes," Atticus says. "But Felix thinks she might like cars better."

"We'll change it to race cars next time."

"There won't be a next time," I warn, catching Felix's thoughtful frown in the mirror.

"Daddy, you have a great idea. Changing a password sounds—"

"No!" My voice rises in my struggle not to laugh. "How about you rehash your presentation?" The light turns green, and I make a slow left turn.

"We've got it, Daddy!" Atticus exclaims. I don't have to look to know his wide smile must be in place. "'Four scores and seven years ago'..."

"'Our fathers brought forth on this continent a new nation,'" Felix chimes in.

"Do we have to hear the whole poem again?" Eden groans. But the boys dismiss her.

"You and Mimi will be proud of us tomorrow," Felix adds once they finish.

"I'm always proud of you guys." Their enthusiasm expands in my heart. "Looking forward to hearing your presentation tomorrow."

After another left turn, the school comes into view with ivy creeping up its walls. I slow to join the line of cars in front of the old brick building. Parents and chauffeurs alike drive close to the drop-off by the gym entrance. All the kids are dressed in the same white button-down shirts tucked into navy bottoms.

As we stop at the curb, a shift in Eden's demeanor to sullen sends ripples of concern through me. This habit, budding over the past six months, gives a signal of her inner turmoil. Keeping the car idling, I stretch my right hand back to clasp her smaller one, offering a squeeze of support. "Is everything okay, sweetheart?"

Her reflection in the rearview mirror gives a nod. But her gaze avoids mine, which speaks volumes. "I have a math test."

"You'll ace it. Remember our review session last night?" Will my attempts ever be enough to ease her anxieties? Her fear has no real foundation. Yet it seems to dig roots deeper than the surface worries. She's still struggling from her mother's absence in our lives.

The man in the yellow vest ushers us forward. Having held up the car line, I ease forward and suppress the desire to step out and wrap my children in a parting embrace.

"Bye, Daddy," the boys' voices overlap.

"Love you." I stretch over my seat back to offer a smile.

They're already stepping out and closing the door. Their backpacks with cartoon characters swing with youthful abandon.

Eden sighs and rolls her eyes. If only she could communicate whatever is behind her frustration, then perhaps I could help her. "Can I skip dance practice today?"

"But you love dance." I speak over the traffic guide's whistle—a reminder of the queue forming behind us, a reminder I choose to ignore. "Is everything okay?"

"I'm fine." She sounds indifferent before she draws out a breath and swings open the door to step out.

"Love you." My voice rises over the chatter of kids' voices, and Eden responds with an "I love you" as she slams the door.

The kids blend into the sea of uniforms, my boys already lost from sight, but I glimpse Eden merging with the stream. Lately, the gap between us seems to widen with unspoken words and missed opportunities. Driven by another urgent whistle, I pull away, a weight on my chest. My kids are growing up so fast, each stage presenting new challenges with their evolving needs and desires. I might pull off parenting the boys, but I'm not so sure about Eden.

Is it ever enough to be the best dad for them? And what does it truly mean to be a good father? I'm thirty-seven, and I've grappled with this question since I was four. With only my mom's resilient spirit as a guide after my dad vanished from our lives, the last thing I want is to mirror his absence.

Shortly later, I park in my alternate designated spot alongside Family Sphere Tower. I'll park in the garage after this network meeting. I'm normally punctual, but today's agenda leaves me minimal time to review the three candidates our human resources team vetted as possibles for a position on our new reality family show. Now, my business partner and I must select one of them today.

My phone rings in my coat pocket as I step out of the car. Mom's contact flashes on the screen.

Besides the kids' school, hers is the only call I can't ignore. I press the device to my ear and close the door. The crisp March breeze plays through my suit as I cross the parking lot. People filter in and out of the eleven-story glassed-in structure to merge with the sparse crowd on the sidewalk.

"Jay." Mom's voice soothes as always. Though she named me Jason, she only uses my given name to emphasize a point, then I'll be Jason Carson Sterling.

"Morning, Mom."

"I'm on my way to pick up Eden from school."

"Why? What happened?" My grip on my phone tightens. "I just dropped them off."

"The school called. She threw up." Her tone carries the same worry now clenching my stomach.

The bustle blurs. "Why didn't she say something earlier?" I pause at the entrance. The automatic doors slide open in invitation, but I'm rooted to the spot. "I just don't get it."

"Don't be too hard on yourself. She's eleven. Much is going on in her mind, plus all those unanswered questions about her mother."

Acknowledging the truth doesn't ease my twisting guts. As for the kids' mother, that's *not* a topic I bring up to the kids.

How unsettling that my daughter can't even tell me when she's sick. Perhaps her asking to skip dance meant she was sick?

"Perhaps it's her age." I retreat a step to allow a woman to pass, then do a double take. Dressed in a tailored navy pantsuit, a beverage in one hand and a cream handbag in the other, she strides with attention-grabbing confidence. Glossy dark hair cascades over her shoulders, the perfect frame for delicate features in flawless olive skin. Our gazes lock, and a flicker of something unspoken ignites. I'm not sure why I'm flabbergasted, but I force the intrigue away as my mother's voice reels me back.

I clear my throat, and my fingers find the tension at the back of my neck. The piled-up tasks at work pale in comparison to my daughter's well-being. "I'll try to leave early today."

"She'll be okay." As a retired ER nurse, Mom doesn't gloss over the practicalities. "Focus on your workday. The boys still need to be in school for the rest of the day. I'll call if you need to step in."

Today, of all days, when my presence at the network is nonnegotiable, I'm thankful for my mother's support. "Keep me updated."

"Of course, sweetheart."

"Thanks, Mom." What would I do without her? Life, especially when juggling single parenthood and a CEO's responsibilities, seldom offers respite. I thrust the phone into my suit pocket and push through the glass doors, a façade of composure in place. But beneath that lurks the fact that Eden didn't feel comfortable sharing her discomfort with me. Am I falling short?

My mother has been my unwavering support, raising me single-handedly as she worked full-time. Now retired, she still volunteers at the hospital. Nonetheless, she prioritizes taking care of my children. Despite my attempts to find a reliable nanny, no one has matched her standard of care. She deserves a break, but the right help seems out of reach.

Entering the lobby, I exchange a customary nod with the security guard. And Sally, usually the beacon of morning cheer, is preoccupied with people at the reception desk. I rush past to catch the elevator before it closes. I'm pushing the button to close the doors when heels click against tile. I quickly press a different button to keep the doors open.

The woman in the navy suit enters, a guest lanyard around her neck and a disposable cup still in hand. Our eyes lock again, and a flutter spirals in my stomach once more.

Maybe I'm staring and I'm the reason her foot twists as she steps onto the granite. When I reach to steady her, I collide with her cup. It tumbles to the floor, brown liquid splashing onto my shirt.

"Ugh..." The heat from the spill seeps close to my skin. Almost ignoring the discomfort, I pick up her cup. Funnily enough, none of it splashed on her. The doors close, and we ride up.

"I'm so sorry." Her shaky hands rummage for something in her handbag. A tissue, I realize. What she needs is to take the cup from me, but she doesn't.

I bite my lip to contain my impatience. I'll snap should I speak.

It wasn't her fault. Though if she hadn't been carrying coffee, this incident could've been avoided.

"If I get the mop, I can—"

"We have a cleaner for that." Without looking at her, I stiffen my jaw. My daughter is sick, and I'm late. I have no patience for this.

The elevator deposits us onto the executive level, and the woman mumbles an apology and adds something about being on the wrong floor. When she remains in the elevator to head back down, I can't shake the suspicion she's one of the three candidates we're interviewing this morning.

If she's this clumsy, she's not what our network needs.

CHAPTER 2

Jason

Dropping the coffee-stained cup into the trash bin beside the elevator, I greet my assistant, Beatrix. Under the recessed lighting, the glow reflects off her porcelain skin as she types something.

She glances up from her computer and winces. "Looks like you've been mud wrestling." Her Dutch accent thickens as she snickers.

"Seriously?" That's just Beatrix. Sometimes, I tolerate her jibes. A competent assistant, she's been with me since my company's inception ten years ago. She was recommended by my mom, whom I trust, and now, she's like the sister I never had. I ask her to report the spill in the elevator before someone slips and sues the company.

In my office, I rummage through the closet for another shirt among the many I keep around for unexpected media appearances. My fingers work the buttons, and the shirt warms me.

A knock sounds at the door as I slide behind my desk. Beatrix steps in, her peachy silk blouse tucked into a black pencil skirt. "Coffee today?"

"I'll skip coffee today." I power up my desktop. I usually drink a cup before I leave home and another when I get here with time to spare.

"I know you like extra reminders of the schedule. Your meeting with Solo Parents Unite is Friday evening."

"Just because I started the organization doesn't mean I have to go to every meeting." I peer at my computer as it goes through updates. "My kids have a game on Fridays."

"I know that, but you can just stop by for the intro meeting." Unfazed by my grunt, she outlines other meetings lined up for the week. She knows I need these reminders since my home life occupies my thoughts more than my schedule.

A realization hits me. I tear my gaze from the updating computer. "What are you doing here on your birthday?"

She smiles, content. "I figured you'd be lost without me today with all the interviews you have. My boyfriend will be back from his work trip tomorrow. That'll be a better day for celebrations. They delivered your flowers to my home this morning. Thank you."

I'm so blessed by her dedication.

"Your meeting is in fifteen minutes, by the way."

I draw out a breath. I still have some time. "That's why you should let me be."

After I type my password into the computer, I right-click the mouse to open the folder Beatrix has organized with all candidates sorted by their respective interview times. I reviewed their résumés, but I haven't watched the video clips. At least the other executives have done so. Still, I'd better refresh my memory on the paperwork and candidates.

Valentina Diaz.

I skim her profile. Thirty-three years old. Born in Venezuela and raised in Brooklyn. An NYU graduate with dual degrees in Psychology and Feature Journalism.

Impressive.

Began as an intern at a premier national newspaper. Navigated her way through the media industry to become a field reporter delivering international crises. She also covered practical health guidance and psychological advice. Her skill set extended to digital media proficiency, a critical aspect in this industry.

She bounced around a lot in the first few years of her career. Hmm.

But her fluency in three languages, including Spanish and French, is a valuable asset in broadcasting to families who communicate primarily in those languages. Beyond her professional commitments, she volunteers at a middle school, teaching English (ESL) to immigrant kids and their families.

Her recommendation letters and recent job history carry praises for high ethical standards, an innovative approach to storytelling, and the capability to analyze and empathize with her colleagues—a trait probably enhanced by her psychological insight.

Then I see Starwatch. Her most recent employment. Bells ring in my ears, and my growing admiration halts.

Starwatch? Heat courses through me, and my throat closes off. Good thing I didn't bother putting on another tie after ditching the coffee-stained one—It would be stifling right now. Starwatch is a cable channel known for its streamlined content, including that ridiculous show. A knot forms in my stomach.

Valentina was the host of *Get Your Life on Track* or whatever the name is. I've never taken an interest in the show, mainly to avoid confronting the lies it might've fed my ex-wife. This is the show that prompted Daisy to abandon our family.

My finger hovers over the mouse. My gaze glides to the window. Valentina was on the show for four and a half years. Doesn't matter if she was the host all four years. She was at the helm during the time it most influenced Daisy. Night after night, I'd hear the TV from the other room proclaiming "You've got your life on track," followed by snippets of the show that seeped into our two-bedroom apartment.

Enough with pursuing résumés. I push to stand, take my tablet, and leave for the meeting. By the time I reach the sixth-floor conference room, anger has clouded my judgment.

"Finally." Chris lifts his wrist to eye his watch, and the recessed lighting catches the silver strands in his gray hair.

"Thompson." I dip my head, sit across from him, and place my tablet on the table. Being late leaves no time for relaxed banter.

"Hey." Axel raises his water bottle. He's our production director, overseeing the new show's content and execution. His presence in the final interviews is crucial.

I manage a wave to our chief content officer and the HR manager. The latter individual usually doesn't say much, but when she speaks, we all make sure to listen.

Beatrix brings me a bottle of water, just like all my colleagues have in front of them. "Thanks." I let her know we're ready for the candidate. "Let's get this over with."

"Everything okay?" Chris arches a brow.

My indifferent comment—a departure from my usual preference for a thorough vetting process—must've piqued his curiosity. Although I consider him a partner, my ownership of 70 percent of the shares positions me as the primary decision-maker. However, I always value his insights as an equal.

Beatrix ushers Valentina in and introduces her. Valentina's demeanor is poised, and she glances at me before greeting everyone and taking the seat she's directed to at the head of the table.

I barely refrain from reacting with a jolt to seeing the woman from the elevator. The nerve. And how could someone who thrives on sensationalism think she could align with Family Sphere Network's principles?

Beatrix positions herself at the small desk alongside us. Her fingers hover over her laptop, ready to document the meeting minutes.

"Thrilled to have you, Ms. Diaz." Chris flashes a friendly smile.

Axel nods, his expression neutral yet expectant.

The pleasantries seem unnecessary, fluff that contrasts the verdict formed in my mind.

Although I had standard questions prepared, I don't bother looking at my iPad. "Are you aware our platform isn't a stage for the sensational?" My cold tone surprises even me.

"I'm aware, Mr. Sterling." Valentina's professional smile remains unwavering. "I respect Family Sphere Network, and having an opportunity to interact and engage with couples and families is something I've been eager to explore."

Everyone around the table nods as she elaborates on ways she intends to make a difference with her work.

Chris leans forward. "Ms. Diaz, could you explain how your background in psychology might align with a role as a host for our show?" His question doesn't foster the doubt I want him to have.

Her gaze meets mine, and her continued composure under my critical eye intensifies my skepticism. I don't give her a chance to answer, saving everyone from getting fed whatever lies she's scheming. "How can someone immersed in the sensationalist world pivot to embody the family-oriented values we cherish? Perhaps you could enlighten us on how peddling rumors on Starwatch has prepared you for serious journalism."

Defiance sparks in her dark eyes, and I shift on the padded chair. It's as though she can see right through me, through my skepticism.

"My experience with the show at Starwatch taught me the power of media and its impact on lives." She purses her lips, then fiddles with her pearl necklace. "I aim to use that influence to be clearer in informing and empowering rather than sensationalizing."

I let out a mirthless laugh. "To inform and empower would be a big change for you. Your show has been tearing couples and families apart."

"Have you watched my show?" Her confidence steady, she fixes her gaze on me. Unsettling. She's one of those people who can't be trusted. "Maybe you should revisit a specific segment you might be referring to."

Off guard, I swallow, seeking time to come up with a snarky remark.

But Axel points at her with his water bottle. "I watched your show when it was at its peak. My sister's favorite, actually. She started her own salon thanks to you."

"I'm sure her endeavor had more to do with her business confidence." Valentina ducks her head, her confidence wavering for the first time.

Chris beams at me, obviously pleased by Axel's testimonial about the so-called candidate.

"We can't rely on Axel's personal opinion alone."

"Any more concerns, Jason?" Chris asks.

Why can't anyone see what I see? Under the table, I fold and unfold my hands.

"If this is about the accident we had in the elevator, Mr. Sterling—"

"If you think I'm basing my professional judgment on a coffee spill," I cut her off. I've lost control in the boardroom. "Then you don't know who you're dealing with."

"Ms. Diaz." HR ventures a question, and I shift my focus to the buildings towering outside, not interested in anything else Valentina Diaz has to contribute. My decision is final.

After everyone else has posed their questions and she has responded, I see no point in prolonging the pretense. "I'm afraid we can't offer you the position."

"Jason," Chris hisses.

"Sterling." Beatrix speaks in a hushed tone almost at the same time.

I disregard them as Valentina stands.

With her dignity undiminished by the overt rejection, she flings her handbag on her shoulder and offers a curt nod. "Thank you for your time." Her gaze catches mine, holding it longer than necessary, stirring a twinge for my hasty judgment. "I hope Family Sphere continues to uphold its integrity."

It's for the best. Having her on the team would only resurrect memories of my failures as a husband.

Her exit, poised and graceful, leaves a palpable tension. Chris is the first to speak. "Sterling, you care to explain what that was all about? She was our top candidate."

The HR manager nods, and so does Axel, adding, "That's why we scheduled her interview first."

"That wasn't the Sterling I knew." With a frazzled look, Beatrix takes me in as if I'm a stranger. "Is she your ex-girlfriend?"

"No!" She's attractive. Under different circumstances, I might consider asking her out—if not for my responsibilities.

"Next time, perhaps phrase it as, 'We'll get in touch after we've conducted the other interviews,'" my HR manager suggests with her usual tenderness and diplomacy.

Axel and Chris don't relent until we adjourn. Their confusion haunts me as I retreat to my office. My body is too stiff, and my mind awhirl. Unable to think straight, I move to the window. The clamor of New York carries in the crisp March air, its noise quiet compared to my thoughts. I thrust my hands into my suit pockets as unease unravels my composure.

Valentina Diaz is beautiful, intelligent, and unapologetically confident—my polite way of saying proud. Her dignified departure and parting words linger. Consumed with prejudices, I hadn't considered the earnestness she embodied.

"Have you actually watched my show?" Her challenge burns through me, her fiery gaze imprinted in my memory and her words clear and unyielding. I recall hearing bits and pieces in the background whenever Daisy listened to the reruns. But I never engaged with the show beyond dismissing it as gossip-filled and unconstructive. Perhaps it's best to let my team handle today's remaining interviews. Given my current emotional state, I'm in no mood to make a fair judgment.

CHAPTER 3

Valentina

I always prided myself on never letting anything dampen my spirits again. While growing up in Brooklyn under my feisty mother, wallowing was never an option. Yet, my resilience seems insufficient now as I slam the taxi door and step onto the chalk-adorned sidewalk. Normally, I'd pause to admire the whimsical artwork the neighborhood kids create. Today, my mind is crowded—so much so I nearly collide with a cyclist. With a jerk backward, I avoid what could have been a painful encounter.

Chin up, I inhale the crisp morning air to regain my composure. Still, with each click of my heel on the concrete pathway leading to our two-story brick home, my shoulders sag under the weight of humiliation I just suffered. Leafless shrubs along the pathway graze my slacks as my mind replays Jason Sterling's voice. "I will not hire you." While not his exact words, he expressed them as though I was a malicious influencer snooping to bring him down. His blue eyes flashed as if fueled by revenge against an adversary.

Before the interview, I'd considered him handsome with kind eyes based on his profile photo on the network website. His subtle smile and square jaw would have every woman's head turning as he walked into a room. I'd been distracted by his looks the moment I saw Jason, forgetting whatever the receptionist told me and I rushed for the same elevator.

I wince over the coffee spill. No wonder we had a terrible first impression. Either way, his reaction was stronger than that coffee. How could anyone in his position harbor such anger? And yet, beneath his voice, I sensed a hidden weight, even as I found comfort in challenging him, perhaps because I recognized the resentment he carried—a recognition from one damaged soul to another. Could I, without even knowing it, be the source of his irritation? Had my

17

show at Starwatch struck an unintended nerve? I'd submitted the best scripts from the last three networks I'd worked for.

I've never exerted so much effort to muster confidence as I did in that boardroom. And now, I'm utterly exhausted, and it's not even eleven o'clock. Shaking my head to clear it, I try to savor the crisp air penetrating my suit—a fashion decision made in the hopes of presenting a professional, polished appearance, even at the cost of leaving my coat at home.

I'd been so confident of securing the job today. Now, I'm jarred almost as much as I'd been from betrayal when my ex-boyfriend broke my trust and altered the course of my career.

"Hello there, Val."

I pivot toward the voice from a two-story house similar to mine. My neighbor, still in his black robe, pauses from clipping his withered shrubbery.

"Good morning, Pierce." I step toward him and manage a smile, the kind reserved for the outside world that perceives me as confident.

"Are you okay?" His gray brows draw together, his dark-brown skin harmonizing with my lighter tone.

"I'm fine, but if you stay out much longer, you won't be. It's too chilly for yard work." I rub my arms on my shoulders and nod at the clear sky. "It should warm up later, though."

"I've got a jacket under my robe." He rests the clippers at his side. "Why aren't you wearing a jacket?"

I dismiss his question with a wave before his free hand ushers me closer.

"Can you believe spring is here?"

"It sure is." Pierce and his wife, Joan—our closest neighbors since we moved here when I was five—boast the most vibrant potted plants on our row. Although now the pots on their porch and sidewalk sit dormant, they'll be vibrant with blooms in two months.

I'd delve into gardening too, if I could manage to squeeze it in between my relentless job hunts.

"Look at this."

I lean in to inspect the sprouting buds. Hope blooms anew. I breathe it in, hold it in. "I've been longing for spring."

Maybe the new season will bring in the change I need. Perhaps even a new job opportunity.

Pierce's eyes shine. "I hope you didn't hear that caterwauling last night? Our cat, Spunky, got into a bit of mischief. I think he must've been chasing a mouse along the bookshelf, but he knocked over Joan's aloe vera plant. The way he carried on—yowling and howling—you'd think the spiky plant attacked *him*."

The diversion into pet stories, or anything else for that matter, offers a welcome respite. But Joan's voice soon floats from the window, summoning him for their midmorning snack. So I turn toward our home. In the detached single-car garage, my gray Civic awaits long family trips. Otherwise, the subway or taxi's more convenient to get around the city.

Leafless shrubs flank our weathered porch steps. In a month or so, the leaves will sprout and breathe life into the landscape again. Once I punch in the code, I swing open the wooden door and step into the comforting warmth of home and the aroma of fried food, vinegar, and freshly made tortillas. The TV blares where my brother, Carlos, perches on the worn brown sofa, his dark hair tousled. Dressed in a navy-blue Yankees jersey, he's engrossed in a baseball game or perhaps a rerun as he bites into an arepa dripping with cheese and meat.

"If Mami doesn't stop serving you lunch for breakfast, I might have to buy that treadmill after all." I raise my voice over the TV. I should consider working out at home or joining Carlos in running and kickboxing, which won't cost me anything. With my time in the spotlight winding down, I might as well cancel my gym membership.

Carlos wipes cheese remnants from his mouth with the back of his hand. "Did you get the job?"

Two years my senior, he prefers working as the scheduler and accountant in our mother's nanny agency, as opposed to the unpredictability of the outside world. Following his divorce two years ago, he moved back in with Mami, making visits with my nephews infrequent after his ex-wife moved them to Chicago. "When do you start?"

I slide off my heels, the hardwood floor cool beneath my feet. I tuck the shoes on the wooden stand beside my handbag. The old planks creak with every step. "I wouldn't be back this soon if I'd gotten the job."

"Their loss, *hermana*. They don't know what they're missing." He plates his arepa on the coffee table, the TV apparently losing its allure. With a click of the remote, he turns it off and channels his full attention on me.

Warmth spreads through my chest at his unwavering belief in me. "It's not the best job for me anyway." Not true, but I need to stay strong, act disinterested. I'm not going to vent. My gaze drifts to the tan wall hosting family photos and midcentury Venezuelan art, plus paintings that celebrate the spirit of Brooklyn.

"Someplace better and more deserving will come along."

I need his optimism.

"On the bright side, I got those tickets you wanted to the Yankees spring training in a few weeks. We can invite up to six friends."

"Thanks, Carlos." Baseball is not my favorite sport, but my smile is automatic. I enjoy the atmosphere and catching up with my friends at these games.

"Is that Tina I hear?" Our mother's voice emanates from the kitchen behind the tall TV cabinet. Underplaying it, the busy clatter of pots and pans resounds in comforting familiarity.

"It's me, Mami." I sneak a bite of Carlos's enticing cheesy sandwich before returning it to him and heading toward the kitchen.

Our living room windows invite streams of natural light, and the warm glow illuminates the polished hardwood floors. The cozy three-bedroom house might feel a bit cramped for the six of us—my two sisters, cousin, brother, Mami, and me—but it's home.

I swallow the sandwich bite as I step into the kitchen where she's mixing something on the stove, steam rising around her. The aroma of garlic and freshly made tortillas, stacked high on a nearby plate, envelops me. "What are you cooking?"

As usual, vinegar, some in spray bottles and more in regular bottles, stands ready next to the measuring cups. Whether for cleaning or medicinal uses, vinegar is the one thing my mother never runs out of.

"I figured you might return with an appetite." She secures the lid on the pot and smooths a wisp of dark hair back into her bun. The frazzled escapees help hide her silver streaks. "Had to make your favorite lunch to celebrate the new job."

"I thought I'd land the job too. But green chili would be a great comfort food right now." I no longer need to watch what I eat since I don't belong in the spotlight anymore. After eating, I'll take a bath infused with relaxing essential oils to ease my stiff muscles.

Her smile radiates her usual certainty, as if the job's already mine. She wipes her hands on the flour-dusted apron protecting her green dress with its dahlia print. She's plump and short—a stature my sister, Anna, inherited, while the rest of us took after our lanky dad. "Tell me everything about the interview."

"It seems our prayers have gone unanswered yet again." I fidget with my pearl necklace. Now, it feels like a noose. My fingers twitched at the urge to tear it off, but I bottle up disappointment and recount the coffee-spill incident. "He insisted it wasn't the reason I rubbed him the wrong way."

Mami approaches, and her hands cup my cheeks. "Hija, just because God said no, doesn't mean He hasn't answered our prayers."

As I collapse into her arms, the anxiety knots begin to dissolve.

"You're beloved by all the people and families you've worked with," she says. "And their children adore you."

"I only wish I could've extended some of that charm to this man."

She steps back, her eyes reflecting understanding. Having lived in America for many years, she speaks more English than Spanish, although the lilt of our Latino heritage still colors her speech. "Come here, baby."

Her deep-brown eyes gleam as she guides me to the dining table. She sits across from me, the gold locket around her neck catching the light. I don't have to open it to know it carries a picture of my siblings and me—"always close to my heart," as she often says.

"What happened?"

Under her tender gaze, I recount a story different from my other job interviews. "It wasn't a fair interview." I squelch the hurt of having navigated all three stages at Family Sphere to be rejected in the final round. "He looked at me as if I stood for everything he detests."

"I'm sure whatever bitterness you sensed from him stems from somewhere else." Mami traces her finger on a small stainless bottle. "Like this salt shaker's contents, we don't understand what others are going through until shaken to the core. On a brighter note"—her smile widens—"you have a degree in psychology. Maybe it's time to dig into opportunities beyond TV that can benefit from your degree."

Right. I'd almost forgotten why I pursued psychology, especially after Austin's manipulations.

"I gotta say, your recent TV counseling show really resonated with women on their journey of self-discovery." Carlos scrapes the chair legs against the floor as he sits down and sets a plate with the remains of his sandwich in front of him. "But single guys or those happily married might not appreciate being labeled as losers."

I flinch, not just at his words but also at the oversimplification. "I never used the word *losers*." I turn to Mami, seeking an ally. Her knowing look only deepens my unease.

He folds his arms on the scratched wooden tabletop. "That's not what bloggers are saying."

"My message was about empowering women to discover their worth independently." Surely, Mami, of all people, understands this. "You've been our rock, raising us single-handedly, and look how well we've turned out."

Melancholy softens her expression. "Not every man is like your father, *Hija*. Do you think this man rejected you because he might have been offended by your show's viewpoint?"

"He's too bitter to be married if you ask me." I speak from my disappointment rather than as the counselor I should be. "If he were married, I'd advise his wife to make a run for it."

Carlos's deep laugh booms, soon joined by Mami's more reserved chuckle.

Shaking her head, she grips my hand. "I'm relieved you're not working there. But, if you keep up with your dislike of men, I might never see any grandkids."

"Mami means men are intimidated by you." Carlos's lightness belies the gravity of his words. When I swing a punch at his hard chest, he winces, mock groaning.

Still, sadness chills me. The one man I fell for tainted my view of romance forever.

"I wouldn't count on grandkids from me anytime soon." I can barely hear my voice. "Our family isn't the poster child for stable relationships."

"Anna is married."

I snorted at Carlos's reference to our oldest sister. "She spends more nights here than with her spouse. Let's face it. She's on her second marriage, and it's hanging by a thread."

He rubs the back of his neck, then rocks his chair off its front legs. "Well, Rosa's engaged again."

"*Again* being the key word." I can't help pointing out our pattern of failed commitments. No reason to go into our cousin's recent divorce after a dramatic split similar to Mami's fiery response to Dad's betrayal.

"Adding grandkids to this mix wouldn't be wise." I remove my pearl necklace and set it aside. This perhaps symbolizes letting go.

"It's not our fault those relationships haven't worked out." Carlos draws out a breath as he's tipped back. Balanced like that he'd topple with the slightest whack from me.

But the whack I give him is verbal. "That's just the problem. It doesn't change the fact that none of us have had a lasting love life."

"You're the youngest and not married yet. Perhaps you can change our family history." Mami squeezes my hand. "Think of all the redemption stories from the Bible. So often, God used the most unlikely people to make a difference."

I pull away. My path has been more self-directed, straying from any divine guidance. Perhaps that's why I feel forsaken.

"As for work, while you're figuring things out, your skills are always welcome at the agency." She shakes a finger at me. "It's time to jump into a window, now that this door has closed."

"I agree." Carlos licks his fingers, having finished off his sandwich.

"A new opportunity is on the horizon, *Hija*." She's never let us wallow in disappointment. "A woman reached out specifically asking for you. She's heard glowing recommendations from the families you've assisted and was impressed by your résumé and online reviews."

Wait. What? I dodge her shaking finger. "I thought you removed my résumé from the website."

"I planned to once you secured a job. But I asked her for a couple of days to decide, and today marks the second day." Mami beams. "Talk about timing!"

Even the possibility of being wanted for a job—albeit not my dream job—reinjects much-needed confidence. My mother's nanny agency has been essential to our family, providing for us ever since Dad left, covering everything from our bills to college funds, and becoming our safety net every time employment eluded us.

The Family Sphere interview was just one of several attempts to jump-start my stalled broadcasting career this year. Maybe stepping away from the relentless job hunt to spend time with children, letting them brighten these dark days, isn't such a bad idea.

I find myself laughing for the first time today, which feels like forever. Mami asks Carlos to bring the laptop. She manages her agency online and has over sixty employees, excluding my siblings and cousins who step in when needed. Mami and Carlos work from home and rent partial space from a gym when they hold interviews and staff-training events.

"You know, Mami's probably right." Carlos grins. "This might be the break from stress you need."

My mind wanders to my last job and its abrupt end. A new production manager's shift in direction led to my resignation, a decision I thought would herald new opportunities. While the challenge of securing a job in my field looms large, I'm grateful for Mami's agency to bounce back on. Yes, I'm willing to take the next step and contact Judy Flora Turner, the potential employer interested in my profile.

CHAPTER 4

Valentina

Perched at a table near the coffee shop entrance, I cradle my vanilla latte, the cup's warmth seeping into my palms. After yesterday's coffee mishap, I should avoid coffee. Not today, though. I'll blame Mrs. Turner for choosing this spot for our meeting.

It's cute, modern yet rustic, with exposed brick walls showcasing local art. The aroma of freshly ground coffee zaps the air, enough to tempt even the most indifferent passerby. I've visited Manhattan several times, but this coffee shop is new to me. Customers stream in and out, clutching disposable cups, pastries, or both.

I focus on the door, ready to spot Mrs. Turner upon her arrival. My mother emailed her about my interest in the job, and Mrs. Turner called within an hour, eager for a phone interview. She hired me on the spot and scheduled a follow-up meeting for this morning.

My next sip leaves a faint lipstick imprint on the cup. I settle deeper into the plush chair, surrounded by chatter and the whir of machines crafting drinks.

The bustling environment soothes me until a woman strides in and scans the coffee shop as if looking for someone. Dressed in a cream blazer over black slacks, she must be Mrs. Turner. She pauses, retrieves a phone from her handbag, and taps on it.

Remaining seated, I watch her finger move on her phone. My phone beeps. It has to be her. She slips her phone into her purse and heads toward the counter, choosing the shortest line. While the four baristas keep the lines moving, I check the new message.

Mrs. Turner: I'm here. ~ Judy

At quarter past eight, we're both early for our eight-thirty meeting. Good thing I arrived thirty minutes ahead of time so she didn't have to wait on me.

Once she steps away from the line to await her drink, I stand up, leaving my white jean jacket on the chair to reserve our spot. Drink in hand, I navigate through the crowded coffee shop. Unlike yesterday's tailored suit, today's knee-length teal dress and strappy flats make it easy to move.

"Hello." I greet her.

She turns, her eyes narrowing and lips pressing into a cautious line—an instinctive New Yorker reaction to an unexpected greeting. "Hi."

"I'm Valentina." I smile. "I saw you texting me when you walked in."

"You made good time." Her brow lifts as she adjusts her silk scarf. The elegant accessory complements her refined presence, and her subtle fragrance blends with the aromatic coffee.

"You've made good time too, Mrs. Turner."

"Please, call me Judy." Her voice floats over the sound of steaming milk. Then we shake hands, and the barista calls her order.

"I have a table for us." I beckon once she has her beverage.

"Thank you for meeting me on such short notice."

"It's no trouble at all." I lead her back to our table and pull out a chair for her.

"Thank you." Judy sets down her black handbag and sips her drink. Her brown hair touches her shoulders, and any gray is hardly noticeable. Her blue eyes are kind as they peer into mine. She could be around my mother's age, though her stylish appearance suggests younger.

"As we discussed during our phone conversation, finding a good nanny for my grandchildren is crucial. I haven't mentioned this, but they have no mother—"

"What happened to her?" Concern for the kids' loss has me forgetting my manners and interrupting.

"Not in the way you might think." Judy waves a hand, the nails free of polish. "That's beside the point. But I must say how your reputation precedes you. My friends who've employed your services through Proverbs Twenty-Two Six Agency have highlighted you as the ideal nanny. Attentive and nurturing, they've said. Did you know twenty different reviews mentioned those specific traits?"

Her words warm me more than the latte, and the sweet detail's an espresso shot to my self-esteem.

She nudges aside her coffee. "You're what my grandchildren need."

"I appreciate your kind words." Especially after yesterday's disheartening interview.

"The very reason I wanted to meet you." Judy leans in, her expression earnest. "The schedule. It's complicated... hectic perhaps. Are you flexible enough to commute to Meadowbrook most weekends?"

"That's close to Hudson, right?"

She dips her head. "An hour drive or so. On some days, you'll take the kids from Meadowbrook to school in Manhattan, including during their breaks, and in case they get sick and need to be tended to in their home while their dad is at work." She gives me an apologetic smile. "Staying the night on weekends and during their breaks is a must."

"That won't be a problem." I'm not doing anything else after all. "Just to confirm: Eden is eleven, favorite color hot pink." I tick off one finger, then the next. "Atticus's favorite color is blue, and Felix's is green, eight-year-old twins."

Judy's eyes sparkle. "Great memory." Her smile fades and flattens into a thin line. "Eden's been struggling lately. Even a simple math test sends her into a whirl of anxiety."

I nod, making a mental note.

"The boys have high energy."

"I love high energy." I tinker with my cup, drinking in memories of other kids I've watched in the past.

"To summarize your role..." Judy then clarifies my job description and schedule, which includes picking up the kids from school in Manhattan at 2:45 p.m., getting them to her house, helping them with homework, and taking them to their respective after-school programs. "Some days might require preparing them a meal."

The more I think about this job, the more I relax. It will be a great distraction. Plus, while the kids are in school, I can look for jobs, which is why I have to be upfront with Judy.

"I'm a psychologist, so—"

"You are?" Her voice rises and her eyes brighten. "This is even better!"

"Nannying is not my permanent career. My mother owns the agency, and whenever I'm not employed, I get to help out."

Her brows knit together, and she reaches for her cup. "How long will you be with us?"

"Three months, for sure." That should give her enough time to find my replacement. "Four, if it takes me that long to find a position."

She nods, then flicks her gaze to the big window spilling light into the room. A silence falls between us, merging with the surrounding hum and chatter and the whirring machines.

Pedestrians stride along the sidewalk, their faces marked by the resolve and fatigue of navigating urban life. The occasional taxi zips by alongside other cars, and cyclists weave through the gaps.

"Three months with a good nanny is better than the instability of the nannies we've had recently." Her voice pulls me back.

These kids' nannies have been constantly quitting? That's worrisome. "Um, why haven't the nannies lasted long?"

She lets out a soft chuckle. "That's another thing I was going to mention. Their dad believes I'm the only one, besides him, capable of taking care of his kids."

"Ah." I wrap my hands around my latte cup. The vanilla scent floods my nostrils before I take a sip. It's cooler now, but a perfect balance of bitterness and sweetness, much like my current situation. I want to help the kids, but if their dad is against having a nanny, my job could be challenging. Been there, done that. "What makes you think he'll be okay with me taking care of his children?"

Kindness gleams in her blue eyes. "Because I believe in you. And if you're as good as I've heard, you're going to disregard their dad and do what's in the children's best interest."

"I can do that." I sound more confident than I am. I've spent my journalism career tackling challenges and being driven by revenge. I did the job well, and the ratings spiked until the show's last six months.

"As for compensation..." Judy mentions a figure far beyond what she discussed last night.

"That's a lot." I gasp, my hand finding my chest.

"I'm going to convince you to stay for at least four months." She bats her long lashes. "I'll email you the paperwork by the end of the day."

I encourage her to ask any questions if my résumé and credentials on the nanny website weren't clear enough. Clients who sign up for an account can access our nanny résumés online.

"I'm pleased you're up-to-date with your first aid training." She lifts her cup in a toast, and I lift mine to toast hers. "I'll get your driver's license from you this afternoon. I'm so relieved you're available. My husband and I have a trip planned in less than three weeks."

She flicks her ring finger, and the diamond sparkles. "I got remarried last year, and now Phil and I are ready to travel."

"Sounds fun. What's the destination?"

"We're doing my dream trip—three months in Europe. We're hoping to keep it laid-back, with enough time at each destination to soak up the flavor."

I nod, sipping my drink as she recounts all the countries they'll be visiting.

Then she pulls out her phone, probably checking the time. "I need to get going. My grandkids have a presentation in an hour. Can you meet the kids this afternoon? Maybe come to my house at three-fifteen?"

"Of course."

"Great. I'll text the address. My house will be where you'll spend your afternoons during the week until their dad comes to pick them up."

Commuting an hour from Meadowbrook daily to go to school here doesn't make much sense. Aren't there schools in Meadowbrook? I want to ask, but I don't need to know everything before the first day. Their father must care about their welfare if he keeps thinking the nannies aren't good enough. I wonder what he'll think of me.

CHAPTER 5

Valentina

At three-fifteen, I climb the stairs to a prestigious home in a gated community. The taxi that dropped me off and the traffic sounds are distant beyond the ornate iron gate, as if this community is removed from the surrounding bustle. I set the large tote bag beside the door, adjust the purse on my shoulder, and ring the doorbell.

The elegant two-story brownstone homes are spread apart, and flower gardens and budding trees line the sidewalk. An older couple walks past with their basset hound on a leash.

What kind of jobs do residents in this neighborhood have? This isn't the first time I've nannied in the West Side of Manhattan, but I've always wondered if, even with the money, I'd ever want to live in the bustling city. It's great if I'm working for a TV broadcast, but if I had a family, I'd want somewhere far from the honking cars and blaring sirens.

The door swings open, and I reach for my bag. It contains introductory gifts I picked up for the kids and something for Judy.

"Good afternoon, Valentina." Judy opens the door wider, ushering me in.

"Good to see you again, Judy." Her kindness refreshes me. Too bad I can't say every family I've worked for was this warm and friendly from day one. I let her lead me through a long hallway adorned with modern paintings, our shoes tapping against the marble floor. "You have such a beautiful home."

"My son bought it for me, but with Phil retiring, we will move somewhere more modest."

A lemon scent hangs in the air, the place immaculate, and a smile curls my lips at the sound of children, their voices drowning out the soft background music.

"The kids are supposed to be doing their homework, but it's not going as planned."

We enter a plush living room. A paneled black accent wall hosts a dormant TV, while sage-green sofas cozy up to a smooth coffee table, and floor-to-ceiling windows reflect light off the marbled floor. A room beyond it features a black shelf with books and a table where the kids are seated.

One boy cups his cheeks, his eyes downcast and shoulders slumped. The other glances at us, then grabs a pencil, his hurried scribbles a clear attempt to seem occupied. They are adorable and look so similar. I doubt I can tell them apart. The girl casts a fleeting look our way before burying her head back in her book, her pencil moving slowly. They are all still dressed in their uniforms.

"Guys." Judy claps. "Come meet your new caretaker."

The boy with the pout stands first and walks toward me, looking down. None of them seem excited to see me.

I set my bag at my feet and lower myself to meet his gaze. "I hope I'm not the reason you're sad."

"Felix squashed my paper airplane, and Mimi doesn't want me to do anything." He crosses his arms, a frown creasing his forehead. Sweet thing. If his brother is Felix, then this must be Atticus. Distinguishing them from one another will be a challenge with their identical facial structure, brown hair, and blue eyes. When Felix joins us, I study them both. Atticus has an athletic build, and Felix is leaner.

"I'm sorry about your airplane," I say.

"Atticus hit me." Felix counters Atticus's complaint.

"You stepped on my plane."

"It was an accident."

And now, I'm cast as the judge in this sibling dispute. Judy stays silent, testing me to handle the matter, so the tactics I've developed over the years come in handy.

They continue the argument, and Atticus wants justice.

So I turn to him. "You know what helps me feel better when someone upsets me?" His wide eyes stare at me as I suggest a solution I've employed before, both personally and with other kids. "I go outside and scream at the top of my lungs."

"Will I feel better?"

I nod, and he scurries off toward the kitchen, his frame vanishing beyond the stairs. Judy smiles as I shift my attention to Felix. "Have you apologized to your brother already?"

He shakes his head.

"I'm sure it was an accident, but your brother might want to hear your sincere apology."

After he nods, I ask what grade he's in, and he holds out two fingers. "Second."

"You guys had a presentation today, right?"

"The Gettysburg Address."

"I'd like to hear that sometime."

"I'll do it now." He folds his hands. As he recites, his sister groans from the table. The impressive speech lasts almost two minutes.

"Great job." I raise a palm for a high five.

"It worked. It worked!" Atticus sprints back into the living room. His grin wide, he untucks his shirt. "I feel better. I hollered super loud. I think the neighbors heard."

Again, I put out my hand for a high five. "We'll have to make a new paper plane after your soccer practice."

His brother apologizes for the airplane mishap, but Atticus barely acknowledges it before turning to me. "Are you taking care of us just today?" He seems genuinely curious, and his question reminds me of Judy mentioning the nannies they've been through. "What's your name again?"

"I'm Valentina, but you can call me Val or Tina if you'd like."

"I like Val."

"Eden, hon," Judy calls. "You should introduce yourself."

The girl hesitantly slides off the chair, and her blonde ponytail swings past her shoulder. Her blue eyes reveal her sadness. "I'm Eden." She puts out her hand, and I shake her petite fingers. "But you don't have to worry about remembering my name. Dad will fire you before the weekend."

"Eden!" Judy scolds, but I chuckle. I love how transparent kids are.

"Thanks for the warning." I nod toward Eden, then reach for my bag. I stop her before she walks away. "I have something for you." I retrieve the box kit with a dance skirt and a few girl-pampering items. "Your grandma said you love hot pink."

She takes the see-through box and studies it. Her eyes widen, and her delicate blonde brows wing up. Judy reminds her to say thank you, and she does before walking back to the table. She's tearing the box open and keeping her gaze on the contents, so she must like it.

Just because I've been out of a job in the spotlight for almost a year, doesn't mean I'm too broke to manage a few gifts.

The boys are hovering by the bag. "Anything for us?" they chime.

"A green soccer ball for you." I hand the ball to Felix. "And a blue one for you, Atticus."

"My favorite color." Atticus cheers while Felix assesses his ball from different angles, probably noticing it's his favorite color too.

I'm sure they have plenty of balls, but I didn't know what else they'd like.

"Thank you!" Felix beams, and Atticus rushes to my side, sets the ball down, and hugs me.

My chest expands at the sweet embrace. After the hug, I pull out the final gift and hand it to Judy. I bought it from the coffee shop after she left.

Paper crinkles when she opens the mug.

"'Coffee tastes better in Manhattan.'" She smiles as she reads the words on the cup. "Aren't you a sweetheart?"

"I didn't know what else to get you."

"I love coffee, and it's always the thought that counts."

The boys talk about going outside to play with their new balls, but their grandma halts them. "Best you change out of your school uniforms, and we need to get Eden to her dance class." Judy then turns to me. "I'll give you a tour of the house after we return from the kids' activities. You might like to tag along since this will be one of your tasks. The boys' soccer practice overlaps Eden's dance class."

I nod, and when she asks if I need some tea or coffee as the kids get ready, I decline. Then chaos reigns as the kids get ready. I fill their water bottles while Judy supervises upstairs. Soon, we're out the door and crossing to one of the cars parked along the curb.

Judy calls after the boys as they skip ahead. "Look both ways before crossing."

"Eden, that skirt looks so nice on you." I edge closer to the girl as we approach a white Honda Pilot. She's wearing the knee-length wrap skirt I gifted her.

"Thanks." She tinkers with the waistband.

"And it fits her perfectly." Judy tugs Eden's waistline where the skirt cinches over her black leotard. "It's like Val knew your size."

A middle-aged man with brown skin steps out of the SUV, hastens to the passenger side, and opens the back door.

"Matthew, this is Valentina." Judy smiles between us, and the man extends his hand, which I shake.

"Nice to meet you." I then thank him for giving us a ride.

"Valentina is the kids' new caretaker," Judy explains. "She'll let you know whatever adventures she has planned with the kids and anywhere she needs to go."

"I have a car too." I fold the seats for the boys to slide into the back row. Eden climbs into the middle row, followed by Judy, and then me. "I don't mind driving if you need me to."

"Whatever works for you should be fine." Judy buckles herself in. "Just letting you know you can call Matthew whenever you need a ride."

"Thanks." I arrange my dress over my legs.

As we weave through traffic, car horns and distant sirens create their own backdrop, but I'm tuned in to the boys. Atticus points out cars that would make good airplanes. Felix points out ones that would be good in the video game he'll invent. Eden sits, watching through the window, responding with monosyllables whenever I ask her a question.

If only I could hear her interact with her siblings to get a feel for her personality!

"When you go to Meadowbrook during spring break, you can drive Jay's other car." Judy's voice cuts through my thoughts, and realize Jay must be the kids' dad. I'm supposed to meet him this evening. While the kids' grandma hired me, it's important to get along with their dad. "We'll add you to his insurance."

We park alongside an old brick building. Since I'm seated on the curb side, I step out. Then Judy slides out next before Eden. They embrace before Judy promises to pick her up in an hour after practice.

"You don't usually stay with her?" I ask.

While it's important not to rely on anyone, Eden is just a child. Surely, she'd love to have someone watching and cheering her on during her dance practice.

"I can't be in both places at the same time." Judy winces. She'd probably like to be there for Eden too.

"I'll be fine." Eden fiddles with her skirt. "Dad comes sometimes."

"If you want, you can stay with her," I suggest to Judy, then turn to the driver with his window half rolled down. "Matthew, is it okay if you and I go and watch the boys?" I can handle it myself, but since they don't know me well yet, they'd probably rather have the driver around too.

Matthew's smile is kind. "No problem about that."

"You're sure you don't mind?" Judy touches my shoulder, and I nod.

Fifteen minutes later, I'm on the sidelines while the boys practice in the fifty-degree sunshine. I cheer, clap, and chant Felix's and Atticus's names whenever they get it right. Then they come to the sidelines for a water break.

"You're doing great." I hand out more high fives.

Even though it's not hot, their already somewhat sunburned faces are glistening with sweat. I'd better start stocking my first aid kit with plenty of sunscreen for such occasions.

During the scrimmage, Felix drives the ball toward the goal. I leap up, clapping, urging the ball onward with every ounce of hope. Yet, his kicks lack the sharpness they need, too sluggish and predictable. The alert goalie kicks the ball back, and Felix's frustration manifests. His cleats tear through the semi-golden grass, sending clumps into the air like little tufts of defeat. Beside him, his coach shouts encouragement, pushing him to sync up with his teammates.

I glance around the watching parents and spot Matthew. He stands with the scattered crowd—some seated on folding chairs and colorful blankets, others standing like me. The large field buzzes with the energy of multiple teams weaving through their practices, whistles blowing, and chatter resounding.

A woman with a warm smile and a curvy silhouette approaches, a clipboard clasped in her hand. "I'm the coach's wife. Are you here with Atticus and Felix?"

"I'm Valentina, their nanny."

"Great." She hands me a clipboard with names and dates. "Can you sign up to bring a snack for one of the games?"

I move the tip of the pen to find dates to sign up. There are only two spots left. This Friday and next Friday. I snag the first slot and return the clipboard. "Any particular snacks you need? Any allergies I should be aware of?"

"No allergies on this team, so just something nutritious and kid friendly."

We'll figure something out. I resume watching the practice scrimmage.

After a great evening, we drive back to the dance studio. I twist sideways in my seat to encourage the boys over their skills.

"You know anything about soccer?" Atticus cocks his head. "You ever play?"

"I played all the way into college. My brother taught me the basics." I smirk. "I'm the youngest, so I was eager to try a bit of everything."

A small hand from the back seat taps my shoulder, and Felix asks, "Can you teach me, please?"

"Teach me first," Atticus insists.

Their eagerness warms me. I'm going to like this job better than working for odious Jason Sterling.

We pick up Eden and Judy, then head home. The kids have a snack. Eden hurries to finish her schoolwork, so she can read her book. Atticus settles in to make a paper airplane. Felix pushes to play soccer.

"We can do both." We fold the planes on the marbled kitchen island using the card stock sheets Judy provided. I teach them different variations so they can decide what's easier for them to make on their own next time.

We make extra planes in case Eden joins us.

Before we head outside, I call Eden from the room adjoining the kitchen. She sits with her feet crisscrossed on the comfy sofa, already engrossed in a book. She must have skipped her homework in her eagerness to read.

"I'm good." She waves us off with her dainty fingers.

Judy settles at the island sipping her water.

I arch a brow, knowing well her response. "Want to join us?"

"That's why you're here now." She lifts her glass toward me, ice jingling. "I can get a break."

Felix pushes to play soccer as soon as we finish flying airplanes. I can't say no as long as we have time. I can't play soccer in my flats, though. They're my favorite open shoes, and I don't want them to rip.

On the patio, I slide off my shoes. Furniture forms a cozy oasis on the stone-floored section, surrounded by planters and a white railing. Beyond it lies a charming, fenced-in private backyard—not large, but with enough grass for the kids to play. Two-story homes similar to this one surround us, and taller buildings rise beyond them. The boys are already tossing their planes.

I step onto the grass. Still parched from winter, it pokes at my bare feet. The breeze stirs, whispering a coolness on my shoulders. With the fading sunlight, gone is the warmth and the fifty degrees.

Ignoring the discomfort, I sail my airplane into the air and retrieve it. The boys add sound effects as they run in circles tossing and picking up their planes.

I laugh at the innocence of childhood, getting lost in the kids' world. Then the back patio door slides open. When I turn, I freeze. My stomach tightens, my smile vanishes, and my hand grips my constricting heart. "Jason Sterling?"

His question-filled blue eyes slice through me.

"You?" He frowns, his chiseled jaw clenching, and I feel exactly how he looks when he asks the question I should be asking him too. "What are you doing here?"

"That's Valentina Diaz." Judy speaks from behind him, and I'm glad because I can't find my voice.

Of all the homes I could have been hired in as a nanny, how could it possibly be *his*?

"Daddy's home!" The boys whiz past me to greet their dad.

With deliberate steps, I walk toward the back door where Jason and his mom stand on the patio. No way am I working for this man. Now it all makes sense. He's the man who doesn't like anyone near him or his family. He needs some social skills. What kind of journalist is he without social skills?

I stop at Judy's side. Jason is crouched at his kids' level, hugging them, and I catch a glimpse of his smile. He actually smiles with genuine warmth.

He nods in response to the boys' excitement about their afternoon as they speak over each other. Their happiness diffuses some of my tension. "Val showed us how to make paper airplanes that go even farther."

"She said we can call her Val, Tina, or Va... Vaventina." Atticus trips over his words, mispronouncing my full name, and I stifle a laugh despite myself. "But I like Val better."

"She's going to teach us soccer," Felix chimes in. "Can you play with us, Daddy?"

"We'll talk... about it later." Hesitation slows his words.

Well, I'm just as hesitant to work with you, buddy.

"This is your son, Jay?" I ask Judy as if I hope she'll deny it.

"Yes, this is Jay." She beams at him.

"Short for Jason." He seizes command as the boys tug at his hands. His gaze finds mine.

I stiffen at the tension between us, a silent acknowledgment of our unhappy encounter.

"She's not a nanny, Mom. And she's not going to be taking care of my kids."

"And how many nannies have you interviewed to know who is and isn't a nanny?" Judy plants a hand on her hip.

He clenches his shaven jaw and draws out an exasperated breath. Then his broad shoulders rise, and his crisp white shirt stretches across his chest.

"I'll get going." I start toward the door. Forget whatever promises I made Judy when she warned me about her son. That was before I knew her son was *the grump*.

"Please hold on, Val." Judy snags my hand as I walk past. "Is it okay if Jay has a word with you, please?"

No is on the tip of my tongue, but she gives me a pleading look, eyes blue like Jason's, only hers are motherly and kind. And my conscience niggles. I made her a promise earlier. I nod, unable to form a single word. Did I just do that? Agree to be in the same room with Jason Sterling? Ugh.

Judy then gives her son a warning glare that has him clearing his throat before he instructs the boys to follow their grandmother into the house. "I'll be right there."

The boys groan but don't go inside until they bargain with their dad to play soccer with them. "Val is playing with us too."

I don't bother to correct Felix. But our soccer game won't happen.

Heat rises through my chest. Only one good thing could come out of this moment. I might be able to give Jason a piece of my mind.

As Judy and the kids go inside, I move to the railing and observe the surrounding homes, the darkening sky, and the birds flitting from shrub to fence. Anything is more comforting than looking at Jason.

I should've taken a tour of the house. Perhaps I'd have seen his pictures on the walls and been prepared for this.

CHAPTER 6

Jason

I move to the patio's far end, unprepared for yet another run-in with Valentina. She stands across from me, arms crossed, gaze fixed on the fading sunset. Her fluttery teal dress contrasts with yesterday's sharp professional attire. With her hair pulled back into a high ponytail, her face is more visible. Pert bow lips tinted with subtle lipstick blend into her olive skin. She's a heartbreaker masquerading as the girl next door.

Seeing her laughing and carefree with the boys, her bare feet sinking into the grass, was a far cry from the stern know-it-all I remembered from her TV persona. I shake my head and stifle a mirthless laugh. How, of all people in New York, did Mom find Valentina to be the kids' nanny? Naturally, she's charmed the boys, wheedling into their games like she's known them forever.

Mom's voice had lilted over the phone, raving about the "exceptional nanny" she'd found. Surely, she couldn't have meant this woman. The universe wouldn't send the woman responsible for tearing my family apart here to care for my kids. No way. Not happening.

And I now have to break the boys' hearts and tell them she can't be their nanny. I exhale. Chirping birds and distant lawn mowers underplay our tense silence.

Time to rip off the bandage. I step toward her, stop a safe distance away, hands resting on the railing, and clear my throat to announce my presence. She ignores me as if the air itself conspires to separate us. Her scent—summer flowers and fresh rain—drifts over, tempting yet unreachable.

"You're a nanny and a TV host?" I keep my voice steady.

She huffs and faces me. I tower over her by thirteen inches.

"Some of us don't have the luxury of a single career path."

I hate to say it, but I admire her resilience. She's right. I know little about her, except my ex-wife admired her on-air poise.

"You're not stalking me because you didn't get the job, are you?" She's nothing more than a gossip columnist after all. But there's got to be an explanation for how she ended up here.

"If I'd known who the father was, I wouldn't have agreed to the job." She squares her shoulders, confidence masking an underlying uncertainty. "Now that I know, I quit."

Her flawless English, tinged with a Latino accent, might have been charming under different circumstances. But her grievances with me could end up extending to my children. "Glad we agree on something."

"I need to work where trust and respect are mutual." She steps past me to slip on her shoes. "People like you think the world bends at your whim, making the rest of us feel inferior."

"What do you mean, 'people like me'?"

"Do you really want to know?" She stands, her confidence unwavering. The slight upturn of her lips draws attention to a smirk accentuated by a faint trace of lipstick. "Never mind. I don't owe you an explanation. You're not my boss, Grumps."

"What did you just call me?"

Without a word, she spins on her heel and strides toward the door, her dress swaying with each step. She slides the door open with a flourish, steps inside, and shuts it behind her, even as I trail her.

People like me? Does she see me as one of those egomaniacs in the media industry? I've poured my soul into building my company from nothing, always lifting others alongside me. How disturbing to have someone's perception of me skewed by misunderstandings.

Inside, the playroom to the left of the staircase buzzes. The boys' laughter, usually comforting, now taunts me over the impending awkward conversation—another nanny gone, another explanation due.

I enter the kitchen and pick up a fidget spinner from the island. The handy kids toy helps when I need a distraction, like now as I walk toward the living room where Valentina is addressing my mom.

Eden is still curled up with a book on the sofa. Valentina retrieves her handbag from the bookshelf. Mom is looking up from reading her medical magazine.

"It was very nice to meet you, Judy." Valentina's poised tone and smile remain unwavering as if our earlier exchange hadn't soured the air. "And nice to meet you, Eden."

"My husband is bringing us dinner soon. You should stay and join us," Mom offers, clearly having already embraced the nanny.

The glow of the living room lights enhances Valentina's warm smile. "My family will be disappointed if I don't join them for dinner tonight."

Does she have kids? A husband? I cringe at those intrusive thoughts. If she's a single mother, I just robbed her of a job opportunity—*two* job opportunities. Blood whooshes in my head, and I twist the spinner faster.

"I signed up to bring snacks for the boys' soccer game this Friday." She holds up a hand in apology. "I hadn't anticipated you'd be the one shopping, but I can still take care of it if you need help."

"Don't worry, sweetheart." Mom waves, dismissing any snack crisis—an area where I lag. Where was Mom when Valentina signed up for the snacks, anyway?

"Let Matthew drive you," Mom suggests, but Valentina declines.

"I'll see you tomorrow afternoon." Mom must've missed—or perhaps dismissed—Valentina's subtle hint she wouldn't be around on Friday or tomorrow.

Valentina exits past me with a polite nod, and Eden's voice floats after her, wishing her luck with an undertone that suggests she, too, sensed the nanny's employment would be brief.

The lock clicks through the hallway. Then the door opens and closes, and a pang tightens my chest. I hadn't given Valentina a fair chance for the TV show, let alone shown I might need her for my kids. We hired a host yesterday, though Valentina had the best credentials. I couldn't put up with her at the office stirring memories of Daisy and all the ways I'd fallen short as a husband and father. Having her close to my family is more than I'm prepared to handle.

Before I drop the spinner back on the counter. Mom walks in. Her expressive face is pensive, signaling a conversation that will challenge my recent decisions.

"The kids had a good evening." She pulls out a barstool and plops onto it, her gaze assessing. "They loved Val. I've never felt as sure about anyone as I do about her to take care of the kids. But you've sure run through a host of them."

"The last one was too self-centered." I snort. "Even you thought it was strange the woman asked if there were nail spas in Meadowbrook."

"And the one before that?"

"A speeding ticket."

"Like you've never had one?"

"That was before I was a father."

"You have all the answers, don't you?" She shakes her head, then flashes a weak smile. "Let's focus on Val for now."

"She's a TV host." I rest my arms on the cool marble island. "I don't know how you found her."

"Like I mentioned yesterday, recommendations. Look her up in the mommy groups in the community."

I shift my feet. I should sit, but it's best to remain standing if I need to flee. "Valentina's credentials in journalism and psychology are impressive, but they hardly scream 'nanny.'"

"Jason Carson Sterling." Mom's voice hardens. She only uses my full name in a command for undivided attention. "The effort I put into finding Valentina was no small feat. She comes highly recommended for a reason."

"I get that, but..." *Oh, out with it, buddy!* "She was the host on that show Daisy watched, the one that tells women to leave their husbands." Not exactly, but close enough. I then tell her about my meeting with Valentina at work, minus where I lost control and told her, head-on, I wasn't hiring her.

Mom chuckles and drops her voice as she glances around, cautious not to let the kids overhear. "Honey, don't tell me you're blaming her for *that*. Daisy left because your marriage ended way before she watched some TV show."

Why can't Mom grasp how deeply this still affects me? *I'm your son, and Valentina is a stranger. Hello!* "Still—"

"This is about the kids, Jay." Going no-nonsense, she wags a finger, so I have no choice but to listen. "From what I've heard, Valentina could be what they need right now." She leans forward, her blue eyes softening with the earnestness she's displayed through years of comforting and advising me. That look breaks my defenses each time. "Give her a chance, three months. If it's still not working out when I return from my trip, then we can talk about this again."

I would accept her proposal for anyone but Valentina.

I stand, squeezing the back of my neck, then exhale. I can barely raise my plea to meet the refrigerator's hum. "There has to be other options. Any number of nanny services could offer us someone... not her."

My earlier actions weigh on me. The prospect of hiring Valentina is even more daunting.

Mom's gaze sharpens, her brow arching. My resistance is bordering on the futile. "You want to find someone better suited? Then be my guest. In less than three weeks, Phil and I are off to Europe."

"That's in three weeks?" Time has, indeed, slipped by faster than I expected.

"You'll need someone to watch the kids. Their spring break is around the corner."

The week after Mom leaves. Hmm. I rub my jaw, fingers rasping over the day's stubble as my gaze darts to the fidget spinner. I can't just find someone on a whim, and I definitely can't take a week off to search. And there's no way I can take four months off to care for the kids myself if no suitable person is found. It's prelaunch for the new family show.

After years of raising me and working to keep a roof over our heads, Mom's earned her break. I shouldn't be burdening her with my children too.

"You're on your own." She lifts her hands in a gesture of surrender.

"I... already let Valentina go, Mom." Maybe the difficulty of rehiring her can excuse my earlier decision. I could've handled this better perhaps. "I'm sure she doesn't want to work for me either."

Mom sighs. "Jay, you're the problem in this situation. And giving her 'that look' when you first saw her, as if she'd stolen your snickerdoodles, wasn't your finest moment."

I laugh at the mention of my favorite cookies. "Valentina is not going to work out." Not after I let her go again. "She hates me."

"You're the CEO of a family broadcast. You deal with all sorts of employees and disgruntled viewers." Mom's given up on me if she wants me to stick to this plan. "I have Valentina's address, and you must have her contacts since you interviewed her yesterday. You're going directly to her house, between now and Friday, to plead with her."

"Mom!" I toss my head back and groan. What a ludicrous suggestion. "You mean I ask *her* for an apology?"

"Whatever you want to call it. If you call her, she'll hang up as soon as she hears it's you."

Mom's right, but to apologize and then plead for her help? No way!

Atticus bursts from the playroom, a soccer ball sailing past, with Felix hot on his heels, each kicking their own ball.

"Boys, what did we say about kicking balls in the house?" Mom reprimands.

They pick up colorful balls I hadn't seen before.

"Looks like Mom got you new balls."

"Val got us the balls." Felix clutches his green one.

"Val, yeah." Atticus cranes his head around. "Ready to play soccer, Val?"

I palm the back of my neck. My shoulders edge up. "Valentina's gone for the day, kiddo."

"She didn't say goodbye?" Atticus's face falls.

I'd better divert their attention. "Let's go play soccer in the back for ten minutes." At this point, we'll just have to rely on the porch lights—a dim solution for a much bigger problem.

CHAPTER 7

Jason

Apologizing, admitting fault, seeking reconciliation are all monumental challenges. Yet, as we drive home, the boys' excitement about their time with Valentina and the soccer lessons they anticipate outweighs my grievances. Then a flowery perfume permeates the car.

"What's that smell?" I crane my head to the back.

"Eden sprayed her new perfume." Atticus sniffs exaggeratedly. "Valentina gave it to her."

"She gave her a dance skirt too," Felix adds.

Just great. *I* never considered Eden might be at the age where perfume and stylish skirts would catch her interest. I thought a Gabb phone would suffice for someone her age, but it remains idle unless she's expecting a rare call from her mom.

I signal right onto West Street. Traffic is light, thank goodness. I hadn't even paid attention to Eden's clothes when I greeted her with a kiss as she was reading. Maybe I can engage her now. "What color is your skirt, Eden?"

"Pink." She speaks over one of the boys' yawns.

"Is it something you can wear to dance?"

"I wore it to practice today."

Her brief responses end our conversation. I refocus on the road. Soon, the soft sound of deep breaths fills the car—a couple, if not all three, of the kids have fallen asleep. They need stability. They should be able to come home at a decent hour on days without after-school programs, to a house that feels like home—a refuge from bustling Manhattan. I'm glad we have our place in Meadowbrook. It's refreshing to have a place to lay low on weekends and connect with friends in our community.

Two hours later, after tucking the kids into bed, I retreat to my bedroom, shower, and change into my pajama pants. The house I had designed with a family in mind has eight bedrooms—all on one level for easy access to the kids, except for the laundry room and gym in the basement.

Stifling a yawn, I slip under the covers. Sleep should claim me quickly given the day's events, but as I close my eyes, Valentina's face, her stern expression, and her words—*people like you* and *Grumps*—haunt me.

A wry smile tugs at my lips. I consider myself a happy person, but is that how I come across? Perhaps I have a hard time relaxing when I'm moving from one task to another, but my initial encounter with Valentina might have painted the image of a grumpy boss.

The bedsheets whisper against my bare chest as I turn. If the roles were reversed, would I consider forgiving Valentina if she dismissed me so abruptly? Unlikely.

What's with all the restless energy? I roll to my side. The thin light from the security lamps slices through the blinds. The digital clock glows 9:55 p.m. The silence is too heavy and the need to reach out is overwhelming.

Ethan's kids are likely in bed by now. As the local pastor and one of my closest friends, he's often the pillar the community leans on, yet he manages to keep our friendship free of any moral grandstanding. We met in a support group for single dads in Manhattan. His proposal to move here and build our lives anew incited me and two other guys to join him in buying sprawling land to construct our homes close to one another.

Ethan exemplifies what it means to live with integrity and grace. I should embrace better values, especially being close friends with someone of his moral stature. But I've barely a moment to embrace anything new. Still, he's the one person who knows my background enough to help me navigate this mess with Valentina—maybe even help me align my actions with the better judgment I misplaced.

I reach for my phone from the nightstand and squint against the bright screen in the dark room. I scroll to his name and hit call.

He picks up at the second ring. "You never call on weeknights."

I picture him sitting in his living room, Bibles and research books open for his Sunday sermon preparation.

"Did I wake you?" After all, he might've chosen to go to bed early tonight. I shift to lie on my back, the ceiling invisible in the darkness.

He laughs, a comforting sound. "Since when did that stop you guys from calling?"

"Your fault for being the pastor and inviting me along." I try to keep the mood light. His commitment to his role and to us, his friends, makes Meadowbrook a better place. Though my faith is shaky, he often reassures me that God meets me wherever I am.

"Remember how my mom has been helping me find a nanny?"

"If you find a perfect one, I can't wait to meet her."

I run a hand through my hair. "Apparently, Mom found the one."

"But?"

"I brushed her off because she was a TV host."

"Are we talking about a nanny or a host for your show?"

"Same person." I drag out a breath, then recount the saga, omitting my rash dismissals. "Imagine me walking into Mom's house and going to the backyard to meet the nanny."

"The same person you misjudged." Ethan's voice is cautious yet kind. "God's always teaching lessons. Keeps us humble. After the boardroom incident, maybe He's giving you a second chance to make things right."

"You mean to say this encounter is God's way of humiliating me?"

"You can call it that if it fits." He goes on, reflecting on the coincidence of it all.

"She called me Grumps."

His rich laugh bounces through the phone. "And an egomaniac," he reminds.

Not her exact words. "Worse yet, my mom wants me to plead with her to watch the kids."

"Your mom is leaving for a month."

"Three months." I roll onto my stomach, my elbows sinking into the mattress.

"It's wise to do as your mom asks."

"You mean go and plead with this woman?"

"You know the thing a person says to another when they've made a mistake?"

"Mistake?"

"It's called an apology, Jason."

I blow out a breath and stare into the encompassing darkness. "I thought you'd have better advice," I grumble into the phone, though deep down I recognize the truth. Mom was right, but I'd hoped to sidestep swallowing my pride and making amends—not just for my kids, but perhaps as a step toward healing my own bruised spirit. But still, maybe if Ethan understood my real reservations...

"She used to be the host of that show." I bite my tongue at Mom's reminder that Daisy made her own decision to leave. It's easier to blame someone else for the unraveling of our marriage after the twins were born.

"What about the show?" Ethan probes.

I shift. "That's not important."

"Great." He snickers. "I can't wait to meet this nanny. Congrats!"

"You can laugh now, but wait until you need a nanny."

"I'm not as particular as you." He's smiling. I know it. He benefits from a network of church grandmothers eager to dote on his kids.

After I hang up, reality sinks in. If Valentina agrees to reconsider the job, I'm committed to three months with her, as per Mom's request. I put the phone back on the nightstand and flip onto my back again. Tomorrow is Thursday. Maybe I can stall, wait one more day in hopes Mom might change her mind and find another nanny.

Closing my eyes, I pull the covers up to my chin and try to settle into sleep. But Valentina's image invades again. Her words echo persistently—*Grumps. People like you.*

Valentina Diaz. She's getting under my skin if I can't close my eyes without her popping into my thoughts. I flip onto my stomach again and bury my face in the pillow to block her out. Her appearance, her scent, her lush dark hair... She's beyond attractive. Definitely, one of the most beautiful women I've seen in a long time. That admission forces me to slide off the pillow and cover my head with it. *Sleep, Jason, sleep.*

Her question from the interview interrupts my efforts. "Have you ever watched any of the clips from my show?"

I toss the pillow aside and reach for my phone again.

Who is Valentina Diaz? There's way too much information on the internet. Before I can get through it all, exhaustion takes over. When I sleep, I dream about her.

CHAPTER 8

Valentina

My best friend and I grew up in the same neighborhood, rode bikes together, and went to the same schools until college. While we ended up in different careers, our friendship never wavered. Now and then, we visit memory lane at our favorite street-food spots. Today, it's a hot dog stand in Brooklyn.

I take a sip of water, washing down my swallow of hot dog. I place my water cup on the folding table, my gaze flickering to Leah's half-eaten hot dog piled with jalapeños and hot sauce. "Doesn't it defeat the purpose of enjoying spicy food if you have to down all that water?"

She continues gulping her drink and gestures for my water.

I pass it over, noting the street artists, cyclists, and vibrant city life around us.

"That's better." She sighs and dabs her mouth. Her brown skin glistens in the lukewarm sunshine. "You were saying... your dead-end job search?"

"I have all the time in the world now." I cover my half-eaten hot dog to shield it from the eager fly hovering over our table. As a middle school teacher married to her high school sweetheart, Leah is always busier than I am during the school year. She's also one of the few people I know in a long-term relationship. Perhaps there's hope for some of us to find that special someone.

"Nannying again could pad your wallet." She crumples the mustard-covered napkin into a ball. "Lucky you have that to fall back on."

I chuckle, yesterday's encounter still fresh. "Not if I have to deal with grumpy parents. Guess who offered me the job I'd texted you about?"

"The woman who emailed your mom, right?"

56

I wince. How can I even explain this?

"Another wealthy family in Manhattan?"

"The woman who emailed. She's the mother of the man who dismissed me in the interview. Can you believe it?"

"No way!" She slaps the table, and hot sauce glops from her now-forgotten hotdog. "Did you decline?"

"I quit yesterday before he could fire me." Talking about it makes me hungry. I reach for my hot dog and bite into it fiercely.

We eat in silence until she asks, "What's he like?"

"Annoying." And unfortunately handsome. I finish my hot dog, still irked by his rude treatment.

"Is he a single dad?"

I nod. Sympathy creeps in. What's the reason behind his curt demeanor? Is it because his wife left him? I want to hold a grudge regardless. "Maybe he hates women."

"Is he handsome?" Leah wraps her paper into a ball.

Beauty is in the eyes of the beholder, so I shrug.

"Show me a picture of him from the internet."

I reach for a napkin to wipe my hands, then pull my phone from my purse. The first page on my search appears. There at the top of the screen is his high-resolution headshot. Goodness! His headshot on Family Sphere's site falls short in comparison.

He's more relaxed, his smile warmer. Neatly shaven chiseled jaw. Perfectly fitted navy suit. Crisp white shirt. I don't need a full photo to remember he's tall and broad-shouldered. His hair is longer on top, dark brown with a curl. He belongs in a modeling shoot—okay, more like the popular athletic guy in school who's every girl's dream for a crush. My stomach squeezes.

I wince and scroll down, tempted to click on the many links with intel. There's a gazillion forums about him online.

"Are you going to show me the photo?" Leah leans over and snatches my phone. She uses her other hand to shield the screen from glare and scrolls back up, then raises a brow as if she can read my thoughts. "Wow, look at that jaw, those eyes."

"Handsome or not, he treats me like the bane of his existence." Frustration bubbles over. He didn't even give me a chance for a fair interview.

"It seems his mom hired you, not him."

"How can I take care of his kids if we can't stand each other?"

My last two times in Jason's presence, the tension clogging the air almost suffocated me. "The kids are sweet. I think his daughter is dealing with a rebellious streak, likely due to her mother's absence."

Chin propped in her hand, Leah nods amid the chatter and hum around us. "I have an inkling you find him attractive."

My cheeks heat. "I'm done with men. Even if I weren't, he's nowhere close to my—"

"Type, I get it. But all men are not your type thanks to Austin."

"Not everyone is lucky to find a perfect match."

"Just keep your heart open in case your perfect match comes along."

I snort. "You, my friend, must've forgotten my family history."

She shakes her head, brushing off my retort. "If nannying doesn't work out, our school is looking for a psychologist."

"No way am I going to be a school psychologist." The idea of real counseling is daunting.

"But you've been on TV giving advice. Kids should be easier. Think of the volunteer hours you've dedicated to the school in ESL." She picks up her hot dog and scoops the runaway sauce. "The parents in ESL know you. The principal loves you and would rather hire you than someone unfamiliar who's more experienced."

Of course, I appreciate her faith in me, but I'm not ready to transition from TV to real-life counseling. I am however considering getting out of the spotlight. I just need one more chance to end that career on a good note. "I'll think about the offer, though."

"Pray about it." She licks hot sauce from her lips, then gulps more water. "Your TV job takes a toll on you."

Stressing over researching a topic or story to capture an audience exhausted me. "Maybe God is trying to get my attention."

"Perhaps He's calling you to the career you trained for." Her braids sway with her nod.

When we part ways, I ponder becoming a school counselor for one of the inner schools. I volunteer there two evenings a week during the school year. It might be interesting. I specialized in family psychology, and that includes kids. But I don't want to take over and keep the kids from having someone more experienced in the field.

However, could this be where God wants me to be?

It's been a while since I bothered to pray for guidance. From now on, I need to discern which doors God might be closing, like Mami says, so I can have the courage to climb through the window.

At home later, savory scents of food waft through the kitchen. My sister Anna recounts her day babysitting as we set the table. "That's when three-year-old Lily decided to 'bathe' all her stuffed animals in the mud puddle."

I snort to stifle a giggle.

"Always expect the unexpected with children." Laughing, Mami scoops carnitas and peppers onto a platter. She then hands me the shredded pork platter. "They teach us patience and creativity in their own ways."

I love the transparency of children, even if they test caretakers' limits. I set the platter next to the stacked tortillas on the table. It's just the four of us tonight, but the food is enough to feed ten. I return to the kitchen, passing Anna with steaming green chili.

Mami hands me the diced tomato bowl. "Tina, you should give the job another chance. Quitting isn't in our nature."

I sigh, but it doesn't help as the conversation presses on my chest. "He didn't want me there." A headache threatens to set in. I hand

Anna the tomatoes to put on the table. I need to convince Mami that working for Jason Sterling is beyond my limits.

Before I can speak, my brother strides in. Dressed in his Nets jersey, he points his half-empty Jarritos bottle at me. "I'd work for him, be the best nanny, and show him not to mess with a Diaz." He takes another sip of his drink and starts coughing.

Mami grabs the nearest vinegar bottle and dollops some into a miniature disposable cup. "Drink this, *Hijo*." She thrusts it toward Carlos. "It'll stop a cold before it starts."

"The soda... just went down... the wrong pipe." My poor brother, still coughing, tries to explain between gasps before Mom can shove the vinegar down his throat.

That should've been enough of a distraction, but Anna reverts the conversation. "What were you even thinking, quitting like that?"

"We are not quitters, *Hija*." Mami wags a disapproving finger at me.

Thanks, Anna, for dragging this out.

My family's concerned attention presses in on me. That's how they show their support—never letting me back down from a challenge, always pushing me to reconsider and grow.

We sit around the dinner table, basking in the glow of the overhead lamp, the aroma of garlic and herbs, and the warmth of love. We join hands as Mami begins grace, a heartfelt prayer. "Bless this food to our bodies, Lord."

My chest tightens. I've been sloppy with my spiritual life lately, forgetting how far I've come. How far my family has come. Only God could've brought us this far despite the ups and downs.

Mom goes on, "Keep our hearts and minds grateful and open to each other and Your work."

At her pause, we add a collective amen.

Silverware clinks against plates as we pass platters, each of us scooping up steaming portions. Out of habit to maintain my figure for the spotlight, I keep my portions small.

"You need some more meat, Tina." Mami forks more shredded meat onto my plate, covering my plantains and pinto beans. "You can get back to your diet when you get a TV job."

"Thanks, Mami." No reason to argue. Carlos is seated next to me. I'll slide my leftovers to him.

"Did you ever get that printer to work?" I ask as I stir an ice cube into my meal with a fork to let out the steam. Carlos was struggling to print out a ledger when I left to meet with Leah.

"It was the glue." He pauses from adding meat to his tortilla. "Glue spilled on the desk, and I guess I accidentally put the sticky papers in the copier."

The doorbell cuts through our laughter.

"It's probably a salesman." Carlos draws out a breath, folding his tortilla.

Everyone is ready to dive into their meal.

"I'll get it." I push back from the table, my napkin falling off my lap. I stride to the door, ready to tell whoever it is that it's dinnertime and send them off. But when I swing open the door, I almost lose my balance.

I blink once, then twice through the fading daylight and porch light. Surely, my eyes are playing tricks on me.

"Hi." Jason Sterling waves, his smile sheepish. "I hear this is where we line up to talk to you."

Is that humor I hear? His posture reveals otherwise.

Dressed in a button-down and loose tie, he rubs the back of his neck, wincing as if the day is still bearing down on him.

"Grumps?" I squeak. What's with my voice? My heart leaps into my throat as I attempt a steadier tone. "What... are you doing here?"

I can't find my real voice, and now I'm slightly hot despite the breeze. I grip the door, confused or frustrated—I can't tell which.

"I..."

I'm not thinking straight, so I step back and slam the door, leaving him on the doorstep. Oops, I didn't give him time to finish his reply.

I lean against the door and grip my forehead. I shouldn't have done that. He came for a reason, right? Stomping on my conscience, I march back to the table, unable to steady my racing heart or convince myself I'm doing the right thing.

"Who was that?" My brother pauses his forkful halfway to his mouth.

"Tina, are you okay?" Anna half rises from her chair, reaching as if to steady me.

"You look..." Mami frowns. "Who was at the door?"

"A salesman." I slide back into my chair. Jason is like a pushy salesman showing up unannounced. If he wanted to talk, he could've called. I gulp and glance around our humble house. The tattered chair, dingy sofa, and old family photos crowding the living room walls—things too personal, too intimate for an outsider to see. But he must've gotten the message he's not welcome and left. Whew!

Then the doorbell rings again. Mami gives me that look as she grips both hands on the table and pushes herself up to stand. "I've got it."

Great. So great.

CHAPTER 9

Jason

"I hear this is where we line up to talk to you." I mumble the words again to the closed wooden door. At least the moth flapping over the light finds humor in my line.

I should've expected her to slam the door in my face. Further loosening my tie, I contemplate my next move. The neighborhood is lively with music from one of the homes and cyclists weaving alongside the chalked-up sidewalk.

The evening chill creeps beneath my shirt, and I'm tempted to retreat. After the boys' soccer game, I rushed over here. Pressing the doorbell again, I exhale pure frustration. I loathe this, but I need her answer. If only she'll say no, then I can report back to my mom and let her continue the search.

The door swings open. Good. It's not Valentina. I need to figure out what to say to her.

The woman's eyes glow with a welcome that feels like home. Short and stout, she's older, perhaps Valentina's mother or aunt since her features otherwise mirror Valentina's in subtle ways. She reaches out, her grip firm and her smile broad, inviting. Is this warmth her usual greeting, or does she somehow recognize me? "I'm Paloma." Her accent reminds me of Valentina's heritage. "Tina's mami."

Tina? Oh, right. The boys said they could call her Tina or Val.

"Jason Sterling." I squeeze her hand, calluses indicating her hard work and resilience. "My mother hired your daughter two days ago, but there's been a misunderstanding." Maybe Valentina will overhear and spare me from explaining again.

"I see." Paloma swings the door wide open. "We're having dinner. You should join us."

63

My growling stomach betrays me as exotic scents waft from the house. I ditched dinner with Phil, Mom, and the kids for this. "I need to get back to my kids."

"We have plenty to eat." Paloma embodies the no-nonsense New Yorker vibe. Turning, she leaves the door open and no room to refuse. The dim hallway envelops us as I shut the door and seal us in. "If you want to talk to Tina, you'll need to join us at the table."

The living space is cozy, and the worn brown sofa reminds me of my childhood home in Queens. A TV rests on a wooden cabinet matching the coffee table. Family photos bring tan walls to life, though I barely have time to look as I follow Paloma.

Her voice carries from the connected room. "Jason here has just hired Tina through the agency."

As I approach, tension prickles me. My gaze meets the sets of eyes pivoting my way—all except Valentina's. She's focused on her full plate, flicking her fork through her food with disinterest to avoid looking at me.

I wave at a woman who resembles Valentina and a man with a boxer's build.

"I'm Anna, one of Tina's older sisters." The woman tilts her head toward Valentina, who continues to dissect her plate with indifferent clinks.

"You're the one who cost my sister the job?" says the boxer. He must be a sports fanatic, given he's dressed in a Nets jersey. He stands, protective and confrontational, then smirks as if savoring a personal victory. "Two jobs, actually."

"Enough, Carlos," Paloma intervenes.

Though I'm caught in the crossfire of accusations and familial loyalty, I can't help but envy Valentina, who has siblings to stand up for her. As an only child, I've often imagined such support. Standing here beneath their stares and her indifferent presence, I stiffen as regret pushes me toward the resolution I need.

"Val, why don't you get our guest a plate and something to drink?"

At her mother's question, Valentina draws a deep breath and lifts her chin to meet my gaze. Her eyes narrow, her emotions unreadable. If she's annoyed, I can't tell. She sets her fork down with a deliberate clatter against her plate. "What do you want to drink?"

"Can we talk?" I'm hoping for a moment alone.

"Just get him Jarritos." Carlos pulls out the empty chair on his left side, directly across from Valentina. Despite his earlier edge, he seems more relaxed now as he gestures for me to sit. "My sister is pretty awesome. No wonder you're back, crawling."

"Shut it, Carlos!" Valentina seethes from in front of the refrigerator. She emerges from the kitchen and hands me a bottle of unfamiliar red soda.

I'd have preferred water, but I better not push my luck.

"Thanks," I murmur as she leans close to pop the lid with a bottle opener. Her proximity allows me to escape into the freshness of her fragrance. Aromatic, fresh like rain and flowers.

She leaves and returns with a plate for me, her tight jeans and red T-shirt highlighting her slender figure. As they pass bowls my way, I sample a spoonful from each, curious about the unfamiliar dishes.

"What's this?" I point my fork to a chunk of something brown.

"That's plantain." Softness laces Valentina's tone.

"Jason, you're born and raised in Manhattan?" Paloma shifts the conversation.

"Queens, actually." I then ask how long they've lived in Brooklyn.

"Born in Venezuela, raised in Brooklyn." Carlos salutes with his now empty bottle. His gesture reminds me of my drink, so I take a cautious sip. "In this very neighborhood, Mami started the family business."

"I started babysitting when they were little." Paloma gestures to her kids and shares stories of how her nanny agency started and how her children were always part of the business. She doesn't mention a husband as she shares challenges from her first years as an immigrant. She keeps the conversation flowing.

Then it shifts when Carlos starts in on sports. I catch a basketball or football game here and there, but depending on what my time with the kids allows, I seldom have the luxury of time to watch sports.

His Nets jersey compels me to toss out a casual question about their latest draft pick, and then we're deep in discussion. From football's tight-end strategies and hockey's power-play tactics to debating the merits of a controlled fade in golf and the intricacies of baseball's bullpen management—Carlos has it all down. He rattles off stats and player histories with the ease of a sports anchor, clearly a die-hard sports fanatic with more than enough knowledge to fill a sports column.

As the family converses, I grasp the depth of their connection to this place, and regret hits me for not understanding Valentina's world sooner. This time with her family has given me more inside intel into who she is than any internet search could reveal. She comes from humble beginnings, raised by a down-to-earth family. She's not a vixen or the reason behind my failed marriage.

The clinking of utensils blends with stories about the challenges of entrepreneurship. I'm half listening, captivated by the rich flavors dancing on my tongue and distracted by Valentina.

She maneuvers her fork through her food with a quiet focus, seemingly lost in her world until her gaze rises to mine. Then the space between us seems to spark. Charged with an electric undercurrent, it leaves my palms moist.

"Now that you know how we started our business"—Paloma's voice pulls me back—"I hope you can give us good reviews."

"He can't give us a review when he hasn't used our agency." Valentina's steely look sends a flutter through my stomach.

"I looked you up on the internet." I might as well discuss why I'm here.

Her eyes narrow, and her fork clatters onto her plate. "And?"

Her advocacy for women's independence was brilliantly expressed through fans' detailed reviews, but while she was loved by many, some grumblers, mostly men, left comments saying they felt she'd misguided their spouses. I haven't watched clips of her show yet, so I'd best speak carefully. I'm still afraid I might further dislike her, yet I'm gravitating toward liking her. "I see how some might misinterpret the message."

"Does that mean you're going to hire her for the show?" her brother probes.

"Carlos, Anna." Paloma claps, silencing the room. "Let's give Tina and Jason space to talk."

As they clear their plates, only Valentina's and mine remain.

I grip my bottle, using it as an anchor, taking a deep breath for what comes next. "The kids—my mom thinks you deserve another chance."

"Is that so?" One shapely dark brow rises, highlighting the skepticism flashing in those lively eyes.

"Yeah." My tongue is suddenly heavy. When was the last time I offered a genuine apology? Only to Mom because she doesn't let me get away with anything without demanding an apology. "What matters is your relationship with the kids. We'll need to communicate, maybe even share spaces, and not just when the kids are on break. But as long as you and I are—"

"How do you expect me to take care of your kids when you despise me?" She folds her arms, a *V* creasing the delicate skin above her nose.

I need to do better. My grip tightens on the bottle. "I trust my mom's judgment, and she speaks highly of you. The children need stability. For their sake, can we set our differences aside?"

"There are plenty of great nannies out there."

"Rumor is you're one of the best New York has to offer." I soften my tone. "Maybe it's worth seeing if that's true."

"Is that why you're here?" Her lips twitch. Is she amused by my discomfort?

"I told you why I'm here." Didn't I convey my sincerity?

She rests her chin on her palm. Her posture suggests a newfound ease. "You can't trust me to work for your company, but you're going to trust me with your kids?"

Put that way, it's ridiculous. She's not letting me off easily.

I exhale. "I judged too quickly. Your show—" I can't admit why she rubbed me the wrong way without delving into details. "I should've watched more, gotten the full picture. You could've been a great host for our show." That's gotta be apology enough. "You were the most qualified. But we've already hired someone else, so hopefully, it doesn't come back to bite me."

Her posture softens, maybe in understanding or concession. "I could've acted better too." Is that an apology? I don't need one. "I got defensive and reacted the way any human might. I'm sorry."

Caught off guard by her sincerity, I flex my grip on the bottle. She's being gracious, and now, my reaction at the interview seems harsh. I sip my drink, nodding.

"I'm glad you watched the snippets I added to the application. I worked hard to get the best clips."

"I haven't watched those yet." I spare her why her presence left me restless, prompting a deep dive into anything the internet had to offer about her. "I did my own research."

"So, *you* were stalking *me*," she teases with the accusation I leveled at her at my mother's house. Her eyebrows arch, highlighting her long eyelashes. She's so effortlessly beautiful.

"I'm considering you as my kids' nanny. It's only fair I learn more about you." I try to keep the mood light. At least, she's relaxed while I'm anything but. "We started off on the wrong foot. I'm sorry."

Now that wasn't nearly as hard as I expected.

Her eyes soften further. "Your apology is accepted."

I'd better clarify my intentions now. "I'd appreciate it if you would give us another chance. The boys are taken with you and hopeful you're coming back."

She shrugs. I'll take it as a cautious openness. "If I come back, we need to discuss some conditions."

"Okay, name them." I set my soda aside. I don't deserve the time she's offering me right now.

"I'll call you Grumps until you prove yourself a happier person."

The teasing glint in her eyes warms me. My lips curl, and a laugh escapes, freeing the tension from my muscles. "What's next? Don't tell me it involves having to laugh at your jokes?"

"You have to let me do my job without jumping in to criticize my every move."

"I can do that." I nod. "As long as you're not tying my kids up to a tree or something."

Her lips curl upward.

My stomach flutters again as the tension between us shifts into something lighter, more playful—more daunting. "Also, I don't know if my mom mentioned it, but the kids have spring break in three weeks—actually less than three weeks." I hope it works out for her schedule. "You'll need to stay in Meadowbrook that week."

"Yes, she told me." Valentina falls silent, perhaps weighing her decision.

"Great." I jump in before she decides to turn me down. "Are you free tomorrow? We could give you a tour of the kids' favorite spots in town, places you might want to take them during spring break."

"What time works for you?"

"Would one o'clock be too late, too early?" That should allow enough time in the morning to assist the widow with the tasks Ethan mentioned, followed by breakfast and a catch-up session with friends.

"Works fine." She gestures to my half-eaten plate. "You should finish your dinner."

I hate to waste food, but even without checking my watch, I know I'm pressed for time. "I need to go and get my kids."

Her expression softens. "How did their game go?"

Warmth floods my cheeks. She remembered? "Their team lost, but they had fun." I then thank her for signing up for snacks so I could contribute. "They emailed me a few times, but I kept forgetting to sign up."

She picks up her fork, seemingly embarrassed.

"And thanks for dinner." I reach for my bottle and take another sip. The mysterious drink isn't bad. It's been a while since I drank soda.

"Good to see you changed your mind about Tina." Everyone reemerges from the hallway and wherever they've been hiding. Paloma beams, her chest swelling. "We're all set, then?"

I nod and thank her for the delicious dinner. Then I stand with my half-empty plate and soda bottle.

"We'll put that away." Anna takes the plate and bottle.

Carlos shakes my hand. "I'm glad you and Tina worked things out."

"Me too."

When I say goodbye, Paloma insists I take some food for the kids and my mom. Then she saunters off to the kitchen, calling over her shoulder. "I made some empanadas earlier. They just need to be microwaved."

"They'll be okay." I try to decline politely.

"They haven't tried any of my food," she counters.

Valentina stands up and waves me off. "Save yourself the time arguing. She's not going to let you leave without food."

I give in. Minutes later, I follow her to the door, a bag of exotic food in my hand. I have no clue what empanadas are, but I'm looking forward to trying them. Mostly, I'm looking forward to deepening my connection with this family—especially Valentina.

CHAPTER 10

Jason

The scrimmage on the enclosed basketball court on Ethan's property feels like a clutch game, but it's just a casual Saturday with my friends.

"What time is she coming again?" Russ lobs the question as easily as he sinks a three-pointer.

"Close to one." My neutral tone masks my nerves. I catch the rebound and dribble toward Ethan, passing the ball and pushing thoughts of the nanny away.

Ethan catches my pass on a fast break. His pastor calm brings some perspective to our conversations. Russ, the tech-gadget guru, remains laid back, and Liam, with his architectural eye, adds structure to any chaos. All of us share the bond of single fatherhood, each story a unique play in the game of life.

The space reverberates with the squeals of our children beyond the court. Eden is on a hammock under a tree, lost in a book. My twins are teamed up in a spirited soccer match with friends.

A quick steal from Russ has me driving down the court, my dribbles echoing my racing heartbeat. My pass to Ethan is sloppy—too much spin.

Liam intercepts with an agile step. "Mate, you're off your game today." He dodges my attempt to reclaim the ball. His green eyes and sun-bleached hair glisten, giving away the Australian as a surfer transplant to New York.

Valentina's impending arrival sends another jolt through me, which allows Russ to snatch the pass intended for me, his long arms a clear advantage.

"We're going to lose!" Ethan shouts.

Shaking off the mix-up, I regain possession of my faculties and push the pace.

"What's the nanny's name again?" Liam tosses the question like a soft lob.

"Valentina." Ethan spins the ball at his fingertips, a mischievous glint in his brown eyes. "Did you tell them her name for you?"

My cheeks burn hotter than this game. "So much for pastor confidentiality," I grumble. Now's not the time to update them on our resolved understanding.

"Grumpy, is it?" Ethan throws a fake, his dimples sinking into his cheeks.

"She's going to be challenging." I steal the ball back and charge toward the basket. No one contests as I make an easy layup. "She's really outspoken." A smart-mouth.

Liam, now resting against the chain-link fence surrounding the court, smirks. "How did you convince her to stay after you'd fired her?"

"She fired herself." Not from the host position, but the nanny gig. I pass the ball to Ethan, who's ready to wind down. "She told me I can't boss her around and must let her do the job her way."

"She said that to you?" Ethan chortles, covering his laugh under his elbow.

"You just met your match, mate." Liam's smile broadens as he bobs his sun-damaged hair. "Do we get to meet her today?"

"Eventually." I scan the lane with its leafless trees. In a few weeks, the cherry blossoms will bloom. "She'll be driving past your place soon enough." Our little enclave—designed by Liam and including Ethan's farmhouse and my quiet spot—forms the end of the lane.

The game wraps up. "Daddy... Daddy!" Atticus beckons a change in play.

"Looks like I'm on football duty." I move toward the kids' enthusiastic chorus.

"I'm in," Liam calls out. "What these lads need is a bit of rugby."

While Liam joins the boys, I detour to Eden's hammock. I crouch beside her, tugging at her lopsided braid. "What are you reading, sweetheart?"

She ducks. "Daddy, you didn't do a good job braiding. Don't make it worse."

"I thought you didn't care how it turned out?"

She closes her book but keeps her thumb tucked between pages. "I just don't want it more out of place."

Her soft hair slips between my fingers as I tuck loose strands behind her ear. A swell of fatherly pride warms my chest. I've watched several how-to videos over the years whenever she wants me to braid her hair, but I've never mastered the skill.

"Your braiding's terrible." She shakes a finger at me. "That's why I only let you braid it when we're home."

"Smart girl." My little girl is growing up too fast. A chill grips me. I haven't prepared her to be a teen, but I don't know how. "Want to join us for football with your brothers?"

"Not after that earlier rugby game. Mr. Liam had us playing *forever*." Still, she smiles before returning to her book.

I used to read the same books alongside her, something we did together, but she's a more voracious reader than I can keep up with. Lately, spontaneous games with her seem to be slipping away. "We'll leave in ten minutes, okay?"

She nods, absorbed in her reading.

I leave her lost to her pages and join Liam on the grassy field. Still slightly gold, it already hints at the deep green it will soon display.

We engage in a game of touch football, the rules more relaxed.

"What happened to tackle football, eh?" Liam pants, dodging his six-year-old son in a mock sprint.

"Remind me how we hold the ball, Daddy." Atticus poses for a throw, his forehead shining from his efforts.

"Can we go home and play video games now?" Felix's shoulders drop in a dramatic sag. We're barely five minutes into the game. This kid and his video games!

"Let's enjoy this game for now." I nod.

Liam gives Felix a reassuring backslap to revive his spirits. "Maybe if we played real football."

"Real football it is, then." I switch gears to the more spirited game. We allow some mild tackles, and the kids' excitement level skyrockets, their laughter and shouts resounding now. I chase after Atticus and bring him gently to the ground, his squeals infectious, a perfect uplift on any given day.

"We have to get home and get ready for Valentina." I remind them as we stash the balls in the toy bin under the tree and say goodbye to our friends.

"I can't wait to play soccer with Val." Atticus's small legs match my stride on the smooth paved road as we head back to our house.

"I don't think she'll play today, kiddo." My mind drifts to the fluttery dress she wore while running barefoot in the yard. Of course, that was before she knew I'd be her boss. She's only coming to see the house and the town if she can stand my company long enough.

Felix chats up plans for his next video game conquest. Atticus lays out his intent to adopt a squirrel after one darts across the path. Eden walks beside me, her earlier engagement with her book still lingering in her subdued demeanor.

"What's the point of a nanny when you're going to fire her anyway?" Her serious question belies her age.

"Who said I'm going to fire her?" I pull her into a side hug as we walk. She's perhaps terrified of letting people in, afraid they won't stay. I don't blame her. We haven't had long-term constants in our lives, except my mom.

She rolls her eyes. "You always fire nannies."

With Mom's extended trip, the stability of a good nanny is a necessity. Unfortunately, no nanny has stuck around long enough to settle in. None make it past the chaos of a first weekend at Meadowbrook.

"I like Val." Felix kicks a twig along the path.

"Daddy is not going to fire Val," Atticus inserts.

I hadn't expected them to overhear my conversation with their sister.

We arrive at home, a long structure of natural fieldstone and gray siding. The annex where Mom stays when she visits connects to the house.

Inside, the living room is a battlefield of Nerf guns, toy cars, and scattered darts. I've lost the ongoing struggle to keep order in the house. I have so many other things to manage.

My shirt clings to me, and I feel sticky.

"I need to shower." I clap the way I do whenever I need to express urgency to the kids. "You guys should shower too."

Eden doesn't need further prompting. She's off to her room in an instant, likely to escape into solitude or her book.

"Can I play SteamRush first?" Felix tries his luck with a car-racing video game, already veering toward the living room.

"Shower first." I tip my head toward the hallway on the opposite side. The kids disperse, and I head to my bedroom, the first room in the hallway. Not until I strip off my clothes in the bathroom and step into the shower does my mind wander to our anticipated guest again. She's sharp, smart-mouthed, and keen to challenge me. But ultimately, it's all about the kids. Like Mom said, maybe this time, I can make it right for them.

The water cascades over me. I reflect on the chaotic stream of nannies these last months. If Valentina can handle our life, maybe she's the stability we need. I must give this my best for the kids' sake.

CHAPTER 11

Valentina

Gravel crunches under my tires as I navigate the bumpy country road. A rugged blue Chevy trundles ahead of me, setting a slow pace, but I'm not in a hurry—it's only twelve-twenty, and I should arrive in fifteen minutes according to my phone navigation. I take in the expansive lands and aged trees, their branches tipped with the first signs of budding leaves. The cattle mooing and horses enjoying the fields is refreshing.

Soon, I turn onto Renewed Lane and transition to a smooth pavement. To my right is a clean-cut, modern yet rugged two-story stone house with play swings in the yard. A man with sun-kissed hair scoops up a tricycle in one hand. He pauses, smiles, and waves. Every car I've passed in town, every home I've seen with people outside, I've been greeted with friendly waves and smiles—so different from the city.

Further down the road is another two-story home. The road then meanders through swatches of land boasting budding trees and patches of last year's leaves. I follow its curves past a charming two-story white farmhouse radiating a timeless nostalgia.

Near the end of the lane, my phone announces my destination across from the farmhouse. A sprawling single-story stone house with a three-car garage. I can already picture playing with the kids on the grass and planning summer picnics under the trees.

Excitement bubbles up. This setting is the change I need for a time. I park and take in the spacious yard and abandoned scooters.

As if he's aware of my arrival, the front door swings open, and Jason emerges. He's dressed in gray sweats, and a navy T-shirt clings to his broad shoulders. He seems at ease in his house shoes. His scowl and hooded look aren't welcoming. Yet when his gaze finds mine, my heart still stammers to a halt before racing.

He waves.

I manage a nod, then step out of the car.

"I see you found the way just fine."

"Following a truck going ten miles under the speed limit helped. Hard to get lost in a town this size, though one wrong turn and you're back where you started."

He chuckles, and my stomach somersaults. "That would be Chuck. You'll run into him from time to time."

I can leave my handbag in the car. This isn't Brooklyn where someone might break in if they spot any sign of valuables. I reach into the Civic's hatchback and pull out a duffel bag of my extra supplies. Bringing a few things on day one could make a solid impression.

Jason sprints over and grabs the bag. "You're just scoping out the place today, right?"

"Doesn't hurt to be prepared." I catch the end of the bag. "Got something in here for you." Best to hand it over now, away from curious little eyes that might wonder why I'm giving their dad presents.

I unzip the bag and pull out a clear box. His fragrance of eucalyptus and some fancy conditioner warms my senses. His hair, slightly damp, is subtly threaded with gray at the temples.

"I wasn't sure about your shirt size, but this should fit." I extend the shirt enclosed in a clear box toward him.

He takes it, his lips curling upward to soften his chiseled features. "My shirt didn't have smiling tacos and peppers." His words dissolve into laughter, and my heart feels lighter.

"You're a family TV company, right? It might come in handy for family events."

He shakes his head. Warmth flickers in his eyes. "I didn't expect you to replace my clothes. It was just coffee." His thick eyebrows lift in a playful arch. "Or was it intentional, Ms. Diaz?"

I suppress a smile. At least, he's taking it lightly. I shopped for today's attire from one of my cousins who sells specialized merch and couldn't resist the button-down.

I wave to the yard again. I love the mature, yet still bare trees. "This is beautiful. I like your town too."

"I'm glad you like it." He leads me along the path lined with budding and evergreen shrubs. "You'll be spending quite a bit of time here." His voice carries over his shoulder without him looking back. "Nice T-shirt, by the way."

"Thanks." I smooth a hand over my shirt to ensure it's on straight so the airplanes hover above the cars with the gaming console in between. "When I saw this, I just had to get it."

My Converse shoes pad the hardwood as I follow him inside and down the hallway. Frameless contemporary artwork tries to outdo the kids' drawings taped haphazardly around it. We emerge from the hallway into an expansive kitchen. I sidestep a basket filled with toy cars and airplanes next to a play carpet sprawled across the floor. Nerf darts and random toys scatter the area.

I had Grumps pegged as someone who maintained strict order, but if he allows such playful chaos, he might not be as uptight as I thought. Since the house isn't clean and he hasn't said anything about me taking off my shoes, I feel at ease keeping my Converse on.

He drops the bag in the kitchen, sets the shirt on the island next to a plate with a half-eaten slice of toast. Then his gaze wanders toward the living area. The house smells like cinnamon—a rare aroma in Brooklyn, but one that reminds me of apple cider.

Beyond the kitchen comes soft sounds from the TV, and as I crane toward the inviting plush sofas bathed in the generous light from large windows, two brown-haired heads peek out from behind a sofa.

"Guys, Valentina is here. Come on."

The way my name rolls off Grumps' tongue stirs my tummy into a flutter. It's the first time I've heard him say it so naturally, and it feels intimate.

One of the boys bursts from behind the sofa, grinning wide. I take a moment to identify which twin it is as I stride toward him and meet him halfway. "Atticus."

"Val!" he chirps.

"What have you been up to?" I lower myself to his level, expecting a high five, but he wraps me in a heartwarming hug.

He then steps back, eyeing my shirt. "You got airplanes in a video game?"

"I heard you and your brother talking about inventing a video game with airplanes."

"Don't encourage it." Jason's voice rasps from the kitchen. His features are soft, a stark contrast to his grumpy CEO persona. He lets out a chuckle. "The aviation part and car racing, yes—the video gaming, no."

"Let me show you my airport." Atticus's enthusiasm warms me as he shares stories about his setup, a birthday gift from his grandma. In the background, Jason nudges his other son to turn off his video game.

"But, Daddy, the remote died, and I didn't even play yet."

I cackle as I kneel on the hardwood floor, then wince when a figurine jabs me through my leggings. It's an ice cream figure. I place it on the make-believe airport's ice-cream shop. I drove past cute shops just like that. "It reminds me of your town."

"We'll take you to our favorite soda shop when we go into town." Atticus beams, adding another piece to his scene. "Can you play soccer with us today? And can we..." His words tumble out as he suggests all the things I can do with them today. My cheeks are already aching from smiling at his cuteness.

Trailing Jason, Felix joins us wearing a sullen expression. I rise to greet him with a high five. "Hi, bud."

"Hi." He slaps my hand weakly, apparently not happy about having to abandon his game.

"What's with the long face?"

Jason ruffles the boy's hair before Felix ducks. "Try pulling this one away from his video games." Jason then nods toward the hallway. "I'll fetch Eden."

To shift Felix's mood from digital discontent to real-world play, I stand and walk toward the kitchen. "I brought some equipment. Maybe we can hit the park later. It's nice out." Sunny and upper fifties.

"What did you bring?" Atticus hops up, darting to the bag.

"Is it kites?" Felix perks up, and they hover around me while I unzip the bag.

"Kites are a good idea." I'll have to bring some next time. Unsure of what Eden might enjoy, I tossed in an assortment of the sports equipment we keep around the house. Maybe something will stick.

"Check this out." Atticus pulls out a tennis racket, and I wonder aloud if there's a court nearby.

"We've never been to it." Jason calls from the left, Eden in tow. "But we have one in town."

"Daddy and his friends built one for the town," Atticus boasts. "You build?"

"If putting bunk beds together counts." Jason rubs the back of his neck. "Otherwise, by 'build,' the boys mean my friends and I contributed to the community for a tennis court."

"Hello, Eden." I wave, still unsure how to connect with this girl who offers a nod and a timid smile. Is she always this reserved? Her hair is tied in a crumpled braid. "I brought you some books."

Judy had said Eden was into all kinds of books. Perhaps this will give us a connection.

"They're in my handbag in the car. Preloved—favorites I clung to from my childhood."

Jason nudges Eden. "What do you say?"

"Thank you." A flicker brightens her blue eyes.

The boys dive into the bag, hauling out a volleyball net along with a jumble of other gear.

Their sister joins the fray and eagerly picks up a ball. "Volleyball?"

Her keen interest has me grinning.

"You really came prepared."

That sounds like Grumps' approval. My gaze rises to meet his ocean-blue eyes. I place a hand on my hip for support after all the bending and sorting. "I didn't mean to create such a commotion."

"Welcome to my world. It's all competition around here."

He's probably only this nice around his kids. Struggling to hold his gaze, I let mine drift to the colorful artwork magnetized on the fridge.

"Want a tour of the house?" His arm sweeps to gesture to the hallway, so I follow as he leads. A ball whizzes.

"No kicking balls in the house, guys," Jason says.

We stride along, and their gleeful laughter fades behind us. His presence looms at my side. Our interaction, once strained, now flows into an uneasy normalcy. We pass open and closed doors, our footsteps resonating off the polished hardwood floors.

"How was traffic?" He must sense the awkwardness, hence slicing it with a question he could've asked earlier.

"Your town has more traffic than Manhattan."

"Is that so?" He shoots me a sideways glance, and I chuckle when he seems to get my joke.

At the end of the corridor, we enter a spacious room bathed in daylight from a large window. He gestures toward the scattered toys. The shelves brimming with books overlook the disarray. "This is where the kids play if we're home long enough. The boys spend a lot of their time here, as you can see."

I'll have to introduce some chore charts. I move to the window, the woods visible beyond the enclosed structure at the far end of the yard. I shade my eyes to assess the gate and leafless shrubs. "You guys have a pool?"

He nods. "I usually open it in mid-April. Heated and enclosed, it serves as a communal gathering spot for our friends and their families on Renewed Lane." He hooks his hands in his slacks pockets. "You'll find each house boasts a different recreational feature. One has a basketball court, and..." He lists the amenities at different homes. "Should you be here when the pool opens, the kids aren't allowed in the deep end."

I pick up a stray toy and toss it into a bin. There are way too many Legos strewn across a table and the floor. I'll have the boys clean it during their break. Poor Eden couldn't even read in this room if she wanted to cuddle up in the plush pink chair in the corner.

"How deep is the pool?"

"Three feet at the shallow side. Nine at the deep end."

"Do they swim with you?" Perhaps I could foster their confidence in the water. "I was a part-time swim instructor in high school when I wasn't nannying."

He gives me a look—pure contemplation, maybe even a silent challenge against any contradiction.

I meet him head-on. Somehow, I keep my hands from gripping my hips and my stance from widening with my challenge. "Don't you think it's better to teach your kids to swim safely under your supervision rather than keeping them out?"

His lips part as if to counter. Then he closes them and leads me back to the hallway. "All the rooms are on this floor."

Judy had mentioned he'd had his house custom-built. "Why didn't you add an upstairs?"

"I wanted to be on the same level as the kids. When the boys were little, I didn't want them falling down the stairs—too risky."

Who'd have thought Grumps had such a protective nature? I bite at my lower lip to keep a grin from spreading. He shows me a smaller room with a desk and computer. Books clutter two shelves. "If you ever feel like reading away from your room, feel free to utilize this space."

"It's your office?"

"I try not to work from home. If I do, though, and don't feel like working in my bedroom, this is an option."

We walk past a couple of bedrooms, stopping at Eden's room. Subtle pink walls form a backdrop to a bed laid neatly with fluffy hot-pink pillows and cover. At the next room, I reach for the knob of a partially open door, revealing two unkempt beds and a tangled mess of shoes and clothes. Aviation and spaceship posters overlook one bed while race cars appear ready to zoom off the posters above the other. "Wild guess. Boys' room?"

He ducks his head, gripping the back of his neck again. "The house cleaner comes once a week to help tidy up. And to shop if you need any groceries."

"I don't mind shopping for myself."

We pass more rooms, and I inspect any photos I see. They're mostly of the kids. I don't see any pictures of their mother or Jason. Judy's photo is nestled among them, the only adult captured under glass.

"That used to be Felix's room." He points when we pass another room. "But he wanted to bunk with his brother."

"That makes sense." They probably find comfort in each other's proximity.

He then gestures to a room near the start of the hallway, close to the kitchen. His room. He doesn't open the door. Instead, he moves across the hall and swings open another door. "This will be your bedroom. It's the only spare room with an *en suite*."

It's far too close to his room. He seems to catch my hesitation. "My mom usually stays in the annex, and she has her things there, but maybe you can switch?"

"This will be fine." I'd rather not disrupt their arrangements. I'm only here temporarily. It's not like this is where I belong.

"Or you could use one of the other rooms without a bathroom or even the living space in the basement."

"This room will be fine." I swallow whatever doubts I have. At least it has a bathroom, and we can avoid bumping into each other as we enter and exit our respective bedrooms.

CHAPTER 12

Valentina

When we head back, the kids have vanished from sight, but their voices drift in through the kitchen window.

He slides open a patio door. "The backyard. I'll show you the basement when we come back in."

My smile broadens as the boys struggle to set up the volleyball net, their sister helping.

"Val, can you show us how to play this game?" one of the boys calls out.

"Volleyball," Eden corrects.

"Of course." I nod.

"Let me first show Valentina around real quick." Jason waves his kids away, guiding me closer. "There's a trail in case you want to bike into town."

"Can we bike into town?" Atticus bounds over.

"Not yet." Jason starts across the pebbled walkway.

As we cross the open space, water trickles.

"Is that a stream?"

"It's a brook," one of the kids shouts. Apparently, they've abandoned their setup to trail us.

A boardwalk crosses it. The creek's wide calm waters and rocky edges reminds me of a family camping trip with our outdoorsy friends. I pick up a few flat stones. "Do you guys ever skip rocks?"

"How do you skip rocks?" Eden asks, and the boys edge closer to gather their own stones.

I flick one sideways through the air, and it skips across the water. "That's how you skip a rock."

"Show me, show me!" The boys bounce out excitement, skipping around much like that stone.

"Your dad can show you." I don't want to overstep.

But Jason shakes his head. "I've never tried that."

I wouldn't know either if I hadn't gone camping for years. I help them find smooth flat rocks and demonstrate the flick of the wrist required for skipping rocks. It turns into a playful lesson. Eden flashes a shy smile as her stone does several jumps over the water.

"Your turn, Grumps," I encourage when his kids plead with him to join in.

He picks up a stone and gives it a go. It barely hops once before sinking. Rubbing his hands together, he calls it quits.

"You should try again."

He rolls his eyes. "I didn't realize we were having a competition."

"We could turn it into a competition if you'd like." I laugh, grateful he hasn't really shown his grumpy side today.

With the kids skipping rocks, he tries a few more times. He's a pro by the time we're finished, though I tell them the actual world's record is 88 skips.

We continue walking along the bridge, and he points out the way into town. "The road will deposit you behind the library parking lot, and you can't miss Main Street from there."

We make our way back, and the kids dart ahead. The boys dangle off nearby pine branches.

"What did I say about climbing trees?" Jason demands.

"Don't you think it's best to let them climb in your presence? That way you can teach them the right way rather than keeping them off it."

"And you know this how?" He raises his eyebrow.

"I was once a kid." I tug at a flimsy tall shrub along the edge. "I'm not convinced, but you might even have been a kid too."

"Miss Know-It-All."

At least Grumps' tone is light.

Shifting my focus once we're back in the yard, I offer to help Eden who's fiddling with the volleyball net. It's a portable net with adjustable-height aluminum poles, which makes setup and storage easier.

"Have you played volleyball before?" I inquire to engage her.

"There's no time for volleyball." She scowls and kicks at a clump of grass. "We're always away commuting to and from school. I don't even know how I get time for dance."

"We'll play some volleyball during spring break—and today, of course."

Her shy smile rewards me.

Soon enough, we're all caught up in volleyball. I show them imaginary court lines, net, and where players typically stand. Using the ball, I demonstrate the correct stance—feet shoulder-width apart, knees slightly bent, hands together. As Jason leans against the tree, I have the kids practice the motion without the ball first, then use the ball to bump back and forth with Eden helping.

The boys, eager to get the game rolling, soon start kicking the ball, playing soccer instead.

I invite Jason to join us, and like the competitor he seems to be, he splits us into two teams. "Boys against girls."

"You're sure about that?" I eye his teammates, who now are chasing each other in a game of tag.

"Afraid of a little competition?" he challenges, then summons his boys.

"Dad, Val and I are going to take you boys down." Eden swings the ball, practicing the basic skill of serving. Wow, that girl is a fast learner.

Jason gets into the game, anchoring his sons' efforts.

"You sure you don't want Eden to rescue your team?" I taunt between volleys.

He leaps for the ball when Atticus kicks it instead. Then Jason laughs, wiping sweat from his brow. "We're managing just fine."

The banter continues.

"Dad," Eden chimes in. "If us girls win, you gotta let us all have ice cream for breakfast tomorrow."

"And if the boys win?" Jason attempts a serve. The ball lands on the grass at his feet, and Felix kicks it.

She snorts. "You know you won't win, Daddy!"

The game blurs the lines between competition and camaraderie, making for a spirited afternoon. By the time we finish, the kids declare they're starving.

Jason suggests I join them for an early dinner. "It'll give you an opportunity to explore the town and meet some of the locals you'll soon become familiar with."

"I can't refuse." I'm also curious about this slice of small-town life.

Inside Brook's Diner, Grumps appears more relaxed and genuine compared to his urban persona. The cozy setting with its cutesy vintage posters brings out a different side of him as he chats with locals and calls them by name. A friendly server gives the boys crayons and coloring pages, and they settle into their seats. Eden opens a book but closes it long enough to order chicken tenders while the rest of us order burgers.

"You should try their fried pickles." Jason nods at me across the table. Before I say otherwise, he tells the server to add the pickles to our food. "You can try and see if you like them."

Fried pickles? My stomach curdles. "I can't wait."

"Who wants a soda?" he calls out as he heads across the room, drawing giggles from his children. Grinning, he makes a show of operating the vintage soda machine. He exaggerates his playful movements when the kids come over and drop in coins as he twists the handle.

Once the machine dispenses sodas and each kid has retrieved their drink, he beckons me over. "Want to try operating the machine?"

"I wouldn't do any better than you."

He still hands me coins from his pockets, and I slide them into the slot. With dramatic effects, he spins the handle. His smile, so sincere and unhurried, warms my heart.

We walk back to our table. I twist my grip, the condensation from the soda can cool in my hands. "You're a natural here."

"It's a nice change from the city's constant rush."

This relaxed version of Jason is the kind I want to see every day. But how long before Grumps reemerges?

CHAPTER 13

Valentina

My first day with a new family always feels like a new start. Despite my experience, each family introduces unique dynamics. With Jason Sterling's family, I still have to win him and his daughter over.

My stomach tightens as I close the car door and wave to Matthew. I glimpse the boys through the tinted windows as the chauffeur pulls away. Eden stands beside me on the sidewalk in the gray leotard and the hot-pink skirt I gifted her.

"We're earlier than usual." Her skirt sways as we head toward the old brick building. She's pulled her hair into a loose ponytail.

My fingers itch to gather it into the sleek style I assume dancers wear. But we're not at that touchy-feely stage yet.

"I didn't want to risk being late on my first day." I adjust my handbag and guide her toward the ramp. We don't need to take the ramp, but we have fifteen minutes to spare. "Maybe we can wait inside if they've opened the doors early."

Afternoon traffic murmurs beside us.

"Remind me what kind of dance is it again?"

Eden shrugs. "Pop. I've been dancing since I was five, maybe four? It was Mom's idea." She winces, then stiffens her shoulders. "Dad still thinks it's my favorite thing to do."

"You don't want to continue?"

"There's no time for me to try anything else."

"Have you told your dad you'd like to try something new?"

"It's fine." She hurries toward the metal double doors.

In my short time around Jason, he's proven himself a dedicated father who would do anything for his children—even hire me. I stride forward and pull open one of the heavy doors. At least, it's unlocked.

Inside, the smells of an old building and floor polish tints the air. The space resembles a hall, its walls painted off-white. Metal folding chairs stand stacked in a tall pile to one side. In the center, about fifteen chairs form three rows, each set a considerable distance from an elevated stage where thick curtains drape the sides. Someone on the platform tinkers with a stereo.

She pivots and waves. "Hello, Eden. You're early today."

Eden nods and half smiles when she looks at me.

Scrambling through my purse for something to pass the time with Eden—a phone or book?—I find nothing.

"This is where you'll sit if you want to wait." Eden gestures to the empty chairs. "Though very few parents stay for practice."

I sit in the front row and pat the chair next to me for her to join me until more students arrive. Maybe I can learn more about her. "What have you read recently?"

"I finished *Wind in the Willows* at school. I'm going to start reading one of the books you gave me next."

"When you finish the first three books, maybe we can binge the movies."

"I'd like that." She swings her feet, and her black dance shoes scuffle the polished floor. "Where do we find the Chronicles of Narnia movies, though?"

"Leave that to me." I continue with random questions. Apparently, she has a couple of friends at school, but they are as busy as she is with after-school activities and live too far from Meadowbrook for a weekend playdate.

Other students trickle in.

She stands and slants me a look. "You know you didn't have to come."

"I might not be a dancer, but I enjoy watching."

"Okay." She pivots to follow other girls and boys onto the stage. Her ponytail flips over one shoulder.

The instructor engages the students. Then Meghan Trainor's "Better When I'm Dancing" energizes the room, and the students spread out to begin their routines.

Eden moves with fluid grace. Despite her expressionless face, her movements convey joy and freedom. Absorbed in the scene, I don't notice the parents behind me until I hear their chatter.

I crane my neck and spot two elegant women deep in conversation. On the back row, three more women sit spaced apart from each other, each engrossed in their thoughts or devices.

The studio's atmosphere transitions to a quieter, more reflective mood with a slower melody, highlighting Eden's graceful movements and flexibility. Out of the corner of my eye, I see someone walking toward the seating area. I turn.

It's not just anyone—it's Grumps.

All heads must be turning toward him. If the dance instructor's pause to glance his way isn't indication enough, the subtle shift in the room's focus confirms it.

This powerful aura surrounds him, and I can't help but look his way. His straight posture and strong squared jaw command attention. He forks his fingers through his dark-brown hair, short on the back and sides but showing more length to the top. Although rumpled, it still looks right.

My heart stutters, ramping up as whispers flutter behind me:

"Speaking of handsome men."

"I've never seen his wife here before."

If they've seen him enough to comment on that, then he must come to his daughter's practices fairly often.

His gaze lands on the stage, his face softens, and his chest puffs out. Eden seems to spot her dad, and that oh-so-sweet shy smile tips her mouth. I peek behind me again. He's smiling the genuine smile he seems to reserve for his children alone.

When he moves to sit, he notices me, and his expression falters. His stare is potent, holding my attention, and the heat of it tingles along my skin. Electricity bounces between us, even as I refocus on the stage.

Despite the availability of empty seats, he settles into one beside me. The faint scent of eucalyptus and an expensive cologne wafts off him, and the scent warms me to the core.

He's the definition of off-limits, everything I should avoid. Yet, my pulse dances wildly under my skin. Handsome men are no strangers in my life. So why does Jason stand apart, a thrilling and terrifying presence?

He's not the hero from a fairy tale, not with those eyes that know too much sorrow and hide fear perhaps. And, if I learned anything from Austin, it's never to let myself get carried away. Falling in love for me again would be getting carried away.

"You're supposed to be with the boys." The music barely veils his scold.

I glance at him before refocusing on the stage. "How are you today?"

I'd expected him to ask how my first day on the job is going. But I shouldn't push my luck with this grump. "Matthew is with the boys at their practice." I try to ignore the tension Jason brings with him. "I didn't know you'd come. Thought Eden could use the company."

"Matthew's not supposed to watch the boys during soccer."

"He didn't mind." I'm striving for calm the way a counselor would.

"I don't care whether he minds or not," he retorts.

It takes all my willpower not to turn and give him my fiercest glare. "Matthew has been working with you for four years now? If your mom trusts him with your kids, I figured you'd trust him too."

"You asked my mom's permission?"

That's it. I foist off a controlled smile. "She hired me."

His jaw clenches. "From now on, communication needs to be between us, not through my mom. She isn't babysitting the kids anymore."

I hold his gaze, and we stare at each other.

I might explode from internal turmoil. Still, no way am I letting him think he can bark at me whenever he feels like it. The air between us crackles with unsaid words.

"Do I make sense?" This time, his voice is a hushed whisper, and a slight softness glosses his eyes.

This man... Well, thankfully, he doesn't make falling for him easy. The urge to unleash every pent-up thought gnaws at me. I hold back and speak through gritted teeth. "Point noted."

Seething, I'm tempted to bolt and hail a taxi. But I can't afford to leave such an impression. I'm here for Eden, so I won't storm off midperformance.

His stomach rumbles.

On instinct, I reach into my purse for an energy bar and pass it to him.

He shakes his head. "No thanks."

We sink into a strained silence. "Rewrite the Stars" starts. I recognize it from one of my favorite movies. The words remind me of Mami telling me I can rewrite our family history of unstable relationships. She's wrong, though. I'm not going to be the one breaking our pattern.

The kids sweep across the stage. Eden is radiant when she looks at us and especially at her dad before slipping back into her routine. Despite the frost between us, I'm aware of Jason's nearness. This warmth he radiates affects me more than I care to admit.

His stomach growls again, and I shove an energy bar onto his lap.

"Jason," a woman calls from behind us. She waves when he turns around. "I'm Liz. Remember me?"

"Nope."

With his curt response, I focus on the stage. I have no need to see how Jason handles the flirtation.

The woman persists. "Are you usually here once a week? I mean, I don't come as often, but... I've seen you a few times."

"I don't keep track of how often I'm here."

Jason dismisses her with terse disinterest. Then a wrapper crinkles. Ha! He's tearing open the energy bar and biting into it. His intense focus, whether from disinterest or just his nature, rebuffs the woman.

Soon, his thumbs begins moving on his phone, perhaps texting or emailing.

The dance session ends. Jason stands and meets his daughter halfway as the kids leave the stage. He puts out his arms for a hug. Eden looks around, clearly shy, and goes for a quick side embrace. Perhaps she's getting to that age of not wanting affection in front of her peers. Mom never dropped us off at school or activities. We took the bus, so I never faced those moments of hugging a parent in public.

We step aside so people can pass, but Eden jitters in place. She unfolds a flyer about the end-of-year performance.

"Wow!" Jason glances at the paper. "You get to make introductions?"

"They forced all of us to audition." Her face falls. Apparently, her dad's more excited than she is.

"That means you had the best presentation." He scoops her into another side embrace.

I brave tapping her hand. "If you can dance the way you do, then introductions should be a walkover."

Her face softens, and her chin rises. "Thanks for coming."

"I know how hard dancing can be."

Parents and kids swirl around us.

"You danced before?" Jason arches a brow.

"And it went down in the books as a spectacular failure," I quip. "Nerves had me tumbling headfirst during my first performance."

Eden laughs, and I even catch Jason's fleeting smile.

As we leave, he mentions his earlier text to Matthew to bring the boys straight home after soccer. "You and Edie can ride with me."

"Aren't you going back to work?" She grips his hand.

"I thought we'd get home early tonight." He bends to her level. His tenderness belies his gruffness with me. Then at his SUV, he opens the passenger door, and the gentlemanly act surprises me. Maybe there's more to him than his stern façade.

He reaches back and opens the door for Eden. That softness in his movements seems reserved just for her. Once he slides into his seat, he peers over his shoulder before he backs out and starts driving. "How was school today, Edie?"

"Same as usual. Mom's coming to Meadowbrook on spring break."

"Your mom told you that?" Why does he sound so skeptical? His whole body seems to stiffen as he weaves through traffic. Even his knuckles whiten on the steering wheel.

"She texted." Through the mirror, I glimpse Eden checking her phone as if making sure she got it right. "She'll come any day during our break."

"Of course she texted." Jason seethes under his breath. His chest heaves, and his jaw clenches as if he's battling with something internal. "I just don't want you to..."

Clearly, his relationship with his ex is strained. Does he still love her? Not my business, but the unsettling of my stomach says otherwise.

For a while, the only sound is the SUV's steady thrum and the city's distant buzz.

Then he draws out a breath and shifts the conversation to me. "Will it still work out for you to come by on Sunday?"

"I'm planning on it." Judy walked me through the house routine earlier today while I helped with laundry and other chores as she prepared for her trip. Although I'd thought I might stay every weekend in Meadowbrook, it seems I'm not needed unless specifically requested.

When we pull up to the house, I'm ready to make a quick exit, but Eden scooches forward in her seat and blinks shy-eyed at me. "Are you staying for dinner?"

And there I am, caught between my desire to leave and my fear to disappoint her.

Then Jason nods. "The kids will love it if you stay."

His neutral voice says I need to remember our original arrangement.

Right, I'm here for the children, not for any personal entanglements. Maintaining this boundary helps me focus. Jason Sterling is off-limits. If we can reach a cordial understanding, that will do.

CHAPTER 14

Valentina

The cool evening breeze brushes against my cheeks as we step into Central Park. The smell of fresh-cut grass and distant popcorn wafts through the air. It's my fourth day at work, and already, Eden, Atticus, and Felix are weaving into my heart. They don't have any after-school activities, so we have enough time to spend an afternoon together before I fulfill my weekly volunteer commitment at Lstars School this evening.

"Race you to the big oak!" Atticus, ever the enthusiast for anything that involves rapid velocity, challenges his siblings. He's off before I can blink. His feet pound the path, kicking up the earthy smell of disturbed soil.

Felix, who always prefers to discuss his next game invention or to race cars on-screen rather than race himself, surprises me by joining the chase, his laughter bouncing along behind him. "Wait up!" he shouts, not quite as swift but every bit as spirited.

Eden hangs back, her arms crossed. She's hit that age where enthusiasm battles the need to appear uninterested.

"Not a fan of racing today?" I nudge her elbow.

She shrugs. "Maybe I'll just watch."

"How about we find a good spot to sit? You can judge who touches the tree first." At her nod, we make our way to a nearby bench.

As we settle, her gaze follows her brothers, and her lips curve. "Atticus thinks he's a jet."

"Yeah. He has more energy than all of us." When he narrowly beats Felix to the oak tree, I clap. "And Felix isn't far behind. Looks like his gaming skills are translating to speed."

Eden laughs, the sound clear and carefree, a rarity for her. "He's lucky I didn't run. I'd win for sure."

I laugh with her, grateful for the moment of connection. "Next time, you'll have to prove it."

"Maybe."

The setting sun casts a golden glow over Central Park, illuminating playing children, bikers, and walkers. Signs of spring abound among the budding trees and almost green grass.

The boys jog back, faces flushed.

"Did you see that? I was superfast!" Atticus beams, and a fist pump expresses his excitement.

"You were like a rocket." I put up my palm for his high five, then do the same for Felix's. "And you were right on his tail. Impressive!"

Felix's eyes light up. "Next time, I'll beat him."

We play five hundred next, a game I introduce to the kids using the football I brought along. Intrigued, even Eden wants to play. But it doesn't seem I'm holding the football right based on Atticus.

"Daddy says your hand should form a *V* when you hold the ball." He uses his hands to show me how I should grip the ball.

Then Eden and Felix chime in to guide me on my stance and hold, and I end up learning more about football basics from the kids than they do from me. At last, I glance at my phone. "Yikes, guys, it's almost six, and I need to be at the middle school by seven-fifteen." It's my last night for ESL this season.

They groan, not ready to let me cut our fun short.

"How about we grab some ice cream on the way home?"

"Sounds good to me." Eden shrugs, and the boys sprint ahead.

"Can we get different flavors?" Atticus asks as we exit the park.

"Of course. You guys can pick your flavors."

At the stand, the kids take their time with their choices. Once everyone is happy with sprinkle-filled ice-cream cones, we walk home. Their laughter and the distant strumming of a street musician create a melody sweet to my ears.

I use this time of closeness to mention chore charts. When they ask what they are, I explain. "We'll make some during your spring break."

The kids lick their ice-cream cones as we stroll. The boys' faces are a sticky mess, but they need to shower soon anyway. I like that we can walk to the park and shops and restaurants here. Not that I can afford to shop here, but seeing small businesses thriving fascinates me.

A tap on my fingers pulls me back, and when I look down, it's Eden's pinkie. Her linking her pinkie to mine feels like a victory. Maybe, just maybe, I'm starting to fit into their world, not just as a caregiver, but as someone they could trust and enjoy having around. The thought warms me more than the setting sun, promising more shared smiles and park walks in the days to come.

That's how the following week unfolds. On days when the boys don't have soccer practice and Eden doesn't have dance, they prefer going to the park. I try not to make ice cream before dinner a habit, especially after hearing an earful from Jason last Thursday when Atticus said he'd eaten ice cream and wasn't hungry.

We fill our time with games, first practicing how to hold a volleyball at Eden's request and then playing soccer and football with the boys. They've sure got an impressive understanding of football!

My second week wraps up at the boys' soccer game on Friday night. Saying goodbye to them until Sunday saddens me. It seems they feel the same. Atticus clings to one arm and Felix to the other, both pleading with me to join them for the night in Meadowbrook.

I haven't stayed the night in Meadowbrook yet. I could've last Sunday. But after watching the kids while Jason and his friends gathered for guy time, I returned to Brooklyn to see my nephews. That was the only evening their mom was in town for Carlos to see them.

Plus, Judy and Phil just spent time in the quaint town with their grandchildren before leaving on their long vacation.

"We'll see her on Sunday." Jason assures them as I slide into the taxi parked in front of Judy's Manhattan house. While Jason and I haven't sat down to talk since that day in the studio, we tolerate each other. At least, that's my hope. It's hard to tell with him. One minute, he's smiling and watching me play with the kids in the backyard—the next, he's moody and brooding. Like two days ago when I was about to leave after taking a glass of water to Judy.

We collided in the kitchen doorway—me stepping out, him stepping in. In our clumsy dance to avoid each other, my water ended up on his shirt.

"What's with your clumsiness?" he seethed.

Intoxicated by his scent, I forgot my blunder and teased, "Takes a klutz to know one, Grumps."

We survived that mishap. We can survive whatever else happens.

Either way, I'm looking forward to spending more time with the kids in their small town.

***

Jason

Sunday afternoon gatherings are hit or miss with friends, depending on how we each handle our chaotic parenting schedules. It's always a highlight when we can make it happen.

I'm settled into a lawn chair. A chilly breeze sweeps over the flickering campfire in the open space by the road and carries the kids' laughter from behind us.

Closer to my house, Valentina has become the focus, blowing bubbles that drift like dreams until eager hands pop them. The children surround her, their happiness evident with each bubble they burst.

"What happened to the cheese dogs I brought?" Russ's voice cuts through my thoughts, and I wave him off.

It was chaotic when he dropped off his contribution—minutes before Valentina arrived. I even attempted picking up the kids' toys from the kitchen and living room so it would look cleaner than the last two times she came over.

"You should be glad to eat whatever you're handed." I sink my teeth into a hamburger with a satisfying crunch of lettuce.

"I see you didn't turn this into charcoal this time." Ethan holds up his burger, his smirk directed at Russ.

"The flames got out of hand last week." Russ shifts in his chair, his long legs too close to the fire ring. I remind him of his near disaster with the steaks last month.

"I'm just glad we have Valentina watching the kids today." Liam bites into his hot dog. His superhero cape from entertaining the kids earlier still drapes his shoulders. "I can eat this in one go without having to stop for a rescue mission."

I lean back. The cold water bottle in my grip offers a mild relief from the fire's residual heat.

Across the lawn, Valentina commands the kids' attention with the ease of a seasoned entertainer. Something about her just draws them in—like iron to a magnet. Normally, one of my friends' nannies would be handling this, rotating each Sunday. But last Sunday and today with Valentina present, it's only fair to have my nanny help out. After all, I never actually had one, except for when Mom and Phil stayed the weekend and helped.

Valentina is now settled on the grass. A toddler content in her lap, she applies bug repellant to another. Something tugs inside me over how attuned she is to the kids' needs. Even Eden, who's been keeping one eye on her phone for a call from her mother that I doubt will come, seems drawn into the scene, distracted for a few hours.

My friends' voices float in the background, but my focus is on Valentina.

She springs into action, comforting a little one who tripped in their eager play. Her laughter rings out when another child taps her head.

Without realizing it, I've let a smile form on my lips.

My boys haven't stopped talking about her for days. On our drives to or from Manhattan, her name always comes up.

Eden hasn't shown much emotion. But she's been adamant about wanting Valentina to join us for dinners at my mom's house before leaving for the day.

I've taken a different approach—acting gruff to keep things professional. It might come off as rude, but I'm still figuring out how to act around her. And I doubt I'm handling the delicate balance well, caught between admiration and the need to maintain distance.

"She's got a way with them, hasn't she, Jason?"

I nearly jump in my seat. Across from me, Ethan's grinning. My cheeks warm—and not from the fire's glow. I divert my gaze to my plate and snatch up my half-eaten hamburger, taking another defensive bite. But then I catch Liam observing Valentina too. His admiring gaze stirs uneasy feelings.

"If things don't work out with your nanny, she might be the perfect backup for my family," Russ comments from my other side. He eyes me for a reaction before he takes a hefty bite from his second burger.

"She's made it through the second week and is starting week three. Trial phase is over, no?" Ethan tosses his empty plate into the flames.

I feign indifference and throw my paper plate onto the flaming log while holding my burger. "The kids need her for now." I might as well be speaking to myself as I eat the rest of my hamburger. Mom will be back soon, and Valentina will return to her other gigs—perhaps even land a position with a more prestigious broadcast than Family Sphere, where leaders don't cook up lame excuses not to hire her.

"She's not just good with the kids, mate. She's easy on the eyes too, eh?" Liam elbows Ethan.

Ethan, our peacemaker and philosopher, merely smiles and shakes his head, then sends me a knowing look. "That goes along with our lesson about the rose."

"Which lesson are we talking about?" Russ leans in as Liam reminds him of our dodgeball get-together last Sunday when Ethan spoke about the nature of a rose, among the many quotes he analyzes about roses.

"To add to Liam's response"—Ethan wags a finger at me—"sometimes we only see a rose for its thorns. But each rose has its unique beauty, protected and waiting for the right person to appreciate it."

"I can't remember why you like using all those rose analogies." I fold my arms, amused by his practical examples. Besides his obvious lesson last week during our game, he's been weaving rose metaphors into conversations so often I've lost track of when he started.

He shrugs. "We can talk more about it next Sunday."

My gaze flickers to the fire. The flames twist and writhe, and his analogy strikes deeper this time. Valentina and I had a rocky start. Now, watching her kindness and patience with the children—a trait I sometimes find in short supply—I'm forced to question my initial judgments.

"Besides your mom, you haven't had any woman or outsider in your house," Liam states. "Does it make you a tad anxious to have Val here?"

"Liam!" Ethan scolds. "Let's not make any assumptions."

"I've seen beautiful women before if that's what you mean." No reason to admit I never had one work this close to me.

But Liam's unfinished question lingers, unnervingly accurate. I hadn't considered the implications when I assigned Valentina the room across from mine. The thought of our paths crossing more intimately hadn't entered my mind. My body tenses.

Russ must've noticed. He claps a reassuring hand on my shoulder. "Don't stress over it, man. She's a catch, but she's here for the kids."

"Yeah." I manage a half smile as the children gather around her for a group hug. "For the kids," I echo, more to myself, willing my brain to align with my words.

"Plus, Valentina isn't Jason's type," Ethan adds as if reading my mind.

"And who's his type again?" Liam smirks, his green eyes glinting. "Never met your ex to know what type you date."

Dread grips me. "Never going back to dating again." My type, if I were to consider it, would be someone settled, not still chasing a career.

"Never say never." Ethan arches an eyebrow, ever the optimist.

The responsibilities as a father anchor my response. "My kids can't be put through that again."

Risking another person walking out of their lives is unbearable. Sure, I sometimes long for companionship, for someone to come home to and cuddle with on the sofa as we talk about our day. Someone to love and to let me experience their love, but that's hard to find.

Plus, my desires are secondary. My kids come first, always. I sit up straighter, but the fire crackling its warmth is a stark contrast to the chill of my resolve.

CHAPTER 15

Jason

Long after everyone's left and gone to sleep, Liam's question about whether Valentina's proximity makes me anxious haunts me. In the dark room, I toss and turn. Besides my mom and then Phil, no outsider has ever stayed in my house. With Valentina here, I sense another presence—like sensing a shadow through a closed door.

Liam's casual inquiry now has me imagining a series of potentially awkward encounters. We could bump into each other in the kitchen or cross paths in the hallway. But it's just a few weeks, right? She's staying each night temporarily, and given how our interactions have gone, she isn't my biggest fan. Maybe she'll be the one steering clear of me.

That's right. We don't get along. Or so I keep telling myself. She still calls me Grumps now and then. It's easier to maintain this grumpy façade and appear disinterested. But then a reluctant smile tugs at my mouth thinking about the funny shirt she gave me with its smiley tacos and peppers. She has a sense of humor. That much is clear.

And then the granola bar at Eden's dance studio. Despite my less-than-welcoming demeanor, she heard my stomach's betraying growls and offered sustenance. And that fire in her eyes during our unintentional staring contest hasn't faded from my memory. It was considerate of her to watch Eden dance. My daughter appreciated it.

Evenings at my mom's have taken on a new dimension. Mom was serious when she declared she was stepping down from nannying. She insisted Valentina stay until I returned from work. Now, the kids want Valentina to eat with us every day. I've ended up seeing a lot more of her than I anticipated, and it's altering my comfortably single lifestyle.

I find myself stealing glances, awkwardly maneuvering around her in the kitchen. Our recent run-in sends tingles down my spine—the heat that flared between us in the kitchen when she came too close and her water spilled on me, a spill I needed to help cool off the intense warmth. Instead of handling it smoothly, I barked at her, calling her clumsy.

Not that she didn't hold her own right back. I smirk.

My annoyance and admiration conflict. Yes, I fear Valentina. With the prod of good intentions, she could chip away at the walls I've built around myself and my family. My defensiveness is about my fears of letting someone new into our lives, isn't it?

I shift to my side, my thoughts drifting to Daisy. My insistence on having more kids drove us apart. She was content with Eden, but I wanted more. Then she left not long after the twins were born. Now, she's toying with Eden's emotions. I have to assume she loves her children, but doesn't she feel anything with regards to the promises she fails to keep?

Thankfully, the boys don't ask about her as much as Eden does.

Although I manage to drift off for a bit, sleep then escapes me again. Now, it's after four-thirty. My day usually starts an hour from now with a morning workout.

I stretch out from under the covers, resigned to my wakefulness—not the best way to start a Monday.

Doesn't help that Daisy is supposed to visit today—a promise so frequently broken that each missed visit erodes more of Eden's hope. I'll stay home today to console my daughter if or when disappointment strikes. But will that be enough? If only there were words to assure her that, even if I'm not the perfect parent, I'm here for her and always striving to be the best dad I can be for her.

To burn off restless energy, I rise at five. I swing my legs out of bed and trade my gray pajamas for workout shorts and a muscle shirt.

As I open my bedroom door, I pause, my gaze falling on Valentina's closed door across the hall.

There's an undeniable undercurrent I'm determined to ignore. After the way things ended with Daisy, falling in love again is a door I can't afford to open—not with my children's hearts and my own fragile balance on the line.

Drawing out a breath, I push tempting thoughts aside and head downstairs to the weight room, the familiar clank of weights and strain of muscle beckoning like a refuge. As I pass the basement living space, a sliver of light ahead catches my eye. Did I forget to turn off the gym light yesterday?

I continue toward the weight room. The adjacent laundry room comes into view on the right. Then I step inside the gym and jolt to an abrupt halt. Valentina, her back to me, decked out in black leggings and a neon green top that clings to her lithe form, is in the middle of a barbell squat. Her long hair hangs from a high wavy ponytail. The attraction resurfaces, stronger this time and more unwelcome.

She hasn't noticed me yet. If she sees me leave without acknowledging her, it'll seem like I've been gawking.

You are gawking, idiot.

Being rooted to the spot dumbstruck isn't helping. She pauses as if sensing someone. Her gaze slips to the mirror, and our eyes lock. She gasps and loses her balance. The barbell clatters onto the thin mat and then rolls to the tile floor. She scrambles to regain her footing but teeters close to the surrounding equipment.

"Snap!" Without thinking, I rush to her side to prevent a tumble into the squat rack.

But I'm no knight in shining armor. I leap forward in two long strides and trip over some dumbbells. I catch her and pull her toward me, but without any balance, we tumble to the floor. My head thuds against the tile. The coolness at my back seeps through my T-shirt, and Valentina's warm weight presses against my chest. Then my heart thunders as shocked big brown eyes peer into mine, our hearts beating in sync.

"Are you... okay?" I manage to say. My hand cradles her back in a death grip, and the electric tension sparks more heat than any morning workout could produce.

Snap. I yank my hand away as if I'd touched fire.

"I'm sorry," we both blurt.

Then she stands. 'I—I didn't expect anyone else to be up this early,' she stammers, touching her cheeks, which makes me suddenly aware of the heat in my own face.

"I usually have the place to myself." I pull up to stand, feeling a tug of something lighter, almost like amusement, amidst my frustration. "Looks like we need a schedule."

Her laughter rings out, clear and comforting. "Or a bigger gym—if Grumps doesn't mind sharing."

I find myself grinning. I shift my foot like a dumbstruck schoolboy with a crush. Already forgetting my surroundings, I stumble over the stupid dumbbells again. My arms flail in a bid for balance.

Valentina reaches out. Her tentative but steady touch stabilizes me with an ease that contradicts our earlier tumble.

My gaze glides to hers, and I forget what I was going to say. The gold specks in her brown eyes dance in the light as heat radiates between us.

A wry smile tips her delicate looking bowed lips. "Guess we're both a bit clumsy today."

I open my mouth to respond with something witty. But the words—whatever they would have been—dry up, and I find myself rubbing my neck instead. I should grab some water from the dispenser since I'm suddenly parched.

"I'll leave." My voice is hoarse. Yep, I definitely need water.

"Stay. I'll leave. I've had enough exercise for the day." She turns and glides out the door, leaving me alone with the dumbbells she didn't put away—likely due to our chaotic moment. I rush to fill a glass of water, my throat dry and my mind racing. Only when she's gone, can I breathe again.

To regain my routine, I start with crunches, curl-ups, and jumping jacks, but my workout has no rhyme or rhythm today. Panting and breaking a sweat, I'm lost, unsure how many reps I've done or what exercises I've completed, and frustrated for not having contained my emotions.

By the end, I've overdone it with the leg workouts, feeling the strain as I hobble up the stairs. The shirt clings to my damp skin. Normally, I'd strip it off and toss it in the laundry, but I'm not thinking straight. I don't feel like trekking downstairs again.

I emerge into the kitchen.

My boys chatter away, still in their pajamas but buzzed with Valentina around. She smiles, engaging with whatever story they're spinning. Perched at the island, they hunch over a painting project while Valentina leans against the counter, holding an egg—probably for their craft project. Beside her, a steaming cup of coffee by the running coffeepot adds to the rich aroma scenting the kitchen.

As I observe this domesticity, my stomach churns against a curdling mixture of contentment and disquiet. And the morning's events linger, dissipating but still hovering like the steam rising from the coffee.

"Daddy." Atticus's voice jolts me. "Val is going to make the hard eggs like you do."

Now in a yellow T-shirt and jeans, her hair wet and clinging to her face, she must've been rushed out of the shower by my boys' eager knocking. She's so effortlessly beautiful and fits so naturally into our kitchen.

Her gaze seeks mine, and concern scrunches her features. "Did you pull a muscle? Need some ice?"

Is she hinting at my age? I laugh it off. "Ha ha. I can handle a workout."

She chuckles, then holds up an egg. "Does he mean hard-boiled eggs?"

"Fried, but hard." I move behind the boys, ruffling Atticus's, then Felix's sleep-rumpled hair.

"We're decorating our chore charts today."

"Chore charts, huh?"

Blue stock paper shaped like an airplane has Atticus's name on it and wooden clips with specific chores written on them. The green card stock shaped like a video game controller must be Felix's. She's tuned into the kids' likes and activities with impressive ease.

"When we finish our chores, Val is going to reward us." Felix grips a red marker and colors one of the circles.

Valentina sips her coffee.

Catching her eye over the rim, I mouth, "Good luck with the chores."

She mouths back a thank you, then salutes with her cup. Hmm. She's using my favorite mug. Interesting choice.

"I'll fix the eggs, if you want to get ready," I offer.

She fills another mug with coffee. "Cream or black?"

"Black is fine." I pull out a package of sausage links. Hmm, that bottle of cream wasn't in the fridge before. She came prepared for the week. I like that.

As I move to the stove, she hands me my coffee. "I'll cook. Enjoy your coffee. Gotta do my job so I don't get fired."

Memories of our meeting in the elevator surface. Coffee was involved then too.

As if reading my mind, she quips, "I'm not going to spill coffee on you."

Her fingers brush mine as I take the steaming mug. The brief touch sends a ripple through me. "I've almost forgotten that incident," I lie.

"What incident, Daddy?" Felix pipes up.

"How's that chart coming?" I take a careful sip of the coffee.

Valentina smiles, asking how I like my eggs.

"No need to make mine." I'm still reeling from how natural this is, her making coffee, fitting into our home. "I'm used to taking care of myself, and I need to hit the shower."

I lift my cup. I'll take it with me. I need to collect myself. I'd planned to take the day off to ensure Eden is okay, almost certain her mother will let her down again. But Valentina can handle it, and it's best we give each other some space.

CHAPTER 16

Valentina

Standing in the guest bathroom, I braid Eden's hair, warmed by her letting me. Today, I wove my hair into two French braids while Jason was saying goodbye to his kids. Once Eden saw me, she wanted hers to look similar.

The boys have scampered off to pick up toys in their room, and this moment lets me recover from the gym encounter. I hadn't anticipated starting my first morning in Meadowbrook wrapped in my boss's arms. With the way my heart raced and his eyes bored into mine, I'm surprised I didn't pass out from desire.

Then later when he appeared in the kitchen, his shirt clinging to him, exuding a subtle eucalyptus aroma and the scent of a healthy, active man. His mouth had curved into something close to a smile and sent my heart fluttering. Was there a crackle, a spark between us? Or did I read too much into it?

I'd come from the basement intending to hide in my room until he left. But once I finished showering, the boys were pounding on my door. I'm grateful it was locked.

Though Jason didn't ask for breakfast, I made him scrambled eggs. He ate while standing and chatting with Eden before rushing off.

"You're good at braiding." Eden speaks up as I finish the second braid.

"You have beautiful hair." I wag the end of her braid. "Makes the task easy."

Her chin tilts up, and through the mirror, her soft smile reveals her sadness. "Daddy always braids my hair." She winces. "Not nearly this good."

My heart squeezes. She had her hair braided crookedly the day I came to check out the house. "Not many dads can even attempt a ponytail." Does she know how special her father's effort is? "Your dad deserves an award for braiding your hair."

"Thank you for fixing my hair."

"Happy to do it anytime." We're bridging a gap.

She slides off the stool and tilts her head to one side, smiling at her reflection before her attention shifts to the array of essential oil bottles on my counter. She reaches for the rosemary bottle. Squinting, she reads the label.

I wave at her. "Twist off the cap and take a whiff if you like."

"What's all this for?"

"I add some to my shampoo and diffuser. They are natural with a clean scent. I also used them to make the bug repellent for our outdoor gathering yesterday."

She sniffs at my candles and bottles, then peppers me with curious questions.

I point to the rose-scented candle she seems fond of. "You can have that one if you'd like."

"Thanks!" Her face lights up and so does my heart.

"Let's go see what your brothers are up to." I wink. "Maybe we can catch them before they find any mischief."

She scoops up her candle. "Are you going to show us how to do laundry?"

"We don't have to do it today." I carry the stool out of the bathroom and set it beside the bed.

I had Eden work on her hot-pink, dancing-girl-silhouette chore chart earlier. Her room is impeccably organized, contrasting the fun wreck in the boys' room.

We follow the chirpy noise to the toy room, and a barrage of Nerf darts whiz past. The boys have constructed yet another fort and are firing across the room. Eden squeals, ducks, and yells at her brothers when they fire at us. We dive for cover.

Then I scout the chaos for ammunition, hand Eden a Nerf gun, and pick up stray darts from the floor. "Load that." I distract her from lashing out at her brothers. I find a Nerf gun for myself. Soon, we're engaged in a dart battle, our laughter mingling with the playful combat.

When our skirmish winds down, Atticus, still brimming with energy, asks, "Can we play soccer?"

"I'd rather play video games." Felix elbows past him, a hopeful glint in his eyes.

Time to channel their energy into something productive. "Gaming will be one of the rewards if we can tackle our chore chart."

"I want to make paper airplanes. We can play with them after too." Atticus's imagination is already taking flight.

"I already got my reward." Eden pats the part between her braids, then offers to assist her brothers in organizing the toy bins. We agree to regroup in fifteen minutes after I rearrange some kitchen cabinets.

Back in the kitchen, I swing open a medicine cabinet—a messy one. I remove the containers, curiosity getting the better of me when I inspect the expiration dates. Most of the medicines and vitamins are expired.

I pull out my phone to jot down the names for a future shopping list. Then the vibration on my phone flashes a text message.

Jason: *I need your help to distract Eden today. Their mom is supposed to come, and I know it won't happen. She likes Sips and Scripts. Perhaps you can take the kids there sometime today.*

What a good father. My chest squeezes as I type my response.

Valentina: *Will do, Grumps.*

Jason: *Use the credit card on anything you need to get the kids wherever they need to go.*

Valentina: *On it.*

He sends a thanks, and I pocket my phone, smiling though not sure why.

He got me a credit card last week, but I haven't needed to use it yet.

Eden had wanted to show me Sips and Scripts, a coffee and bookshop, but the shop was closed when they gave me the town tour. Perhaps we can add more stops along the way to increase the fun.

With a plan forming, I secure the vitamins and medicines, halt my tasks in the kitchen, and head back to rally the troops.

I reenter the room to moderate progress, largely due to Eden's diligent efforts. The boys, eager as ever, are already itching to play outside.

"Maybe you can give me another tour of your town." I don't have to mention why I added visiting town to our list today.

"Mom's coming today." Eden reaches for her phone from her hoodie pocket and checks it before sliding it back. "We need to stay here."

"That's what you said on Christmas break." Atticus tinkers with a Lego before adding it the airplane he's constructing on the table.

"She never comes here." Felix punches at an iPad-shaped toy as if expecting it to erupt noise.

My heart heavy, I keep my expression neutral. Poor Eden seems to be the only one waiting.

Childhood memories flood me—times I'd waited for my father, only to be disappointed. But at least he had the decency one time when he waited for us at the bus stop after school to tell me it was best if he didn't attempt a custody battle against Mami.

"What if we play outside for a bit?" It's a good time to transition to the next task. "We just need to get one more thing off our chore chart first."

Today is chillier than yesterday. So I tell the kids to put on extra layers. And to Eden, I mention a stop at Sips and Scripts, and her eyes light up. "You can bring your phone. If your mom calls, you can let her know where we are."

The boys start debating what game to play next, but I steer them toward tidying up first. "Things will go faster if we work together."

My plan for cooperation devolves into chaos as Atticus turns dish rinsing in the kitchen into a water fight, and Felix creates a bubble mountain over the sink. Only Eden manages her task efficiently, loading the dishwasher with practiced ease.

Almost twenty minutes later, after our kitchen task, we head out to play soccer with the boys. Eden joins in, and we play different soccer drills, most of which they already know.

"Will your brother teach us cool soccer skills?" Felix asks.

I hadn't offered that, but Carlos wouldn't turn down a chance to play sports. "Sometime, I can invite him over." With Jason's approval.

After our game, we head into town, and I park Jason's Audi in the open space by the antique shop.

As we walk along the quaint street, friendly faces greet us, the air fresh with the scent of spring despite the overcast sky. We pass a nail salon, and the diner where we ate last time emits an enticing aroma of grilled food from across the street.

The boys skip ahead, Felix nearly bumping into a passerby walking his border collie.

"Boys, slow down!" I call out after them.

"Here it is!" Atticus shouts while Felix waves us toward a charming coffee shop with a rustic wooden sign swaying in the breeze, labeled "Sips and Scripts."

When we enter the bookshop, the smell of coffee and old books envelopes me, the combination is a hug to the soul. People lounge at tables, and shelves packed with books line one wall. A woman, around my age with honey-brown hair and a warm smile, slides a book into place on a shelf.

"Hello, Eden." She smiles, then greets all the kids by name.

"Hi." Eden's fingers flutter a timid wave before the woman asks what books she's interested in getting today.

While the boys dart to a corner table scattered with Legos, their earlier energy not yet spent, I introduce myself. If she knows the kids, then she knows Jason. "I'm the kids' new nanny."

"The boys couldn't stop talking about you for the last two weeks."

Maybe she's Jason's girlfriend? A twinge pinches me, but her genuine smile shoves away my discomfort.

"I pretty much know everyone in this town. I'm Willow."

"Nice to meet you." I return her smile. "I take it you're born and raised in Meadowbrook?"

She nods, and I ask what she does in town.

"I work here. My family owns and runs this bookstop—I call it that because this coffee shop is *not* a bookshop, as you can see." She points dainty pink-tipped fingers to the bookshelves, some with empty spots. "You can borrow books, swapping them with whatever ones you don't need. I'm also a host for the local radio program."

She then ushers me to the counter as a man in his twenties whirls a creamy pink concoction in the blender, making a smoothie for a waiting woman.

"What would you like to drink?" Willow asks.

I already had my coffee and breakfast, but I reach for my wallet. She waves me off. "It's on the house."

I don't feel right taking pastries and coffee for free when she offers the kids hot chocolate and pastries. I have a fifty-dollar bill in my wallet, so I put it in the glass tip jar. Most expensive coffee I've had, but I don't mind supporting a small business.

"You don't look like a nanny." Willow slides into a chair at my table while Eden browses the nearby bookshelf. The boys are sipping their drinks at the Lego table. "Is that what you've always done?"

I chuckle. "I often help out at my mom's agency, but I'm supposed to be a family counselor."

I sip my drink and so does she. A congenial buzz drifts our way from those occupying the tables, some reading, others chatting over beverages.

As our conversation unfolds, I discover she, too, has an associate's degree in psychology. "I have no experience, but don't tell my listeners I haven't a clue what I'm doing."

"My lips are sealed." I make a show of sealing my lips with my hands.

With her so easy to talk to, we're soon laughing. She then tips her head to the corner where three women glance our way before looking back at their table as if they weren't inspecting us. "This is Gossip Central here. Don't get offended when whispers go around about you. It happens in our town."

I inquire about her radio show and the town. I'm tempted to ask about Jason, but I won't sabotage our first meeting. I just made a new friend in town.

Soon, Eden drops a stack of books on our table and asks me for suggestions. "I'm going to start these when I finish the third book in the Chronicles of Narnia."

As I assess her stash, she pulls out her phone. Her face falls before she slides it back. Her mom better call this time. While I help Eden narrow down her book options, Willow gets us a bag, and I promise to donate some books to her shop. Before we leave, I ask for kid-friendly activities in town and get some ideas.

With a promise to return soon, we head back to Main Street. Then I present bowling as an option to the kids and laugh at their excitement.

We don't go too far before the boys sidetrack us to lunch at Brooke's Diner. Before they gravitate toward the soda machine, I encourage them to eat first.

Our server is fast and gets cheeseburgers to the boys while Eden and I share a basket of chicken tenders. We are both not as hungry.

As the kids mix their own drinks, Eden checks her phone, her eyes lighting up with hope each time. Only to dim.

"My mom won't be coming today," she finally shares. Resignation drains her earlier optimism. "She said she'll just surprise me some day this week."

Despite her brave front, her evident disappointment hurts.

"Let's take one day at a time." I can't assure her that her mom will show up.

As if there's a joint connection between father and daughter, my phone beeps with Jason's text. He's checking on how Eden is doing.

I reassure him all is well. At least I hope Eden will pull through the rest of the day.

An idea sparks as we walk out of the diner. I hope this will lift her spirits a bit. Only God can lift her spirits, which I plan to talk about later and to pray fervently for. But a temporary distraction could suffice. "How about we get our nails done before we go bowling?"

"For real?" She wiggles her bare nails, her smile hesitant. "Mimi took me to get my nails done on Christmas break."

"It's high time we did it again."

The boys aren't excited, but I entertain them with videos—airplane ones for Atticus and a gamer talking about Minecraft buildings for Felix. They take turns using my phone while Eden and I have our nails done.

By the time we leave, Eden's smile is genuine and bright. Then we hit the bowling alley. We're not home until late afternoon.

The familiar warmth of home greets us. Jason is there, working on his computer in the kitchen. Something smells good, even though I'm not hungry. My heart spirals, and my body temperature kicks up as our eyes connect. An unspoken bond passes between us before I lean against the counter to make way for the kids rushing to greet him.

"Daddy!" They envelop him in a group hug. His sweats lower slightly as the boys tug at him.

"You came home early." Eden lingers when the boys skitter off.

Jason's arms remain wrapped around his daughter. He kisses the top of her head, obviously worried about her. "Finished all I needed, and here I am."

"Val took me to the nail salon." She displays her azure nails. "I got the same color as Val."

He grasps her hand and tips it side to side, then holds it up by her face. "This shade of blue brings out your eyes."

His genuine affection for his kids provides a sense of protection and reassurance. He glances over at me, his eyes conveying a silent thank you.

I smile back in acknowledgment of our effort to keep the day positive.

"Dinner is ready whenever you are." He tips his chin to the two pots covered on the stove.

I think it's pasta, but I can't be too sure. "We'll just get the kids to clean up first."

He winks, and my stomach flutters. I'd better go find the boys, because I'm sort of in trouble. I can't afford to be attracted to Jason. He's another heartbreak waiting to happen.

CHAPTER 17

Valentina

Swiping a cloth across the counter, damp with Mom's trusted vinegar solution, I begin the routine at a new house. She packed me off with three bottles, insisting, "The counter always needs to be sanitized." To combat the pungent vinegar smell, a mist of lemon essential oil sweeps over the surface, transforming the kitchen air with a refreshing citrus scent. Nearby, I've lined up a collection of essential oils for cleaning, for the diffuser, and for homemade concoctions like bug repellent and sunscreen.

The pasta and chicken dinner, Eden's favorite meal, was delicious. The kids chattered on over their day's stories while their dad listened. Afterward, I requested they help clear the table and load the dishwasher. "Your dad made dinner, so we get to clean."

They helped without any fuss. Then following some games and story time, the boys asked me to join them as their dad told another story. Once he finished his captivating storytelling, I wished the boys good night and returned to the kitchen. Eden had already gone to her room, and Jason seemed to be heading there as well after tucking in the boys.

Approaching footsteps catch my attention as I hang the wet washcloth on the stove.

A flutter kicks up in my chest when Jason appears. Suddenly self-conscious about my outfit, I glance down at my sweats and yellow T-shirt where the sun shines out of the words *It's summertime*. My professional PJs.

"Hey." He enters the kitchen.

I can only manage a soft hey in response, gripping the counter for support.

He sits on the stool at the island, and I sit across from him. The corners of his mouth curl up as he rests his strong arms on the marble countertop. "Your braiding skills make me look like I didn't get any training. She'll never let me anywhere near her head again."

A laugh escapes. "You have your daughter's heart. That's what counts."

He gives me a thoughtful look, his blue eyes sincere. "Thank you for today."

"Your kids make it easy."

"I hope." His gaze drifts to the essential oils lined up on the counter. "The boys couldn't stop talking about your Nerf battle with them, and Eden couldn't stop looking at her nails. Sometimes I forget she needs to do all those things."

His doubt and uncertainty stings. Can he not see he's doing an incredible job with his kids? "If all fathers in the world did half the job you do, Grumps, many kids would be in better shape." I mean every word.

He shakes his head. "Eden still thinks her mother is coming any day this week."

"I'll do my best to distract her." That's a promise. Now, I'm eager to know more about him. "Why'd their mom leave?"

His laugh rings hollow, void of any amusement. He drags a hand down his face, but can't wipe away the weariness etched deep in the lines around his eyes. "I tried to blame your show for it."

A knot clenches in my chest. My show aimed to empower women to know how to do things on their own and to claim independence, *not* to fracture families. A heaviness settles on my shoulders as his words place a burden of unintended consequences there. "I'm sorry."

"It makes it easier if we have someone to blame." He speaks softer, an undercurrent of reassurance flowing through his words. "I finally listened to bunch of your shows' reruns. What you say is clear to those who need the message."

My muscles tighten, bracing for a caveat that never comes.

Instead, he smiles faintly. "I like how it motivates women to gain their confidence."

"I guess it did a lot of damage." I'm still cringing.

"Daisy was going to leave with or without your show." His eyes lock with mine, earnest and clear. I almost imagine he can sense my inner turmoil. "You didn't tip any scales that weren't already tipping."

The words massage my taut muscles, his assurance a balm. Yet the sting lingers, the guilt reluctant to fade.

I curl my finger around one of my braids as silence envelops us, thick and heavy.

He shifts on the stool. "I worked hard to give her the luxurious life she wanted. I started Family Sphere and ended up spending more time working there than with her and the kids. The twins were overwhelming for her."

I hold my breath. Any sound might fracture his openness.

"She suffered from postpartum depression after the boys were born." His voice, fragile and laden with regret, is barely a whisper now. "Our marriage started to slide down a slope from there." A leaden pause precedes his next words. "She left on Eden's seventh birthday."

"Oh, Jason." Compassion overwhelms me. I can't bring myself to call him Grumps, so I reach out to cover my hand over his on the table. "How terrible Eden must feel."

He looks off in the distance.

"Did you go after her?" Maybe she just needed a break. "Perhaps talk things over?"

"She made everything clear when she called to say she was done." His eyes reflect the unspoken sadness now permeating the air around us. This poor man. "Having kids was my idea." He swallows. His gaze locks on the chore charts magnetized to the fridge. "I'll never again persuade anyone into doing something they don't want to. She left. That meant she wanted to be left alone. I respect that."

I wouldn't know how to counsel his family offhand. "I don't even know what to say."

"Enough about me." He shifts, noticing my hand on his, so I retract it, my cheeks warming. "What about your family? You talk a lot about your mom and siblings in your shows, but not your dad?"

I missed having my dad around, but by God's grace and Mami's overwhelming love and support, my siblings and I turned out fine. "I was about Eden's age when my mom kicked him out."

Jason's eyebrows pull together. "Why?"

"Dad cheated on her, and she went all crazy." I shake my head, the memory vivid and sharp as if cut from glass. "When he pulled up, Mom was waiting on the front steps with cans of spray paint in hand. My poor dad remained in the car, sensing something wasn't right."

"Paloma came after your dad with spray paint?" Jason's brow arches, but a rumble like a chuckle threatens to burst from his chest.

"I think Dad was hoping to apologize when he lowered the car window. But Mom started spraying his face before he could get the window up. Then she sprayed the word *cheater* in red paint all over the car and some other words I wouldn't want to mention alongside them. She topped it off by almost blacking out the windshield and telling him not to ever 'blacken the driveway or her doorway again.'"

The absurdity unfurls a laugh from deep within me. I struggle to continue, clutching my stomach.

Jason leans back. His deep laugh mingles with mine, dissolving into shared amusement.

"Now that vehicle must've been a great headline for a gossip column," he says, still laughing.

"Right?"

"My father's absence is not as fun a story to tell." Humor softens his words. "We have something in common."

"Definitely not grumpiness." I shake a finger at him.

"Obviously, you're grumpier." He winks, grinning. Who is this man? "We were both raised by single moms."

"Both hardworking and passionate about their children," I add, a thread of connection tightening between us.

As Jason shares more about his life, the space between us fills with an unspoken understanding, a mutual respect for the struggles and strengths of single parents. I find myself more drawn to his story, more invested in his life. With each word, a bond grows, rooted in shared experiences and nurtured by collective resilience.

But we both know the ache of an absent parent. I'm determined to do my best to distract Eden from her mother's absence. That reminds me. The day after tomorrow, I have tickets to a Yankees spring training game, an outing the kids might enjoy. I'll see what Jason thinks.

The following day, Eden requests we play volleyball, so we string up the net, transforming their yard into a makeshift court. Her enthusiasm is palpable, her eyes alight. However, the boys, still caught in their soccer habits, send the volleyball sailing far with ambitious kicks instead of controlled passes. Eden frowns and rebukes them, frustrated by their disregard for the game's rules. Eventually, I redirect the boys to a corner with a soccer ball, leaving Eden and me to focus on her volleys and passes over the net. I also guide her again through positioning her hands for a bump, the footwork for a serve, and the motion for a proper set.

"Like this?" Her form improves with each pass.

"Exactly like that!" I clap as she manages a particularly good serve. With her enthusiasm infectious, the yard feels like our private court.

"Maybe I'll play volleyball when I don't dance anymore."

"You definitely should." I toss the ball for another serve. "You should tell your dad. He can look into some recreational leagues that don't require much commitment."

"I don't want to disappoint him." She pauses and pulls her phone from her sweatpants pockets.

I try not to wince at her constant checking for a call that might never come.

***

Valentina

Wednesday is game day. With Jason's permission, I take the kids first to Mami's house, where her excitement energizes the kitchen. She teaches them to make tortillas. Her hands pat the dough as she guides the boys' smaller, clumsier ones. "Like this, just round and flat."

Thuds of dough hitting the counter accentuated the kids' laughter.

"We're going to make some chicken quesadillas." She ushers me to guide the kids in rolling the tortillas flat and cooking them before she shows them how to lay the cheese and chicken between the freshly made tortillas. "It's all about balance in flavor and making sure every bite is as good as the last."

I'm inspired to take pictures.

As they cook, Mami regales them with stories of her childhood in Venezuela, including impromptu soccer games in the dusty streets with cousins and family gatherings where she learned these recipes. And I go through all sorts of pre-game security measures so the kids don't get lost and know what to do should we get separated. "In your pants pockets, you each have your dad's number, mine, and Carlos.'"

"And the security guards?" asks Atticus, so I again tell him they will find a staff member at the game should they need to make a call.

Carlos, ever the enthusiast, is bent on preparing the kids for the game after lunch.

"I can't believe you've never caught a ball with a glove. T-ball is not real baseball." He peppers his lessons with amusing details about baseball's finer points. "Before the game, we have to get you guys some merch." He shakes a finger at them. "You're not a Yankees fan without a jersey."

"Leave them alone." I roll my eyes. "They are Mets fans." Or so Jason told me when I requested to take the kids to the game.

"Either way, kids, you'll look like real fans when you show up in the right gear."

So, before we head to the stadium, we stop by Carlos' buddy's street stall for baseball merch and deck the kids out in brand-new Yankees jerseys. I chuckle. My wardrobe already houses three jerseys in different sizes, gifts from a few of the countless games Carlos has dragged me to over the years.

It's not hard to use up the six tickets between me, the kids, Carlos, and Leah, who happens to be on spring break. Her husband has to work and isn't interested in going to baseball games anyway.

As we settle into our stadium seats, excitement buzzes around us. The smell of hot dogs, peanuts, and fried foods permeates the air, adding to the vibrant atmosphere. I worry the kids might find the training game dull, and Eden's frequent phone checking confirms my fears. However, the boys' enthusiasm brims over when the game starts. They barrage Carlos with questions about every play. He explains with animated gestures and a broad smile until even the most mundane plays seem thrilling.

"Didn't realize she's so attached to her phone." Leah, seated at my side, whispers into my ear over the cheer around us.

I turn to her so Eden doesn't see me mouth, "It's a long story."

"And you're still in a standoff with the dad?"

I breathe, unable to sum up what Jason is. He's protective of his family, which makes him a winner. "He's not that bad."

Leah's brow arches. "Care to share more about that transition?"

Eden taps my shoulder, asking for a soda when a beverage vendor passes by, saving me from the conversation.

By the time we head home, we're all worn out. But at least, the drive unfolds quietly, the steady hum of the engine blending with the rhythmic breathing of all the kids asleep. Eden's breathing is calm, her fingers still curled around her phone—clinging to the connection she seeks. If only I could reach out to her mom, I think perhaps, I could persuade her to visit, even for an hour. A pang tightens around my heart as I steal a glance at Eden's peaceful face in the rearview mirror. Somehow, I must do more for her.

The following day, Ethan, the pastor, requests my help watching his kids while he visits a church member in the hospital. With all the kids together at Jason's house, we fill time with painting and free time to play. After Ethan picks up his kids, I take Jason's kids into town for a shopping spree. We pick out Eden's Easter dress and grab new clothes for the boys as Jason requested.

We wrap up our outing at Jump and Hop, an indoor trampoline park. While the boys throw themselves into the lively chaos, enjoying boundless thrills, Eden's mood doesn't match the vibrant atmosphere. Eventually, she joins me on one of the benches lining the jumping area where adults observe their kids.

"Everything okay, sweetheart?" My fingers trace the end of her ponytail.

Her gaze flickers to the phone in her lap. Resignation soon clouds those sunrays of hope. "Just waiting for my mom to call."

"The week's not over." I rub her back in soothing strokes. "Maybe she'll just surprise you." Even as I say it, I'm holding onto hope myself, silently pleading she'll come through.

Eden's half smile wobbles, uncertainty shadowing her usually bright eyes. *Sweet thing. Please, God, protect her heart.*

While the kids clean up before dinner that night, I update Jason about the day and Eden's continued hopeful anticipation. After the meal, he devotes extra time to her, letting me take over tuck-in duties with the boys. They are a bundle of energetic charm, their eyes wide as they plead for bedtime stories. Atticus insists on an airplane adventure. Felix wants a video gamer to be the hero.

Good thing I took creative writing classes in college. I weave their requests into a story, drawing from everything I learned about narrative structure and character development.

When I finish, Jason must still be in Eden's room. Her light's still on. Exhausted and needing time to pray for this family, Eden in particular, I retreat to my room.

During my prayer time, inspiration strikes. I used to write in my gratitude journal when I was in high school, and it helped me focus on the positive rather than the negative.

Gratitude is on the tip of my tongue when I wake the next day. So as we sit around the kitchen island before going swimming, I introduce the theme of starting each day with a grateful heart. "I'm going to start writing in my gratitude journal again." I tell the kids how I used to keep a journal. "Each time we count our blessings, we're less likely to focus on what we don't have."

"I want a journal too." Atticus lifts his swim towel, and Felix echoes the request.

"When can we go shopping for journals?" Eden asks.

I check the clock. "I suppose we could go before swimming."

We're loading the Audi with a beach bag and a cooler of snacks. At the jumping place yesterday, we heard about a new adventure pool one town over. The kids are excited to check it out, though it's cloudy with a chance of rain or snow.

As I swing open the back door to usher the kids into the car, a sleek sedan pulls up and parks behind my Civic in the driveway. The driver rushes to the back and swings open the door.

A sophisticated woman and a distinguished gentleman step out. Both appear to be in their sixties. They approach with smiles that don't quite reach their eyes.

"Glad we caught you before you left. Look at you all so grown." The woman waves painted-black fingernails, and her heels click-clack the pavement.

I hesitate, my hand on the Audi's driver's seat door. "Kids, do you recognize our visitors?"

"They're our grandchildren." The woman's formal voice doesn't have kids rushing toward them.

The boys are hesitant when I coax them to greet their grandparents—at least I assume they're Daisy's parents. The twins offer quick, obligatory hellos before sliding into the car.

Eden, however, pauses longer. "Where's Mom? Have you seen her?"

"Darling, we haven't seen Daisy in months." The woman gives a dismissive wave, then focuses on me. "You may go, miss. We'll take the kids out for the day."

Eden looks back at me, her body language tense and cautious.

"We'll bring them back tonight." The gentleman waves me off, expecting compliance.

I have a dashcam mounted on the Audi's dashboard. If they are planning to kidnap the kids and me, the police will have a starting place. "They're not going with you unless I come."

They must've been here before. Why would Jason tell them where he lived if he didn't want them close to his family?

"No need for you to come along." The woman rolls her eyes as if I insulted her.

"I need to call and ask Jason first." Although I was looking forward to spending time with them at the pool, it's important they see their family members. I dial Jason's number, but it goes straight to voicemail. I wince as I turn back to the couple. "Sorry. I can't let them go without permission."

The woman advances, black nails tapping her hips. "They are our grandchildren," she repeats.

"And I'm their nanny." I keep a steady tone while Eden moves around me to get in the car. "Their dad didn't tell me you were coming."

"They're our grandkids, for Pete's sake!" the man snaps.

They don't seem so enthusiastic to rush to you. Keeping that to myself, I apologize again when the woman snaps and says something under her breath. I cross my arms and close the back doors so they get the memo and march off to their car and drive away.

Jason calls back two hours later. Standing by the window in the adventure pool area, phone pressed to my ear, I recount the incident. The kids' joyful squeals echo off the glass, a sharp contrast to my tension.

"You did the right thing." Jason's voice cuts through the cacophony. "They disappear for years and think they can just show up whenever without notice. They were the same when Daisy was growing up, always traveling overseas and leaving her behind in school. She used to say she felt more like a doll they took off the shelf and played with now and then, than a child they had a relationship with. A good nanny does what you did."

I blink, absorbing his words. Was a compliment tucked into his frustration? And was I glimpsing a bit of why Daisy didn't know how to be involved in her own kids' lives?

He thanks me again, his tone lighter. "What escapades are you up to today?"

"We're at the adventure pool." I glance back to the towering splash section where the kids splash and play with other kids.

"Sounds like they're having fun." He can't miss the kids' happy shrieks in the background.

A smile spreads across my face. "They are."

"Are you swimming too?"

My heart flutters. Is he flirting or genuinely interested in knowing what's going on?

"Are you being a nosy Rosie, Grumps?" I keep myself from overly breathing through the phone as I'm gasping for air.

"Just keeping tabs on my kids' nanny."

"What a good boss." I twirl a strand of my hair with my finger. My gaze drifts to the play area where the kids are still having a blast.

"Just doing my job." He lets out a chuckle. "Make sure you're having fun too, okay? It's not all work." His voice is soft, the most tender moment I've ever experienced with him. Warmth rushes through me. I must be dreaming.

Then he adds, "See you at home."

"Okay." I'm still breathless. This easy exchange does nothing but deepen my attraction to my boss, to the wrong man.

Could it be that this family is where I belong? For this season in life anyway. Could it be why I'd not considered looking into the counseling job at Leah's school?

When we leave the pool, the kids plead to return the next day. With spring break almost over, I promise to bring them back tomorrow afternoon. This indoor pool outshines our local pool. Only twenty miles away, it will serve as a perfect reward to motivate the kids to keep up with their chores. This week, Felix has barely asked to play video games. We've been too caught up in our activities for him to think about sitting behind the console.

The next day, I'm in the pool playing catch with the boys. A few minutes earlier, Eden had stepped out, but I keep glancing over at her. She's checking her phone again. I hurl the beach ball toward the boys. As they leap and Atticus snags it midair, my attention is pulled back to Eden.

Her expression crumples, and she flings her phone into the pool.

"Eden!" I shout, my voice cutting through the noise.

I tell the boys to keep swimming. Then I make my way out of the pool. "Sweetie," I call out as she wraps her towel around her shoulders, her lips trembling. My heart sinks. The boys and their new friends beckon me, but I ignore them, rushing to Eden, who's beside a bench. "What happened, sweetheart?"

"She's not coming."

"Oh, honey." I reach to pull her into an embrace, but she stands stiff, that determined look in her eyes. I recognize that posture all too well—the effort to appear strong in heartache.

"Can we go to Sips and Scripts after this?" she asks.

"On the way home, sure." I'll do anything to help her forget this moment, though I'm not sure the bookstop will still be open.

I head back in the pool to retrieve her drenched phone. If we bury it in rice, we might be able to resurrect it. But right now, I'll make the rest of the day as light and enjoyable for Eden as possible, anything to ease the sting.

Throughout my media career, a desire to prove myself—to show someone out there I have what it takes—drove me. It wasn't about doing my best. It was about being the best, surpassing expectations not for my fulfillment but to validate my capabilities.

Now, I want to give my all for a different reason. This shift isn't about others' perceptions or external validations. It's a genuine desire to excel from a place of personal integrity and passion. However, while liberating, this doesn't guarantee success.

As we drive back, snowflakes dance through the sky, painting the world in a wintry spectacle despite April beginning on Monday. How unpredictable nature is, much like my own circumstances.

With snow, traffic seems worse. It's nothing compared to New York's real traffic, but the road demands my full attention. The twins chatter in the back seat, infusing the car with their lively energy. Eden sits in silence, even more subdued than usual.

Then the car jerks. I grapple with the steering wheel to maintain control. An airbag deploys and smacks into my face. The force rocks me to my core. My heart races, adrenaline surging as the kids shout.

A stunned moment passes before I realize we've been hit from the side—my side.

"What happened?" Eden shrieks.

"I–I don't know." I put the car into park, turn to look in the back, and draw out a long breath. Their faces may be fear-struck, but the kids are alive. I assess them for injuries, every bit of me shaking. "I'm so sorry, sweeties."

"I want my dad." Eden snuffles.

I dial 9-1-1, but emergency services are already enroute. I try to push my door open, but it's stuck. I need to get them out of the fumy car! I slide past the steering wheel to the passenger door and open it before letting the kids out.

I embrace the kids, and the boys cling to me. Pensive, Eden stands aside. The snow flurries have stopped and barely stuck to the ground, but it's frigid. From the back of the car, I get the blanket I'd put in for emergencies, and I wrap it around the boys. Since Eden has her hoodie over her wet hair, she should be okay for the time being.

A man checks to see if we're okay. He, too, appears unharmed though shaken. After one look at his car, I thank God he survived. Our SUV's robust build must have spared us from a worse outcome.

I contact Jason next, updating him.

"Are the kids okay?" His frantic voice rises. "Where are you?"

"The kids are fine," I insist.

The twins' small hands clutch my arms for comfort. Eden, just a short distance away, appears much further away, so aloof and detached.

"Can I talk to Eden?" Jason asks.

When I hand the phone to her, she responds with brief affirmatives. Then a snippet of their conversation sends a chill down my spine. "She was talking on the phone."

What? I try to focus on comforting the boys.

Soon Eden hands back the phone, and Jason's voice hardens. "How could you be distracted when driving my kids?"

"What?" My chest heats as Eden avoids my gaze. "You think I'm that reckless?"

My body trembles from the chill air, the crash's impact, and the accusation. The emotional pain stings more than the physical, though.

A fire truck and paramedics arrive.

"The first responders are here. I gotta go." I'm done with this man. I take back the last promise I made to myself before any of this happened.

As a police officer takes the report, the man who hit us admits his fault, which is a small solace.

Paramedics insist on checking the kids and me. Although dizzy, I claim I'm fine as my frustration with Jason outweighs any physical discomfort.

When he arrives, the kids rush to him. Once assured of their safety, he turns to me. "Are you okay?"

I nod. My head pounds with each beat of my heart.

We linger at the scene until the tow truck arrives. Then he instructs the driver on where to take the Audi. Before we leave, I move our items to his car. I also take the dashcam with me.

As we drive back to their home, Jason scolds me again. He arrived after the police report, so he still thinks I'm at fault. "If anything happened to my kids—"

"They're fine." My head throbs with each word, my patience fraying.

"Still, I expected you to be more careful." The grave words boom in my ears, perhaps magnified by the lingering car crash. "I should have never let you drive them anywhere."

I rub my temples to soothe the intensifying ache, but his words cut deep, harsher than I think he realizes. I bite the tip of my tongue and focus on the dull pain spreading across my skull.

"I just—"

"Stop yelling at Val!" Atticus shouts through the tension. A squishy ball sails from the back seat.

Jason ducks and swerves before straightening in the lane. "Who threw that? Atticus! Felix!"

"Val is nice!" Atticus's hoarse defense tugs at my heart. I know Eden didn't mean to accuse me. She had to take her anger out on someone.

Tears prick my eyes as I turn toward the boys. Streetlights illuminate their faces. My heart swells at their terrified looks. "It's not good to throw things, even if you're upset." I address Atticus, my voice as shaky as the rest of me. "Especially not to hit your dad."

He remains silent, so does everyone in the car. Despite the chaos, his support touches me, but the wedge between Jason and me grows heavier with each mile.

By the time we pull into the driveway, I'm overwhelmed. Tears blur my vision as he parks. I hand him the dashcam footage, then step out.

The boys burst from the car and rush to me. "Stay with us, Val." Atticus wraps his arms around me.

Felix tugs at my other hand. "Can you stay the night and go to the Easter egg hunt with us tomorrow?"

"Your daddy needs some time with you." My voice cracks like static on an old TV. It's hard to leave, hard to deny their pleas, but I need space to clear my head.

Eden heads into the house without a word, her struggles evident.

When I'm finally in the comfort of my car, tears obscure my vision as I drive away. "I thought I was bonding with the kids—and

Jason." I shudder a breath, speaking to God this time. "Was I not supposed to reconsider when Jason came to my house, Lord?"

Gratitude insists a small voice.

Right, I should count today's blessings.

No one suffered serious injury tonight. The boys had a good time at the pool. They don't want me to leave. Those are positives to make the day's entry.

Whatever other good things came out of the day, perhaps God will reveal later.

I'd slacked on job hunting this week, caught up in the family I was serving. Maybe it's time to refocus, to reconsider the counselor position at Leah's school if it's still available. Spring break is over, and they've likely found someone. Still, it's worth checking. It's time for a new start where my efforts are seen and valued. But where?

What if this is where God wants me, and He's testing me to see if I can depend on Him rather than take off to another dead-end job?

I can't tell which is which. But I'll never let anyone make me feel less worthy than I am. And I'll never let anyone assume they have power over me. First, I need to quit once again.

CHAPTER 18

Jason

Making a mistake in front of my kids leaves me vulnerable to their requests. Sensing my guilt, the boys push their luck tonight. They persuade me into letting them have cereal for dinner, coax me into watching YouTube videos on folding paper airplanes with Atticus and racing a car in a video game with Felix, then wrangle me into building a fort in their room way past their bedtime, the manipulative rascals.

Eden, on the other hand, reacted differently. After I insisted she eat something, she retreated to her bedroom and shut herself away.

Now I'm lying under the makeshift fort on the boys' rug with Felix on one side and Atticus on the other. The usual toy clutter is absent from the floor. Valentina's chore chart and reward system have made an impact. The tidiness doesn't ease the heaviness on my chest—not only from the scare but also from my behavior afterward.

I want to ensure the kids have overcome the scare. Plus, steering the conversation toward their day distracts me from my concern, though Atticus saying the other driver admitted he caused the accident does not help my guilt.

They chatter about the fun indoor pool in the nearby town. Felix recounts the splashing and the sheer joy of the water, while Atticus dives into the various activities they enjoyed this week. "I loved cooking with Val's mami."

"Carlos taught us how to catch a baseball with a real glove before the game," Felix adds.

While my mom is incredible with my kids, she's not keen on herding them on one adventure after another. It's too much work for a grandmother.

Meanwhile, Eden is probably dealing with her mother's latest letdown. She'd apologized for chucking the phone after Daisy texted that she wasn't going to show up.

I need to clear the air even with my kids. I clasp Felix's fingers in one hand and Atticus's in the other, drawing them close. "You know how I say adults get scared sometimes?"

"Like when you screamed so loud when I cut off your finger with a knife?" Atticus's soft hair tickles my neck as he leans into me.

"That was an accident, and you didn't cut off my finger." Lesson learned. No sharp objects in reach of eager little hands during cooking sessions. "Anyway, I was scared when I heard about the accident, and I didn't handle it well."

Atticus slips his hand from mine and rolls onto my chest. Those big blue eyes blink down at me. "I don't like how you were mean to Val."

"That wasn't nice," Felix adds.

My chest tightens further. "I know. I'm sorry." It doesn't excuse my harshness. "I shouldn't have yelled at her."

"When you're mad, it helps to go outside and shout." Atticus presses down into my chest as he shares this nugget.

"And you've tried it before?" A slight smile cracks my lips.

"Yes. Val told me. And it helps." He couldn't be more sincere or endearing.

"Val is very nice." Felix speaks slowly, as usual weighing each word first. "We had the best week ever."

"I'll try to make it right."

"Is she coming back?" Felix's underlying fear grips my heart.

"I hope so."

In my anger, did I let slip any words suggesting Valentina was fired? How can I mend things this time? She's had a long week, and she deserves the weekend off.

I need to make amends. But how? I, at last, tuck the boys in.

The driver's door took the brunt of the impact. Valentina must be dealing with physical discomfort like headaches or whiplash on top of everything else. There's so much I need to say, and I'd drive to her house right now and apologize if I could. But I'm tied down.

Heart heavy, I approach Eden's room. Soft sobs escape the crack beneath her door. I rasp my knuckles on the door before letting myself in.

"Honey?" My chest tightens at the sight of her forlorn figure curled under the hot-pink comforter. I rush to squat at her bedside. I tuck the tendrils of her hair behind her ear.

"Can I talk to Mimi?" She sniffles, not looking up.

"Right now?"

"Mom didn't come. She lied."

"I know, baby."

Like I do each time, I harbored some hope Daisy would follow through.

Eden pushes the comforter down to her waist and sits. "I'm sorry for throwing the phone in the water."

"It's okay." I sit and hug her, feeling her tremble. "I can get you another phone."

"I don't want a phone anymore." She wiggles free, grabs the soft stuffed giant giraffe from her bedside, and hugs it in her chest. "What's the point?" Her sadness goes beyond a missed call.

I understand her need to disconnect from the constant letdowns. Opting not to bring up the car accident now, I focus on comforting her. I trace my thumb over her cheek, smudging away the dry trail of tears. If only I could smudge away the hurt as well!

"I'm your dad and I love you. You can be assured I'll always be there for you. I'm not going anywhere, okay?"

She draws out a sigh.

"The accident." She eyes the stack of C. S. Lewis books next to a candle on her nightstand. "It wasn't Val's fault."

"I know."

She frowns at me.

It's on my tongue to tell her she owes Valentina an apology. But I need to ask Valentina's forgiveness first.

"Can I go to bed now?"

Her nightstand clock displays 12:40. It's so late. Good thing it's Friday, so we can all sleep in.

Not sure what else to say, I lean in and kiss the top of her head, savoring her fruity shampoo and hints of Valentina's aromatic oils. Then I wish her good night and step out of her room.

When I settle in my bed, my thoughts drift to Valentina. In a mere three weeks, she's become a part of our lives, fitting in as if she's always been here. Her diligent care extends beyond the kids. She's even managed our health better than I ever did. She organized our vitamins, replacing the expired ones and setting out daily doses for us all, complete with little labeled cups—a small but telling gesture of her thorough care.

I turn to my side, unable to turn my back to my mom's advice, given when she'd sat across from me and demanded I apologize to Valentina face-to-face. I'll drive to Brooklyn sometime this weekend, but right now, I reach for my phone.

She needs to know I'm sorry. I don't want her to quit. I need her. My kids need her.

I've not managed to express how valued she is, not only as a nanny, but also as a part of our family. I hope I haven't messed things up beyond repair.

I'm still tired the next morning, but the Easter egg hunt will make a good start for Saturday. So we're soon at the park for the community event Ethan's church organizes. Despite the cloudy skies, the air's abuzz. Laughter enlivens the background as kids dart around. Their baskets swing alongside them in their hunt for colorful hidden eggs.

Eden's seated on a bench by an evergreen tree, her head buried in a book. Around her, other kids run and laugh, yet she remains still. Maybe she's outgrown these egg hunts or maybe something's bothering her. Either way, her withdrawal casts a shadow that feels even deeper against the gray hues of the midmorning sky.

"How are those burgers coming?" The clap of hands and familiar voice pull my attention toward Ethan, and I refocus on my task as smoke rises from the beef patties.

"Still going." I flip a few burgers, leaving the ones still too pink to cook longer.

Nothing seems to get past Ethan though, one of my best friends and also my pastor. Yes, my faith is flimsy, but Ethan is still my pastor. Now, he's dressed in a hoodie bearing the Meadowbrook Community church logo, matching the one on my red apron and those worn by others manning the grills. Liam and Russ are also in charge of grilling, while some church members set up tables where food will be served.

"I'd hoped Valentina would join us today." He thrusts his hands into his hoodie pouch. "I ran into her at Sips and Scripts, and I extended an invitation when she watched my kids on short notice."

His soft tone hints they spoke on a more personal level. Unease churns within me, and I bite the inside of my cheeks, flipping a burger that's still too pink to flip. Why didn't Valentina tell me she'd watched Ethan's kids? None of my kids told me either. But again, they've all been so busy.

"Anything you want to talk about?" Ethan grabs a platter and steps closer.

"It's complicated." And yet he is comfortable enough with Valentina to invite her to events while I'm still struggling to cross from professional to casual level.

"Sounds like an interesting complication." A knowing grin spreads across his face. "You know, I'm good at managing complications."

I lift my spatula toward the bustling crowd. "Aren't you busy enough today?"

"That's what I have you guys and all the church volunteers here for." He lowers his head, his gaze meeting mine squarely. "Boys said you might be looking for a new nanny after all."

"They told you that?" I scan the swarm of kids for my own.

Ethan then launches into my apparent domestic upheaval and how I lost my temper and caused Valentina to quit.

I chuckle. "I apologized to those rascals."

"And you apologized to Valentina, I believe?"

My heart sinks. "She didn't text me back."

"Perhaps you need to kick up that apology." Keeping his voice low, he glances around as if to ensure our conversation remains private. "I'm under the impression she's going to be more than your nanny."

"What do you mean?" I play innocent, but I know what he means. I set my mouth in a firm line, but my next words don't sound convincing even inside my head. "She's not my type."

His smile widens, sinking dimple holes in his cheeks and aggravating me further. "Why did you go all stiff and clench-jawed when I said I ran into her at the coffee shop? Or was it because she watched my kids for a couple of hours?"

I exhale. The grilled-meat aroma turns my stomach, the thought of having a burger now unappealing.

Someone calls for Ethan, and he turns to leave, displaying a smirk only a pastor privy to his flock's secrets could wear. "Remember that lesson about the rose and thorns!" he calls over his shoulder.

I'm attracted to Valentina, and my kids like her—even Eden does, despite her struggles to let her in. I have the same hesitation, but maybe it's time to open that door.

Somehow, I make it through the community event. Then to cheer Eden up, I make a stop to the Sips and Scripts. As she wanders between the shelves, her pace is slow, almost reflective. I watch her, a chasm widening between us as my attempts to engage her fall short. I try calling their grandma, hoping a familiar voice might cheer her up, but the call goes to voicemail. We've only talked to her once since she left. With her and Phil moving from one country and city to another, communication is limited.

The day drags on, and around six, Eden complains of a stomachache, which might explain her quietness. She retires to her room, her face pinched. Her emotional state tugs at my heart as I follow her. What has Daisy done to distress our daughter like this?

"Can I borrow your phone?"

"Of course." I hand it over and return to play with the boys. After almost thirty minutes, I leave them occupied with their Legos in the playroom and return to check on Eden.

She's lying face up and lowers the phone as I enter. "Did you know Val advocates for women to be bold and independent and rely on themselves?"

The proper way my daughter explains it gives a new perspective to Valentina's show. I sit on the edge of the bed.

"That's why she wanted us to learn to do our laundry and chores. So we don't have to depend on Eliana doing it for us all the time."

She has a point there. But it's good to have a balance. "It's important to accept help sometimes."

"Have you watched her show?"

Valentina must've told her about her life in the spotlight.

I nod. I watched segments among the many hours I spent on the internet reading bloggers and comments about the show. But I don't tell Eden about my odd first meeting with Valentina.

"Can I... call Val?" She blinks at me, appearing almost fearful of my reaction.

"Okay." I'm still unsure how Valentina feels about us after yesterday's misunderstandings. I've checked my phone throughout the day, but she hasn't texted me back. I'll visit her tomorrow, after church. It's Easter, and the kids are looking forward to the morning church service.

Eden scrolls through the phone and taps her finger on the screen. I hear the phone ringing, perhaps she accidentally activated the speakerphone.

"Hello?" Valentina's voice sounds hesitant and weary. Does she think it's me?

"Val, it's Eden. I–I just wanted to hear your voice."

Her vulnerability breaks my heart.

After a brief pause, Valentina responds in a softer tone. "Hey, Eden. Everything okay?"

"I'm so sorry, Val. I'm sorry for saying you caused the crash when you didn't. I, um, I wanted Daddy to fire you." Eden's hand shakes as tears threaten to take over. I want to pull her into my arms, proud of her for taking responsibility. I can't take credit for her conviction, so I remain still, letting her focus on what she needs to say. "What's the point of you being my friend when you're going to leave? Mom left, and... I don't know what got into me."

"It's okay." Valentina's warmth emanates through her voice.

"Are you mad at me?"

"I'm proud of you for being so brave and owning up to your mistake."

Eden breathes out, her shoulders relaxing. "Can you come here, Val?"

"Go there? Why, honey?"

"I have a question to ask you. It's something I can't talk to Dad about." Eden shrugs at me, urgency still alight in her eyes.

"You know you can talk to your dad about anything," Valentina reassures her. "You're the center of your dad's world, and he'll do anything for you. Do you know you have the best dad in the world? You're so lucky. My dad is alive, but he's never been involved in our lives like your dad."

Eden presses the phone tight to her ear, seemingly unaware it's on speaker.

Valentina considers me a great dad? I don't even feel halfway there yet. My chest squeezes.

Eden glances at me. "He's awesome."

I blink away the tears, my vision flickering like bad TV reception. Now I'm unsure what to do with this private conversation I got myself into.

"I can't believe you said all that. My dad doesn't even like you." Eden has my eyes widening.

"He likes me." A playfulness lilts Valentina's voice. "He just doesn't know it yet."

"Why did you say I don't like her?" The words fly out before I realize I'm interfering in a private conversation.

Then comes a dreadful pause on the other end of the line.

"Oh." Valentina gasps. "Your dad's right there?"

I wince. "Sorry. Phone's on speaker."

Her snort comes loud through the speaker. "Okay. I take back all the things I said about him—if by mistake I said anything nice." She's laughing now. "But it doesn't matter whether he likes me or not. He's your dad. You are his priority."

"Can you still come?" Eden asks again, her voice dropping to a whisper. "It's something I need... a woman's help."

Maybe Valentina could be more than a nanny—a comforting female role model amidst the turmoil Daisy's inconsistency causes.

Not wanting to be an intruder in this private moment anymore, I exit the room and click the door closed behind me. As I walk down the hall, Mom's talk during Christmas break intrudes. Is Eden starting her menstruation? She's only eleven. Don't those things start, like, at fourteen?

I don't know about that, but I'm sure of one thing. Valentina's role in our lives is much needed. Mom is always there for us, but she now has her own life. I need to make things right, not just for Eden's sake but also for the harmony of our entire family. I'd better not be too late to bridge the gap I've created.

CHAPTER 19

Jason

"Can we watch all three movies please, Daddy?" Eden rests her head on my shoulder, her demeanor more upbeat than the last twenty-four hours.

"We'll see." I don't care if we stay up all night. I'm just relieved Valentina is on her way over.

We're seated on one sofa, the boys on the area rug, consoles in hand, their thumbs moving as they add details to their Minecraft house. My gaze keeps drifting through the window for a flash of lights to announce Val's arrival. A steady downpour drums against the pavement. I need to be ready to meet her with an umbrella so she doesn't get drenched on her way in.

"I can't wait to watch the Chronicles of Narnia," Eden chirps, having read the books Valentina gave her—all six in two weeks. According to Eden, Valentina will be bringing three of the movies from the book series.

"Why did you say I don't like Valentina?" What if Valentina thinks I loathe her?

"You yelled at her."

Right, it's black and white. I was unjustly mad at Valentina after Eden's lie and my fear of what could've been.

I tap Eden's nose to lighten the moment. I can't bring this back to her when she's already apologized. "I haven't been friendly to many people... and that includes Valentina." Mostly to Valentina, actually.

Bright light spills through the window in my peripheral, and Eden hops from the sofa. "Val's here."

Her action propels me to my feet. Nerves flutter in my stomach as I rush to the hallway and grab the umbrella. I hadn't realized the boys abandoned their game until they dart past me. I catch them as they swing the door open, restraining their excitement. "We have to wait until she parks her car."

Thankfully, they listen, bouncing their toes on the edge.

Once she parks, we all rush out, kids bounding ahead. I try to catch up, the rain washing over my face—perhaps cleansing some of my past missteps as well. We reach her car as she swings the door open. Then I open the umbrella, not sure why I forgot to use it myself, but I shield her and the kids while they cling to her.

She laughs and pulls them into a group hug. "I missed you too."

"Let's not knock her down," I call out over the rain. The rain droplets on my tongue are refreshing. The air smells clean mingled with her flowery fragrance, and warmth radiates through me. The porch light illuminates her smile, lighting up my heart. She's stunning in her olive-green overalls over a cream shirt, as refreshing as the spring—a time of new beginnings.

"Let's get you inside, okay?"

At my prompt, she disengages from the kids' embraces, and jealousy twinges. No fair that the kids can hug her so freely, and I—

What am I thinking?

"I need to get something from the car." She spins away.

"Hold this." I offer her the umbrella, whispering close enough for her to hear over the rain. "I'll get your bags if you want to head in with the kids."

Her eyes search mine. There's no lightning with this rainstorm, but the moment feels charged with more than gratitude.

"Thank you." A note of something deeper, hope perhaps, imbues her soft voice.

We stand only inches apart, my heart thundering. I pretend to read her mouth through the rain, but truthfully, my gaze is drawn to her sweet bowed lips. Oh, how round and inviting they look!

"Hadn't expected quite a welcome." Her comment pulls me back from my thoughts, and I jolt a step back as well, then swallow, trying to steady my reaction when our hands touch as she takes the umbrella.

She leads the kids to the house. I hurry to the passenger side to grab her bags, moving as quickly as I can from the driveway to prevent everything from getting soaked. Okay, an anxious desire to return to her also fuels my actions.

The following minutes blur. Valentina and Eden disappear into Eden's room with the bags. I change into dry sweats and a T-shirt, then microwave popcorn—the boys' snack request for our movie-binge night.

When Valentina and Eden return, the twins buzz, talking over each other to ensure Valentina isn't leaving, and they include her in everything, even extending an invite to her for the upcoming trip with our friends.

We soon settle into the dimly lit living room where the kids fight for seats, each wanting to be as close to her as possible. Apparently, they've had enough of me.

"There's enough room for everyone." She shifts to the center of the sofa to create room around her. Eden is curled on Valentina's right, the boys on her left. Felix lets Atticus sit next to her after securing a promise that next movie he'll be the closest. I sit on a nearby chair, and no one offers me a place in the queue for a turn at her side.

When the movie starts, the flickering screen captures the kids' attention. Still, they giggle and squirm. The earlier tension dissipates, absorbed by the shared warmth of family time until we're like a complete unit watching *The Lion, the Witch and the Wardrobe*.

During *Prince Caspian*, the second movie, Eden rests her head on Valentina's arm, and my heart further lifts.

Now and then, I steal glances at Valentina. Each time, she catches me. She half smiles and bites her lower lip as if stifling a laugh that still manages to warm my heart. Am I forgiven?

At one point, under the TV's dim glow, our eyes meet. I only manage a whispered thanks, but the space between us, though separated by Eden, is still charged with unspoken words. I need a moment with her to offer an apology.

By the time *Prince Caspian*'s end credits roll, Eden's breathing has deepened, her weight shifting more into Valentina, who has her arm over my daughter's shoulder in a protective cushion that unfurls my heart. Also asleep, Felix leans heavily against Valentina too. Atticus, having had his turn beside her for the first movie, is now sprawled on the side of the sofa, his head on the armrest.

"That's what you get for being popular." I stand and bend over Valentina, then slide my hands under Eden's back to lift her.

"I like being popular." Her voice carries a hint of something deeper, something unspoken that resonates in the space between us.

My hands brush over hers and against the soft cotton of her overalls as I disentangle Eden from her. She smells so heavenly I'm distracted, but I keep my focus on my daughter. The moment I look at Valentina, my eyes will betray me and reveal my attraction—worse if I look at her lips.

The fleeting touch quickens my pulse, so I'm grateful to head down the hall to Eden's room. With my face heated, I just hope she didn't see how affected I was.

I remain composed when I return to get the twins, taking one at a time to their room. By the time I come back, ready to talk, ready to address this tension, she's nowhere in sight. The empty sofa where she sat moments ago mirrors the emptiness in the room, leaving me relieved and disappointed.

I move to the kitchen, run a hand across my face, and brace against the counter, ignoring the twinge at her absence.

The time on the stove lights up 12:35. I can see her tomorrow and talk then. Does an apology need to be a big deal? But for all I know, she could be getting ready to leave. Quit.

That's what I wanted her to do before I rehired her. But things are different.

Not just because of how she affects me. In a way, I'm not ready to admit my attraction toward her. I went down that route in the past, and look where it led me—with my wife leaving us and never looking back. She ended up with one of Family Sphere's silent partners. I never asked whether their relationship started before or after our divorce.

As for Valentina, in mere months, she'll be on her way to her next job or whatever broadcast snatches her. She's confident, intelligent, and likable. Anyone would want her around.

I glance toward the hallway and the light filtering out under her bedroom door.

She wants nothing to do with me. Resigned but needing to speak with her, I take one step, then another toward the hall and her door. My heart lodges in my throat. I press my knuckles against the solid wood for a moment. I need to settle things and ensure she's here to stay longer than today for the kids. I lift my knuckles and tap on the door.

CHAPTER 20

Jason

The bedroom door swings in, and I take a step back. Valentina keeps her hand on the handle. In other words, she can only offer me a moment of her time. She's changed into silk long pants and a red T-shirt with the sun in the front. Her scent, now a blend of something like a tranquil spa, swirls around me, soothing yet stirring a tempest. When her gaze rises to mine, dizziness trips over me, heavy with longing and the aching need to love and be loved.

"What's up, Grumps?" Her playful nickname yanks me back to the moment.

Clearing my throat, I shove my hands deep into my sweats pockets. "Please don't quit." I rasp the words out. "Stay."

Her forehead creases, and her lips part in a silent question. I can't hold her gaze, afraid of rejection. So I glance past her shoulder to the humidifier curling steam into the room and the candles flickering on the windowsill. Her pictures on the wall are blurred from where I stand, but their presence is relief of some sort—they might mean she isn't packing her things to leave.

"Let's talk." Her voice halts my spiraling thoughts. She tips her head toward the hallway to the kitchen, and I lead the way, then pull out a barstool for her. It scrapes against the tile, a harsh, grating sound in the quiet house.

"I considered quitting."

My heart sinks, but I recover when the statement registers—"considered." So I have another chance.

She settles onto the stool and squares her shoulders, that confidence of hers clear. "I'm only here for the kids, Grumps."

"Thank you." That's the most important thing. The kids. My nod is precise as my gaze flits to the rain lashing the windows in the dark. I have so much I want to say, so many confessions on my tongue. I'd better say something before she can unleash something unthinkable like she's done with us.

"I appreciate you coming out tonight." She didn't have to be here, especially in this weather, yet here she is. I search her for signs of discomfort. "How are you feeling? I should've asked yesterday."

"Just a headache, but I'm good." She clasps her hands together on the marble countertop, her knuckles whitening. "Took some meds."

"I'm sorry again." I need to ensure she knows in case my text didn't convey enough sincerity. My phone had shown that she read my message. "I should've—"

"Do you trust me now that you watched the dashcam?"

I shift uncomfortably. "I don't trust myself." I grind my teeth against a raw frustration. Drawing out a breath, I try to calm this turmoil. "Makes it tricky to trust anyone."

My gaze lifts to hers. Hers probes as if to peel back the layers of my thoughts. "I didn't watch the cam, didn't need to. Deep down, I believed you instead of Eden, but I got caught up..."

What am I trying to say? I wrestle with the guilt, what-ifs tangling with the need to trust my daughter—who, in the end, will be with me when Valentina leaves. Isn't that what a good father is supposed to do?

I slide onto the seat across from her. She's perched on the edge of her stool, ready to bolt. Her gaze wanders to the long counter, and mine follows to the glass vials of oils she uses to clean the kitchen and mix dish soap and bug sprays. My home's never smelled or felt better. My kids have never been happier, even if Eden's taken longer to let her in.

Silence stretches as she scrutinizes me. I keep her gaze, this time seeing her sincerity and kindness more than I've allowed myself to acknowledge.

"What are you afraid of, Grumps?"

I blink. "What?"

"You don't trust yourself. Means you're scared of something."

I chuckle, but she's pinpointed my core issue. "I'd almost forgotten you're a shrink."

"Not in the real world. I haven't utilized my knowledge."

Her doubt probably stems from people like me and those threatened by her show. Although it helped many, some of us blamed it for our problems. But she drove here when my daughter needed her, even when Eden was at fault. The least I can do is admit my fears. That doesn't mean I have to look at her when I speak.

"Letting someone into our lives, my family. As soon as we get attached, they leave." The weight I've carried since Daisy left feels lighter with the admission. "I'm also afraid I'll fail my kids and they'll look back and wonder why I didn't do things another way."

My confession hangs in the air. I focus on the aromatic vials again.

At last, she releases a noisy breath. "I'm sorry the kids' mom left you, but anyone else around you—your kids, especially—has no doubt you love them."

Bolstered, I brave looking at her. Her gaze is level, her eyes sincere.

She rests an elbow on the marble and her chin on her hand. "Tell me about your dad?"

Dad? "I barely remember him. He left when I was four." Why does this feel like a session of some sort? Still, the words flow since no one has ever asked before. Even Daisy never brought up my past in any way. "I'd always wondered if he'd stayed, perhaps I would have had a sibling or two. I dreaded playing alone." I share with her the lonely evenings after school, the house empty while Mom worked overtime. "I had friends, but we all had to return to our own homes at some point."

Her mouth folds in a thin line. "You wanted more than one child, so they didn't have to be lonely."

At least she understands how I got here. "I always assumed they'd have two parents in the home—a complete family."

She touches my sleeve. "Your family is as perfect as one with two parents. As long as the kids feel loved, protected, and secure—which they do."

Heat burns behind my eyes, and I blink it away as a weight lifts off me.

I'd better focus on something else before I embarrass myself. She's forgiven Eden, but I still need to apologize on her behalf, and I do. "Eden's phone likely won't work anymore. It's for the best." She doesn't have to deal with checking constantly in hopes her mom called.

"I put her phone in rice at my house. It works now. Wanted to give it to her after I asked you first."

I appreciate her awaiting my approval. "Let's keep it this way. No phone for now." I exhale, desperate for a solution to the endless cycle between Daisy, Eden, and me. "If you were in my position, how would you handle Daisy?"

"What?" She gawks. Ah, so it's her turn to be surprised.

I repeat my question. "I don't want to keep the kids from their mom, but I've got to stop the letdowns when she doesn't show."

She taps her lower lip. "It's necessary to keep open a possibility for her to stay in touch with the kids. Perhaps she can go through you to talk to them—or at least to Eden. She can call you and ask to talk to her kids or make surprise visits without giving them any promises she might struggle to fulfill."

I've been too laid-back. Probably that's why Daisy has walked all over me.

"Are you still in love with Daisy?"

I chuckle mirthlessly. Any semblance of respect for her vanished long ago. I only have enough love left for my kids. "She'll always be connected to me... but love?"

"Do you see yourself moving on someday with someone else?"

"Now and then, I have a desire..." I eye her. Why would she ask, anyway? "You gonna send me a bill now after this shrinking session?"

She chuckles, then waves. "Since you asked"—she shrugs—"don't focus on people who've let you down along the way, Grumps. Thank them. Without those people, without those trials, you wouldn't be where you are today."

That's one of the wisest statements I've ever heard. "That sounds like something Ethan would say." I tip my head. "Makes me wonder if you're a spiritual person."

"Spiritual sounds like practice. I'm more on a spiritual journey, and sometimes I get sidetracked," she says, talking about her faith in God, the ups and downs. "My job hunt and failures reminded me how helpless I am without God's help...It helped me get back on track with God."

Yes, that sounds like Ethan. He always assures me that God meets us where we are and as we are. He made us, so He's aware of our weaknesses and inability to remain faithful while He forever remains faithful to us.

"The point is—focus on what you're doing right rather than what you're doing wrong."

"How do I do that?"

"Let go of the past. Never allow the past to ruin your present. Make new memories for your family... traditions and things that you can do together, monthly, annually, or whatever." She suggests various ideas, including a simple weekly movie night, a monthly hike, or an annual family vacation. "Things that will be a Sterling family tradition for years to come."

"New memories. I like that." Excitement bubbles up. Valentina will be a part of those new memories, one way or another. "I'll start these new memories by being a friend to my kids' nanny."

"That's a good start." She smiles, and my heart all but melts.

I don't want to stop talking to her. I need to savor this unusual moment together. "The boys told me you're all starting gratitude journals?"

"Yeah. I used to journal." A smile curls the corners of her mouth. "A gratitude journal can be a powerful tool for enhancing mental and emotional well-being."

"My mom used to make me write what I was thankful for. Said I complained a lot. I guess I lost track of doing so sometime in middle school." Mom was too busy at work to cope with all the things I needed. "Since I have a counselor at my disposal, what other advice do you have for me to be a good dad?"

"You need to be content that you're doing enough." She makes it sound so simple, yet she carries a challenging intensity. "You shouldn't overparent."

Overparent? "What do you mean?"

"Eden, let's say. She's eleven. Maybe tone down on the hugs in front of her peers. Unless she hugs you first." She shrugs. "Your kids will still love you if you make sure they clean up their messes and do their own laundry. Like I said before, if all the fathers in the country did half of what you do, the kids and the world would be a better place."

I didn't realize I needed this reassurance. Perhaps sensing these personal subjects might be too much, she changes the topic. "How's work going? And the new show?"

"I should've hired you," I blurt out, another form of an apology. "You were our top candidate, but..."

"It's fine. I'm sure the one you hired is doing well."

"The ratings haven't been good." Unfortunately.

Her eyes widen. "Have you engaged in community events? I mean, diverse communities and events. Like in the Bronx, they have a spring music festival that draws families, Queens... no, Brooklyn has a spring food fest—consider diversity in race, age, culture, and financial background. You're a family network after all."

I nod. She's knowledgeable. "How do you know all these events?"

"Did my research before I interviewed at Family Sphere."

I shift, guilt pricking me again as she offers suggestions for different events in detail. She doesn't appear regretful and offers logical suggestions that inspire action. All her ideas make sense. In fact, she's just convinced me to speak at an eighth-grade graduation ceremony in Brooklyn, a suggestion she pitched as a way to connect with the community.

"My friend Leah will be over the moon. A CEO of a family network addressing her students."

My team was right. Valentina was the perfect candidate.

"I am sorry for being a jerk." I look into her eyes, and her half smile makes my heart skip. "Just because I have issues, doesn't mean I should take it out on others."

"We all make mistakes."

"I cost you a job you'd be good at."

"I can be good at nannying too." Her light response assures me of her commitment to us. "And I'm crazy about your kids."

"Does that mean I'm forgiven?" I think I hold my breath for a sign of absolution.

"It depends."

"On?" I lean in, knowing I'm flirting and she's flirting back. Knowing how much trouble we could get into if we don't stop right this second. "What does it depend on, Ms. Diaz?"

"Your behavior."

"Am I behaving right now?" I waggle my eyebrows.

She chuckles.

Warmth spreads through my chest. "I'll take that as a yes." I pause before adding, "And what my daughter said about me not liking you—it's not true. Not in the way she meant."

"I don't expect you to like me, Grumps. I know you let me watch your kids because you think your family is what I need right now."

"And you're what they need." That truth is deeper than I intended to reveal, which must be why she sucks in a breath.

Time to change the subject. "So, you're okay coming along to Long Island in two weeks?"

"I know it's the kids' idea—"

"I, too, would like you to come."

"I'd love to."

My heart soars. Having her with us in my happy place seems just right.

CHAPTER 21

Jason

Valentina stays to celebrate Easter with us. She truly forgave me. Now, as she and Eden enter the kitchen, her presence soothes my lingering tension, and her beauty lights up the morning. Her dark hair cascades around her shoulders, a rich contrast to her white dress with blue print. Likewise, Eden's golden hair swooshes free over her new floral-pink dress.

"You look... beautiful."

"Val helped me shop." Eden's smile reaches her eyes, lighting up her face.

Valentina sweeps her flowy hair aside, and my hands itch to touch the tresses.

I then mouth a thanks. My accountant keeps track of my expenses, so I haven't checked to make sure Valentina is using the card rather than spending her money. Maybe I'd better look into that. For now, I call the boys, and they come racing down the hallway. I let everyone go first, and in the garage, I hold the passenger door to my SUV for Valentina while the kids get into their seats in the back. We're like a family once more.

Being a special holiday, there's no children's service so we all sit together in the church. Ethan speaks of Jesus's resurrection bringing new beginnings. His words weave a gentle reminder of my new beginning. Forgiving Daisy is a necessity, even if she has no idea I'm mad at her. I even convince myself I'm not bothered by her decision to take off and leave us behind.

At the end of the day, she was the one pregnant, and I had no idea how hard being a mom was for her. I have no right to harbor anger.

My heart feels strangely open, vulnerable to the Easter message of redemption and love.

After the service, Ethan insists we stay and chat with other church members for community connection. I've been here a few times, enough to see and greet familiar faces. Several members cast curious glances our way. Some even approach to ask if Valentina is the children's mother.

She's blended into our lives, her role expanding in ways I hadn't anticipated, so little wonder she sparks such assumptions. The question doesn't bother me as much as it might have. Instead, part of me is oddly pleased.

When we leave, the guys and I drive our families to Chuck's sprawling farm for the Easter celebration. Aside from the guys around us, Chuck is our closest neighbor, even though he's several acres beyond us. The breeze is slightly chilly, even with the sun peeking through. Still, my friends and I hover around as our kids feed the goats. My eyes betray me and seek the two-story white house with its blue shutters in search of her.

Chuck is standing behind the grill. Smoke drifts from it as women from church hand him items.

Then Valentina emerges, swinging a spatula, and my heart plummets, then thumps as if it's a drumbeat. With her broad smile, she says something that draws Chuck's and the women's attention. When he responds, her shoulders shake with her laugh.

The sight stirs the admiration and affection I'm grappling with. It's not just her beauty that captivates me—it's her warmth, her ease with everyone.

A slap jostles my shoulder. "Have you told her yet how you feel?"

At Ethan's amusement, I frown to mask my embarrassment. What I feel for Valentina challenges me to confront feelings I hadn't expected. It's exhilarating and daunting.

But I scowl at him and edge away. I keep my distance from him and her for the rest of the outing. But there's no avoiding her later in the comfort of our home as we play board games, eat our dinner, and even journal about our day around the kitchen island.

Then the kids insist we watch the third movie. "We fell asleep before we could watch *The Voyage of the Dawn Treader*." Eden pleads with Valentina, clearly aware she'll yield.

She shrugs, then eyes me for a response. "I wouldn't mind watching that movie."

"If it's okay with you—"

"Popcorn time!" Atticus leaps for the pantry.

Felix holds up a hand. "Let's watch downstairs. I'll set up the projector."

"Felix can set up a projector?" Valentina lets out a low whistle.

"That's my boy." My chest swells. "Anything with electronics, he's always our man."

It's been a long day, and starting a movie at eight doesn't seem right. But I'll go to work late tomorrow. The kids don't have school. It's teacher planning day.

Even with plenty of space to spread out in the basement, all three kids huddle around Valentina, and *déjà vu* sets in.

Then, after *The Voyage of the Dawn Treader*, they insist we watch *Peter Rabbit*.

"Val has never seen it before, but she's read the book," Eden insists.

"Guys." I flick on the lights and try to usher them to their feet. "It's almost ten, well past bedtime, and we've seen the movie already."

The kids make no move to rise.

"It's *Easter*." Atticus folds his arms.

"We shouldn't have a bedtime on *Easter*." Felix gives me puppy-dog eyes.

And Eden cinches it. "Resurrection Day is all about getting up, not lying in any beds or tombs. The bunny stuff is just fluff today, but it's still the *perfect* day to watch *Peter Rabbit*."

The boys back her up. "You've gotta let Val see it, Dad."

But by the time the closing credits roll, all three kids have fallen asleep. Eden on Valentina's shoulder, and Atticus on her other shoulder. Felix is leaning against Atticus, but Valentina's carrying all their weight.

My hands brush over her rib cage as I try to lift Eden. Then my fingers get stuck between the buttons on her overalls. How many of these overalls does she own? I'm frozen in place, strength draining when her gaze lifts, her face inches below mine.

Her free hand covers mine, her breath warm against my face, her fingers aiding to disentangle us with a delicate touch. Our gazes dance, and our breaths mingle in the blaring silence. Her dark lashes frame the sweetest pair of dark-brown eyes, so wide and innocent. Her face alone could bring me to my knees.

"So... sorry." I breathe out, unsure if that's what I'm supposed to be saying.

"It's... okay." Her breath is a whisper.

The fleeting touch and moment send warmth rushing through me, a pulse so strong it robs me of breath. Physically free, I lift Eden, her small form light in my arms, and I carry her up to her room, my heart beating a frantic rhythm in the calm night.

What was that all about?

CHAPTER 22

Valentina

For today's morning devotional with the kids, I plan "The Joy of the Lord is My Strength" to coincide with our gratitude journals. After my personal prayer time at six, I'm ready to start my day.

With my heart soaring, I walk through the quiet kitchen. The silence means everyone is still asleep. After the weekend, I can see good came from an unexpected incident to create a step toward healing for Jason's family and me.

So much for all my self-talk about being done with him. Eden's call and apology vanquished my pride and self-assurance. There's nothing like a genuine apology from a child, not any child but *Eden*. Prickly at times due to trust issues, yet sweet.

She'd been terrified about her periods and upset about growing up. Of course, she was aware of menstruation. They'd even just had the unit in school, and her grandma had the conversation with her prior to that.

"I just hadn't expected it to be this soon," she'd confided, after I talked her through the steps of taking care of herself. We then spoke about growing up and embracing each stage in life as a wonderful gift from God. That allowed me to discuss the accident incident. How to and not to react when we're angry, frustrated, and scared. I might have assured her I'd be a part of her life as long as I'm living. But I hope she understood that didn't mean I had to be her nanny and live in their house.

Now, before the kids wake up, I need to work off some of the Easter food I ate yesterday. Jason might be in the gym this morning or find me there. It's happened twice. A thrill runs through me at the possibility.

How odd a thought. I'm supposed to loathe this man—Grumps. Yet, undeniable attraction causes sparks. I can't say if he despises me.

He's an open book, so I can tell when he's mad and when he isn't. I prefer that over someone who acts all sweet toward you but then stabs you from behind.

Of course, more than that, I prefer the tender moments of this past weekend, well, mostly last night. Those had my mind longing for him to kiss me. My lips tingle at the thought of us kissing. It's all crazy because I disliked him so much on Friday, yet I couldn't stop thinking about him when I went to bed after he texted his apology. I had to picture myself in his position of having my kids come close to getting hurt.

With how much I need to clear my muddled brain, a workout has never sounded better.

When I make it to the dark gym, I should be relieved Jason's not there. Disappointed, I switch on the light and head straight for the treadmill for a cardio warm-up. I glimpse my reflection—my ponytail swishing and my black leggings and hot-pink tank top accentuating my movements. The mirror reminds me to focus on my rhythm, to steady the thoughts and emotions riling me.

The treadmill music helps me pace my breathing as I run. By the time I hit the two-mile mark, my throat is parched, so I head for the water cooler.

Revitalized, I go straight for the punching bags hanging in another corner. Even stocked with all sorts of equipment, the gym looks spacious. Four sets of gloves hang on the hook behind the punching bag. Jason must keep extras for when his buddies show up. I try on several pairs. They are all the same size, roomy, but they'll do.

With the soft mat beneath my shoes, I work through a circuit my brother recently taught me, incorporating strikes and kicks alongside jumping jacks and crunches. Sweat trickles into my sports bra, and my heart rate climbs. But I still need to pull some weights after this.

As I strike a punch and kick, I hear footsteps.

"You do kickboxing too?"

I'm unable to answer, needing to compose myself. My pulse, already fast from the physical exertion, further quickens with excitement. His hair is rumpled, an overnight scruff shadows his jaw, and his black T-shirt clings to his broad shoulders while dark shorts hang low on his hips. I'm mesmerized as he strides toward me.

"Wanna tangle?" He crosses his arms over his chest.

"What do you mean?"

He laughs. "You seem like you can take me down."

Is this some kind of April Fool's prank? "I'm not that good at sparring."

"Makes two of us." He tosses me protective headgear, shin guards, and a mouthpiece, then moves to the center of the room. "Let's see what you got, Diaz."

"I'm going to assume you're not here to hurt me." Properly outfitted, I take my position across from him.

His eyes glow. "You don't strike me as someone who's scared of anyone."

Strike him, I definitely will. Imagine what I'd have given for this opportunity weeks ago! But if he thinks I'm strong and confident, then I've done my job fooling him like I do everyone else. "You sure about this, Sterling?"

"Are you stalling, Diaz?"

I've memorized the key areas my brother drilled into me, so I target those. But Jason is fast and good at this. He blocks my first jab and my second. On my third, he grabs my wrist and twists me around so my back flattens against his broad chest. With my arm wedged between us, my shoulder protests if I try to wriggle out. Worse, he doesn't release me. His breath warms my neck, my knees weaken, and my own breathing quickens. "Is that the best you can do?"

Carlos would have a fit over us combining wrestling and kickboxing and who knows what else. Plus, not setting any rules.

Jason lets go, and I shake out my arm as I catch my breath and compose myself, then face him again. The intensity lingers, sparking a mix of challenge and chemistry.

"I was taking it easy on you." Setting my stance and acting stronger, I fix my gaze on him.

He frowns, maybe concerned I might deliver on my promise. "No hitting my face, Diaz."

"Worried about your face, huh! Trying to impress someone, Grumps?" I strike a jab toward his lower abdomen, but he deflects it. Great. Odds aren't in my favor. After all, the guy is taller than I am and likely outweighs me by nearly a hundred pounds.

"You aren't using your size to your advantage," he chides almost as if annoyed I'm not challenging him more.

"I'm trying!" I protest with a groan.

"Stop circling me. You're wasting your energy."

Fine. Determined, I try for a one-two punch to his chest, but it's futile. In a swift motion, he sweeps my legs out from under me. I end up flat on my back, the air whooshing out of my lungs in a painful gasp. He smirks, leaning over me so his handsome face blocks out the bright fluorescent lights above. I stare up at his full lips, sharp cheekbones, furrowed brows, and I feel electrified. It's the adrenaline, or so I tell myself.

"Is that all you've got?" A devious edge teases his voice. He extends a gloved hand to help me up.

Before he can react, I hike my legs up and wrap them around the back of his knees, bringing him down so he topples beside me. We lie flat on the mat together, breathing hard. My right leg is pressed against his left. "Is that all you've got?" I echo, smirking before I roll over and grind my elbow into his stomach as I push myself up.

With my heart pounding so fiercely, that better be the end of my workout. I leave Jason to continue his session and head upstairs. It's quiet. Thankfully, the kids are still asleep. But little wonder with us letting them stay up until nearly midnight.

Jason catches up with me later in the kitchen while I'm preparing breakfast. His grin lights up my heart. His hair is damp from a shower, and he's changed into gray sweats and a white undershirt. "Need any help?"

"I meant to have you make breakfast since I whipped you, but you have to head to work."

He chuckles and saunters over, joining me as if it's our usual morning routine. The sparks from our mock battle linger in the air, adding an undercurrent to the task.

I have a good feeling about today, and it blossoms into a beautiful day when the kids wake up excited for breakfast and morning devotion. Jason joins us and stays through the devotions. Afterward, he helps the boys finalize their spring break poster boards for their school project. Eden practices her introduction for the recital.

Later, when she suggests we go painting in town, Jason tags along. We get sidetracked by Sips and Scripts, then lunch at Brooke's Diner. Caught up in the moment, Jason even calls his work to cancel the rest of his day.

We return to Manhattan on Tuesday morning, and I drive my car while Jason takes his with the kids, dropping them off at school. Over the following two weeks, I settle into a familiar routine—watching Eden at her dance lessons, helping her memorize the introduction lines for her dance recital, and taking turns with Matthew to oversee the boys at soccer practice. Jason has been leaving work early. On days he can't make it to the kids' practices, he's home by the time we return. I continue to be a part of their family dinners. Twice, Carlos joins us at the park to play soccer and volleyball with the kids, and he stays for dinner. April showers or not, our activities have not been canceled.

One time during dinner in Judy's Manhattan home, the conversation turns to the accident, and Jason asks my opinion on what car should replace the one hit. "The Audi can still be fixed," I suggest, but he insists on something new rather than fixing a car that might be unreliable for the kids and me.

The way he includes me and values my opinions makes me forget about his past grumpiness.

This feeling of family deepens even more during today's visit to the aviation museum. It's Thursday, the second week after spring break, and Jason joins us. Together we explore the displays and histories of various aircraft, snapping pictures. Over the moon wide-eyed, Atticus overwhelms the guide with questions. During our meal at the airplane-themed restaurant across from the museum, Judy FaceTimes Jason, and he lifts the phone.

"It's Mimi."

The kids crowd around, chirping hellos.

"Val took us to the aircraft museum." Atticus and Felix declare while Eden chimes in about the art.

As Jason pans the camera to include me, Judy's face lights up. "Val, I'm so glad you're watching my grandkids. I hope Jason's treating you well."

"Thanks, and he is." I press a hand to my heart, touched by her kindness, then ask about her trip. She looks relaxed, and so does Phil when he pops his head in to say hello. We finish the chat with lively updates and shared laughter.

Friday evening, the kids' pleading wins me over, and I agree to stay the night in Meadowbrook. After tucking them into bed, I wander into the kitchen for water and pause when I see the newly built holders displaying my essential oils.

Jason's footsteps pad the floor, and my stomach dances when he smiles at me.

"You built this?" I tip my head to the holders.

"Built might be pushing it." He shrugs. "It just took assembling with a screwdriver."

"Thank you." My chest swells. How sweet that he thought of organizing my oils.

The next morning when I enter the kitchen, he's already got coffee started. He pours me coffee in my favorite mug and hands it to me. As I sip, the perfect blend of cream surprises me.

He lifts a mug matching mine in a toast to me. "Had to buy another."

"Why didn't you tell me I was using your favorite mug all along?"

"I'm just glad I have great taste in coffee cups." He winks.

When the kids wake, we sit around for breakfast together, amid their cheerful chatter. A sense of belonging consumes me with a warmth I hadn't anticipated, solidifying my place in this unexpected, yet perfectly imperfect family.

Saturday has become the new laundry day for the kids since they've learned to do their laundry. With the boys still playing outside and Eden absorbed in a book in the playroom-slash-library, I head downstairs to run a cycle of my bedsheets and some clothes I wore here last week.

My gaze drifts to the gym's open door. Jason was working out earlier, but the lights are off now. He's probably back to work in his office or bedroom. I turn toward the open door across from the gym, but two steps in, my feet halt. Jason is shirtless, sorting through clothes stacked on the rumbling dryer. Heat creeps through my neck as my eyes betray me, tracing over his hairy chest.

"Having a good morning, Valentina?"

I slap the top of my heated forehead, then swallow. "Oh, I—Sorry, I didn't know you were..." I step back and turn so fast my shoulder slams into the edge of the doorway.

"Ouch!" He's chuckling, isn't he? "No need to run off. I'm all dressed now."

I could just leave, but... whew. My racing heart slows, and I turn to see he has pulled a T-shirt over his head, the fabric stretching taut across his shoulders.

"How's your shoulder?" His eyes twinkle.

I can't contain my stomach flutters. I don't even care about my shoulder. "I came to do laundry." Is that even my voice?

"Don't let me keep you." He folds one of his undershirts and stacks it over a fluffy clean pile from the kids' earlier loads.

Taking a deep breath, I step toward the washer. His scent blends in with the fabric and fills my senses. I reach for the basket and begin loading my bedsheets, acutely aware of his gaze on me. The silence isn't awkward but charged, every shuffle and rustle amplified.

"How did the soccer match go this morning?"

"Eden and I let the boys win." This confined space is far too intimate. My hands shake as I add a soap pod. I focus on placing the laundry in the washer. It now seems like a task I've never done before.

"You're sure you let them win, or did they beat you? Those are two separate things."

I meet his gaze sideways. "What are you implying, Grumps?"

"A fair rematch this afternoon. Girls versus boys." With the challenge arching his brow, he looks me up and down, rendering me speechless. I could get lost in his blue eyes. The world narrows to just the two of us surrounded by the hum of the dryer and the faint smell of detergent. The air seems to thrum with unspoken possibilities. "What do you say, Ms. Diaz?"

"What?"

He repeats his statement since I've lost my hearing temporarily.

"It's not a fair match with three boys against two girls, but—"

A rustle scuffles above us. Then something brown leaps from an open box and sails over our heads before launching itself into the open air and sprinting in a circle.

I let out a squeal and drop whatever I had in my hand. No way! Do I see a bushy tail?

The critter darts up to the side shelf.

"Oh no, not in the house!" Jason dashes to the door and slams it shut, trapping the squirrel inside with us.

I screech. "Why'd you close us in?"

"Quick, open the windows. We need to give it an escape route," he commands over his shoulder and approaches the unexpected intruder.

I snap into action. But as I move to open the nearest window, the squirrel scrambles around in a desperate search for an exit. It's a blur of motion, and my heart thunders while I dodge to the other side. I then run and leap onto Jason's back, wrapping my arms around him. "Get it out!"

The vibrations of his deep chuckle rumble through his body to mine, even as he tries to maintain our balance. "Valentina, you're not helping," he chides through laughter, strides to a window, and slides it open.

What can I say? I'm in survival mode.

I don't see the squirrel now, which strengthens me to slide off Jason's back, my cheeks hot. "Sorry." I heave a shaky breath, then rush to the other window across the room and fumble with the latch. As I guide it open, I turn in time to see the squirrel skitter to the shelf again. I cover my mouth, one hand holding in my scream.

Jason moves around the room, whistling in an attempt to usher the critter toward the windows. Finally, the squirrel leaps through one of them.

I rush to seal the window shut before the critter can reconsider its exit. Then, at last, I cup a hand to my heart, willing it to settle.

Jason walks over, his eyes twinkling. "Well, that was one way to get your heart racing, huh?"

A nervous chuckle escapes. "Definitely not the morning workout I had in mind, but effective."

His eyes gleam as they search mine. My knees are still shaking and weaker now, so I take a step back and lean against the door. I think my whole body is trembling, but I find myself laughing. I survived.

He shakes his head from side to side. "That was quite an adventure."

"Definitely more excitement for today." My heart is still pounding, but my fear has vanished.

"Are you okay?" He steps closer. "I'm glad I had the emergency exit windows installed rather than the usual basement windows."

He seems calm, as if he's handled this situation before.

"Do squirrels get in your house often?"

"Nah. I wouldn't be surprised if the twins had something to do with it. They were fidgeting with ladders and whispering earlier while I was in the gym. They've been talking about having a pet squirrel."

"How in the world did they capture a squirrel?" I shiver and wrap my arms around myself.

"The two of them can get into some serious mischief."

"We'd better get them a dog or cat soon."

Jason takes another step closer. A shadow dulls his eyes. "We had a dog." His voice dips. "It died shortly after Daisy left."

My heart squeezes. "I'm so sorry."

He breathes out, and I realize how close we've gotten once his scent—masculine, eucalyptus, and spicy—fills my senses. He reaches out, and his fingers graze my forehead as he tucks stray strands behind my ear. "I think this all goes along with us making new memories."

His eyes meet mine, the blue so soft, so searching, and my nerves tingle like I'm standing on hot coals. My gaze drops to his mouth. His lips part, and his chest rises and falls beneath his T-shirt.

Footsteps running upstairs snap us out of the haze, and Jason steps back. "We'd better get that laundry and have a word with the boys."

My hand finds my thundering chest. I struggle for breath. Jason and I just had another moment. The warmth of his nearness still lingers all through me.

CHAPTER 23

Valentina

Long Island in April holds a beauty that, while different from the white sand and turquoise waters of Venezuela, feels like a slice of paradise for New Yorkers. The air is crisp, and the breeze, steady and cool in the mid-fifties, carries the briny scent of the sea while rhythmic waves lap the shore.

One of my first jobs after college was as a reporter covering local events and stories, which brought me to Long Island a few times, though never for leisure.

Despite the chill, Jason and his friends are shirtless, their skin glistening as they play beach volleyball a safe distance from where I'm hanging out with the kids. The thumps of the volleyball and the rumble of their laughter mix with the ocean's whisper, creating a lively yet soothing background.

Nearby, Liam, who joined us when his son summoned him to fix a lopsided sandcastle, meticulously reshapes the sand with a trowel. Meanwhile, the rest of the kids build sandcastles while Eden chatters beside me. She scoops more sand with her plastic shovel and stacks it onto her creation. Her running words depict the castle she built here last fall, not missing a single detail of the actual construction. "Daddy had to take another trip into town to get us new shovels."

I nod along, my gaze on her to show I'm listening, though I check to ensure no one ventures too close to the water. Eden's potential as a future journalist shines through as her account paints a vivid picture. Or maybe she'll be an architect like Liam. The sandcastle takes shape under her skilled hands, each mound a testament to her abilities—a story told not just through words, but through the artful sand construction at her feet.

"Happy with that, mate?" Liam stands when his son nods. Then he lingers, slapping the sand off the seat of his shorts.

Since I try to instill manners in Jason's kids and they spend a lot of time with these guys, I'd better chime in. "What do you say to your dad?"

At my prompt, Liam's six-year-old dutifully thanks his dad.

Liam winks at me. "Appreciate you being here and instilling some values into our littles."

"You guys have done a good job of that already." I stand and brush sand from my leggings. The breeze seeps through my light sweater, and I relax, grateful we're not close enough to the expanse of the ocean to warrant any immediate worry. My gaze drifts to the volleyball game, and I catch Jason's gaze across the distance. "You're all great dads."

"It's Jason's turn to cook tonight." Liam lowers his voice, leaning closer, perhaps not wanting the kids to overhear. His green eyes glint, his charm evident in his demeanor. He's tall, lean, and handsome like all his buddies. But his nearness doesn't affect me the way Jason does. "I was wondering if you could help me prank him."

"I don't know about pranking my boss. I'm just getting on his good side."

"He might be a big ol' oaf." His Aussie accent flows as he glances back at the men.

I follow his glance. Jason is staring at me, his focus intense and heated. My mind feels like mush as his gaze holds mine, laden with promises I'm ready to let him make. How is it he can make my skin heat and my heart race from so far away with nothing more than a look?

He flicks his gaze to Liam, then frowns.

Liam tsks. "If anything, it'll be me he wants to harm, not you."

"Liam, get back already," Jason calls. "We need a full team!"

Liam winks, then slaps my shoulder. "We'll talk more about this prank later."

I shake my head, amused yet anxious over what kind of pranks these men might play against each other. But now the kids are arguing, frustrated by their failed attempts to build or whatnot. I'd better dig in to help those who need it.

"What do you think of this, Val?"

At Eden's query, I lower myself. My tights sink into the sand as I inspect her castle. "It's beautiful!"

Atticus shows me his progress on a sand airplane, and Felix showcases his. Liam's, Ethan's, and Russ's kids eagerly display their creations. I smile, encouraging each of them as I ask about their favorite food, colors, and other simple questions. But like most kids, they give lengthy answers, even diverting off topic to what they do on their birthdays. Through the birthday chatter, I sense Eden's silence. Undoubtedly, she still harbors hurtful memories from her seventh birthday.

The sandcastle enthusiasm winds down. Now, two siblings start kicking each other's creations. I summon the kids to join me at the beanbag toss station where we will throw beanbags into buckets instead of the usual targets.

As all the young ones dash ahead, Eden walks by my side, and I take her hand to continue the birthday conversation. My feet sink into the cool sand. "Remember when we talked about starting new memories?"

"I like journals." She swings our hands. "Will you still teach me how to edit videos?"

"I'm looking forward to it." Her newfound passion is for photography this week. She's been snapping pictures on my phone as we stroll to Central Park in the evenings. "What if we celebrate your birthday this year?"

"I don't..." Her steps slow, and her grip tightens. "Dad is... What if—"

"Your dad is not going to leave you on your birthday." That must be what she fears.

"He's busy, and I don't want him stressed."

"Any time your dad gets to celebrate another year of you growing, it's a gift to him, not a burden."

She nods, swallowing. "But my birthday is in June."

"June will be here before we know it."

She smiles. "I guess."

I've decided to extend my stay beyond July. Despite occasional ups and downs, I feel at peace, like I'm where I'm meant to be. I've been praying for guidance and have found my calm.

When we toss beanbags, I glance at the volleyball area where my gaze finds Jason's. Sure, all the guys look handsome under the sun, but Jason... he affects me. Maybe because a heated energy simmers between us.

A tiny hand tugs at me. Ethan's little girl asks for my help to show her how to throw. I lower myself to her level, take her little hand with the soft beanbag, and walk closer to the bucket. Then I aid her to throw the bag in. "Great job!"

She beams. "Did it."

"Do you guys always do this when your dads play volleyball at the beach?" I gesture to the men's elaborate setup with chairs.

"Sometimes Mimi comes with us." Eden brushes a wisp of blonde back from her tanning cheeks. "If she doesn't come, we play whatever they play."

Jason had invited me to play volleyball, but I'd offered to stay with the kids so the guys could enjoy their time. The house is close enough for me to walk the kids back if they get tired.

We continue the beanbag toss and alternate with building more sandcastles when a growl rumbles through the air. I spin around. Jason's limping, his friends scrambling around him.

"Get some water from the ocean!" someone shouts.

"What do we do?" shouts another.

I suck in a sharp breath. "Looks like your daddy's hurt." I touch Eden's arm. "Can you keep the kids calm here while I go help?"

Her blue eyes big and tanned skin blanched, she nods.

So I grab the basket I brought with a first aid kit

Jason is propped up in a lounge chair, his foot elevated and bleeding. As I approach, he turns toward me, while his three frazzled friends hover anxiously around him.

Atticus's voice hollers our way. "If you're upset, Dad, scream."

"Scream, right?" Jason looks at me. "Do you have your phone, by chance?"

"I do." I pat the side pockets of my leggings for it. Whenever I babysit anyone's kids, I always keep my phone handy for emergencies. I get closer to Jason. "I hope we don't need to call 9-1-1."

"I think a piece of glass got jammed in there," Liam says.

Ethan suggests a Band-Aid. Russ suggests Jason soak his bloody wound in the ocean.

"We should first get him back to the house," Ethan adds.

Jason fixes his gaze on me. "Could you call my mom, instead?"

Hadn't he said Judy couldn't be reached unless she called?

"I'll check this out first." I need to be fast to clean his wound. I put the basket down and retrieve the first aid kit. I urge him to tip the back of the lounger down flat. Then, to avoid distractions, I request the dads to help Eden keep the kids away in case some panic at the sight of blood.

With his feet dangling off the beach lounger, I kneel and assess the injury before grabbing a water bottle from the ones Jason and his buddies abandoned on the sand. When I pour it over his wound, he screams—a sharp, piercing sound. As I clean the affected area, he groans rather loudly for such a strong man.

Ugh. "There it is. A shard of glass sticking out a tad from your arch."

"What happens now?" He runs a hand over his face.

"I'm going to take it out like I would a splinter." I focus on his face and avoiding his shirtless chest. "If I can't manage, we'll figure something out."

I pull another chair close and lift his leg onto my lap, keeping the first aid kit on his lounger.

"Is this the time for you to seek revenge?"

"It's a possibility." I rub disinfectant around the wound and toss the soiled cloths underneath his chair. A distraction seems necessary. "Why did you want us to call your mom? Does she still make your doctor's appointments?"

"She's a nurse." He grimaces. "Always there for me."

"I can tell you two are close."

"She's my hero," he admits. "Probably the only one who will never leave me."

I sanitize the tweezers from the kit. "God will never leave you. I hope you know that."

"Sometimes I think He's with me, but I don't know, since I can't see Him."

"God's everywhere around us." I peer at the ocean, then back to his injury. "How your kids make you feel is a good example of how you and I make God feel. We're His children. You also experience God's presence through friends. You have good friends who will stick with you, I'm sure."

I position the tweezers over the piece of glass, being careful. "You have me too. At least, I consider myself your friend."

"But you're going to leave when you find a big-shot job." He sounds genuine, sad even. "You'll forget I ever existed."

As the old rejections linger, my chest tightens. My fingers pinch the metal tweezers on the shard. But the glass slips from their grip, and blood seeps around the wound. "You're not easy to forget. If you want, I can stay in touch. Plus, you have friends to count on."

"I don't like you being too nice to my friends."

"But they're your friends. Why wouldn't I be nice?"

His gaze tingles over me. "They're single and not bad looking."

I stay focused, probing the shard for a good grip again. "I'm single too. Not prone to a good-looking man."

"They will steal you away. They're nicer than I am."

Not sure exactly what he means, I still shiver as butterflies swoop through my stomach. My hand shakes, and the tweezers twang against the glass. That better not have shoved it in deeper. *Focus, girl!*

He grunts. "They don't usually have a beautiful woman in their midst."

Is he jealous? I'm now eager to probe further, flirt with him again. Doing so with Jason is playing with fire. Still, a bubbling excitement takes over any sense of reason.

"You think I'm beautiful?"

"And nice. Kind."

I'm flattered, but he might be delirious if he's telling me this to my face. "How are you feeling?"

"Good. Why?"

"Hmm. Interesting." I smirk, then yank the glass out.

"Ouch!" He groans, blood spurts free, and one of his friends' voice floats from a distance telling him to quit scaring the seagulls.

"It's out." What a relief! "Okay, take a deep breath." I sanitize the area, then wrap a compression bandage around his foot to stabilize it. Moving to his head, I hold out my fingers for him to count. "How many fingers do you see?"

"Three."

I put another finger down. "How about now?"

He captures my hand, his fingers encircling my wrist, his blue eyes tender yet intense. Gone is the breeze, replaced by heat that stirs the butterflies in my stomach. "Are you testing to see if I have a concussion?"

I swallow to mask my affection. "It's not every day you go complimenting me, Grumps."

He tugs me down at the same time as he pulls up to sit, and our faces are inches apart.

"Get used to it." His voice dips. Our lips hover closer, and my heart thuds as our gazes linger on each other. "New memories and starting over, remember?" He then lets my hand go.

I'm lightheaded with desire when I stand. I gotta say I like this new Jason Sterling.

CHAPTER 24

Valentina

The corner lamp spreads a dim light through the room as Ethan strums his guitar and narrates a Bible story, encouraging the kids to repeat the words. While the guys and I sing along, most of the children, sprawled on the soft carpet around me, yawn in their dads' arms.

I shift Ethan's five-year-old to balance her weight on my lap while Eden sits beside me. My gaze flicks to Jason, the only one in a chair because of his injury. I catch him looking at me, but he shifts his focus to the mantel behind Ethan, pretending he hasn't been watching me. The twins are squeezed on either side of his cushy chair, their eyes droopy but turned Ethan's way. Despite the sofas behind Jason, the kids wanted to sit on the floor.

During dinner, I sat across from Jason, not intentionally, but that's how it turned out. Every time our eyes met amid the passing of drinks and plates, I sensed a subtle exchange. Our hands brushed when I passed him a bowl of grilled brussels sprouts, and he murmured his thanks with a softness out of character for Grumps.

With Jason off dinner duty due to his injury, Liam took over. However, Liam pranked him by placing Bubble Wrap under the padding of Jason's chair, which popped when Jason sat, drawing laughter.

"You're all tired." Ethan strums the final chord and sets the guitar by the fireplace.

As the dads help their kids to bed—Jason's two-story beach house has seven bedrooms, enough for all his friends and their families—Eden asks me to read a chapter with her. After bidding the twins and several other kids good night and receiving hugs, I step back into the hallway to await Eden as she bids Jason good night in the boys' room.

"I'll come tuck you in," Jason says.

"Val is going to tuck me in tonight," Eden replies.

Propped up with ruffly pale-pink pillows on her bed, we write in our journals on her bed, then take turns reading the chapter of her new adventure book. It's chapter six, and the girl's on an adventure, slaying dragons along her journey in the woods, yet she's terrified.

The beach photographs on the wall snag my attention. Although it's a vacation home, the room is painted hot pink. Very true to Eden. Jason sure is a great dad to ensure that.

She slides under the covers. A yawn slips loose as she discusses the character in the book. "Courageous people are born that way. You can't just become brave all of a sudden."

Smiling, I shake my head. "Courage and bravery are slightly different, but God can give them to us at the times we need." I feather my fingers through her wispy hair. "Do you know the story of David and Goliath?"

"I heard it in Sunday school."

"David wasn't brave." I twist her hair around my finger. "But he had faith God would enable him to fight the giant."

Eden nods.

"No one is born brave. And courage isn't the lack of fear but rather the choice to act despite it." I release her hair and rest my palm on her shoulder. My hope is for her to be more confident before her teen years. "My mom always said, to be truly brave, you never let anyone trample over you."

"You mean like fighting back?"

I cross my legs, my weight sinking into the bed when I shift to look into her curious blue eyes. "If that's what it takes sometimes to chase off a bully like Goliath, then a fight is necessary." Not that Eden has any bullies, but just in case, she'd better not go fighting her adversaries. "But God tells us to turn the other cheek. It can be hard to have that kind of self-control, but it's the best solution."

I snag one of those ruffled pillows, plant it on my lap, and brace my elbows on it. "My mom once forced me to hit a girl who was always taunting me after school." I'm not sure why I share the personal story I'll never forget from my childhood. "I think she was looking for a fight."

"You got into a fist fight?" Those blue eyes widen.

The ruffles tickle my arms, or maybe something else makes me uncomfortable. I toss the pillow behind me and lean back on it. "It was my first and my last. I won, but I was so rattled."

She chuckles. "I can't imagine *you* fighting."

"You'd be surprised."

"At least you had your mom to guide you." She presses her lips tight.

"And you have your daddy."

"Sometimes there's things I can't tell my dad." She scoops a stuffed pink elephant close to her. "I wish I had a mom to go shopping with and do things other girls do with their moms."

"I know I'm not your mom, but if you ever need someone to shop with, I'm your person."

"Thanks. Are you..." Her forehead creases, and she ducks her head. "Going to stay with us?"

"I'm not going anywhere, sweetheart. Even when I'm not your nanny anymore, you're a part of my life now. I'll come to visit."

"That's what Mom says, but she never comes."

My throat catches, and my next words come out cracked. "I'm sorry, sweetheart." I pat her hair back the way a mother would. "Regardless, just know you are strong, beautiful, and very loved." She has to know there's more love to receive than just from her mom. "God, your dad, your brothers... they love you. You are you. God made one Eden—unique, precious, beloved—and no one will ever take that away from you."

I'd probably better revisit our gratitude theme for today about personal traits. "Remember, 'You're fearfully and wonderfully made.'"

"Psalm 139:14."

"Now that we wrote and reflected on the three personal qualities we appreciate about ourselves, we have to embrace them."

Tears slide down her cheek, and I trace my thumb over her soft face and wipe them away.

"I love my family, and I get mad when someone says something bad about them." Just like her dad, she's fiercely protective of her loved ones. She fidgets with the stuffed animal's long trunk, relaying the traits she'd read me earlier.

"Now try to get some rest, okay?"

She nods.

"Good night, sweetheart." I slide from the bed.

Then she bolts up and wraps her arms around me in a tight hug. "Thank you for reading with me."

Something's lodged in my throat, so I'll sound like a broken record player if I speak. I squeeze her back.

Her breath warms my neck when she speaks. "I want to be brave and confident like you."

Ha! I pat her back. "I'm the most cowardly of all, but I act brave."

"Really?" She blinks at me.

"Really." I nod, step back, and raise the covers for her to slip under again.

"Good night," she whispers, then slides into bed.

I sit again and linger to compose myself, my chest heavy as I pick at a thread on her petal-soft pink comforter. I remain until her eyelids flutter shut. Her breathing is still shallow, but it's time for me to leave. I reach for the night lamp. The click of the switch slices through the hush before I slip out of the room.

The hallway is quiet under the dim lights, but booming laughter reverberates from the guys downstairs in the living room. How nice that Grumps is surrounded by such supportive friends.

My bedroom is upstairs near the ones the children are using, while the guys are sleeping on the main level. It's going to be a short stay. We arrived at ten today, and we leave tomorrow evening.

"Checkmate," one of the guys says, but from the stairway, I can only see shadows through the dim lamplight. Instead of retreating to my temporary room, I walk through the kitchen, slide the glass doors closed behind me, and head for the porch railing.

The night has spread a vast starlit sky over the ocean. The serene backdrop calms my thoughts. Distant homes along the beach gleam, their lights twinkling like fallen stars.

I close my eyes and breathe in the sea air. Today's memories replay before the door glides open behind me. My heart thrums, and I don't have to open my eyes to know. I *feel* him step beside me, and I smell his intoxicating scent of a fresh shower. His presence lingers. I hate how I recognize his scent. Subtle, eucalyptus, it binds me like an ever-tightening rope. He's quiet, and I don't make the effort to speak either. He's the one who came out here. Why is my heart so out of sorts, beating wildly now?

"Jason." My thoughts escape aloud.

"How did you know it's me?" His voice is a rasp, curious.

"I had a feeling." A silence settles again, comfortable yet charged.

"You called me Jason." I've called him Jason before. But he was vulnerable that night and must not have noticed. "Does that mean I've earned the non-grumpy name now?"

I smile into the darkness, mentally revisiting the night he showed up at my mom's house. "Don't read too much into it."

"I'm trying not to."

"I thought you guys were playing chess."

"Not me." When I glance at him sideways, he turns his body to cock his hip against the rail, his full attention unnervingly on me. Everything about him is intense, from the sharp angles of his jaw to the smolder in his gaze—okay, it's only moonlight I'm relying on, but I know how his gaze makes me feel. "Resilience, patience, and reliability," he says. "Some of the traits I like about you."

"I thought we—"

"I know today we're supposed to record our own traits we're grateful for, but I wanted to focus on you. Regardless of my snarky attitude, you've remained strong and patient with me."

My grip tightens on the railing. I need it to keep my balance here. "Patient would be someone who stayed without grumbling."

"I'd be skeptical about you if you didn't complain and took everything I did to heart. Point is you stayed anyway."

"Maybe because I haven't found another job yet."

"I'm sure your mom has lots of families who'd love to take you on." He then winks. "I'm thankful... you saved me today."

"You're too dramatic for someone who majored in business journalism."

"Someone has been busy looking me up, eh?" His tone light, he shifts his foot, and I remember his injury.

"You shouldn't be standing on your foot so long." He's in his slides, and the white gauze I'd put on after he showered is bright under the moonlight.

"Why did you host the show?" he asks. "Your degree could have led you to more opportunities than working at Starwatch."

I sigh. This conversation could mean revisiting my failed romance. I keep my gaze fixed on the sea ahead. "You mean the show that tore marriages and families apart?"

"Not unless those marriages were already on their way down a slippery slope." His voice is tender, soft. "Eden saw your show in a positive light. She was thrilled you encourage women to be confident—"

"Whoa. Wait. You let your daughter watch my show?" No wonder she thinks I'm confident.

He chuckles. "That Saturday after the accident, Eden snagged my phone. I later found her watching segments of your show on it."

He takes a deep breath. "Last time you asked me what I was afraid of." He speaks slowly and deliberately, as if he's been pondering this for some time. "But I never got to ask you what you're afraid of."

My heart thuds against my ribs. Does he know I'm not as confident as I appear?

"It's only fair that you—"

"Letting anyone control my life," I blurt out before I overthink and hold back.

"Would you consider being in a relationship a form of control?"

I love the idea of happily ever after. Deep down, I'd love someone to sweep me off my feet. But the looming reminder from my past shadows such gleaming daydreams. Men can be unreliable, controlling. "Even if I sidestep the other factors, my family history doesn't include happy couples."

"You talked about control." He's looking at me sideways through the moonlit night as if penetrating my defenses. "Were any of your exes controlling?"

"Just dated one person."

"Really?" He sounds shocked, then nods. "Is he why you chose the route for the specific show?"

He seems to have figured it out. "Revenge, I guess, and to prove to him I could handle a show on my own. I also intended to help other women never feel inferior or trapped." Like I felt in that toxic relationship.

"What did he do to you?" His protective concern leaves me vulnerable.

"I went to school to be a counselor. I wanted to help keep marriages and families from falling apart."

He squeezes my shoulder.

"But then I met Austin." I flutter a hand. "He was helpful early on in my freshman year. He was working part-time at Sheer TV and studying for his master's. I was majoring in psychology journalism, and he recommended I add feature journalism while at it." Which wasn't a bad idea to expand my opportunities.

I grip the railing with both hands again, the metal cold and hard against my palms—cold and hard like the memories, like my heart after Austin got through with it. "He might have been planting seeds of manipulation even when we started dating. I followed him to L.A. when he contracted a high-paying photojournalist job. I took a data entry job so I could be close to him. He seemed worth the sacrifice—until we worked together at Sheer TV where he helped me get the job."

I shiver over the toxic work environment. How many times did Austin bash my research when we worked together as reporters for the show—only to take credit for that research, claiming he was a far better presenter than I was? I can still hear him now insisting, "We both benefit when the show's numbers skyrocket." And all those Q-and-A sessions we did together, he jumped in and answered on my behalf when the questions were posed to me.

"The worst part was when he cheated on me with our boss... the gossip in the hallways, and I just..." I cover my eyes at the image of walking in on them in the producer's office with Austin's tongue stuck in her mouth. I swallow the lump that threatens to block my throat. "He wasn't even sorry about it... made it my fault for making rules about intimacy only when we were married."

"I'm sorry." His hand on my shoulder is comforting. "May God help me never come face to face with this guy...." I can sense his defensiveness kicking in when he asks for details about my ex—last name, work history, and his current place of employment and whereabouts.

"Look at you all being protective." I shake a finger at him to keep things lighter than I feel. "At least he taught me videography."

And gave me confidence when I ventured out on my own. I bounced around until I got my show at Starwatch.

"You wouldn't be the person you are today if you were still with him." He uses my earlier remark against me, then shakes his head, exhaling. "You're my family now. You've made my kids happy. You saved me from figuring out nail painting and hairstyling with Eden, and she's been happier and more open with me."

When he traces a loose strand of my hair, goose bumps scatter over my arms. I shift my foot, not sure why I turn to face him.

"You made me see things differently too." His hand trails down my cheek. "Made me realize... maybe I'm not so immune to falling..." He leans in, and his breath fans warmth against my face, my mouth. "From now on, anyone who messes with you..."

My breathing escalates. My lips can easily touch his should I choose to raise my face. "You don't even like me."

"You think I don't like you?" The low rumble of his voice vibrates through my body.

One minute, he's brooding. The next, he's sweet. Breathless, I can hardly get out the words I need. "Hard to know what you're thinking, Grumps."

"Want to know what I think every time I look at you? Every time you pop into my mind when I close my eyes?"

Do I want to know? Unable to speak through my now ragged breathing, I don't answer. I don't need to.

He curls a hand around my waist, and my entire body ignites like I'm seated on coals.

"I was on the phone with my mother when you walked into the Family Sphere building, all confident and beautiful, and I was more bothered and confused when I couldn't tear my gaze away from you. The attraction was instant for the first time in a long time, and then—forget it."

His lips touch mine, and everything blurs but the man sliding his hand to my nape, his mouth warm and insistent against mine. He tastes of mint and chocolate from the ice cream we had for dessert, and he smells of an appealing combination of eucalyptus, cedarwood, and spice. I've been kissed before, but this feels different as I greedily devour his mouth, grappling his shirt, the tiny prickles on his jaw rasping my fingers as I move my hand over his face.

We're panting and breathless when I pull away, needing some air, but still gripping his shirt.

His hands cup my face. We take each other in before I ask myself how we came to this point.

"Aren't we supposed to dislike each other?"

"I haven't kissed a woman in almost six years. Let's try it again. Then I might have an answer." He kisses me again, hooking his arm around my waist, and I melt into him. His fingers trace along my back and into my hair, electrifying every nerve in my body, leaving me floating in a forbidden kiss I've waited a long time for. When I close my eyes, I see stars. Now how can I go back to a professional relationship?

CHAPTER 25

Jason

That kiss! I can't even compare it to any I've ever had.

Maybe because our relationship started on edge or because I'm older now and she's the first woman I've felt drawn to in my adulthood. Either way, I try not to think too much about when I can kiss her again after she gives me *the talk*, saying what we did was reckless.

We fall into a pattern in the next days, my foot recovering in a week since Valentina pampers me when she buys the right shoe and insists on changing the bandages herself. And through it, she becomes a constant in our lives. April slips by unnoticed, yet I can recall every detail about Valentina, including the subtlety of her expressions and the twitch of her lips when my closeness affects her. I remember everything she wears from her snug gym clothes to the cute overalls, fluttery skirts, and breezy dresses.

With the kids in school and during random days off for teacher planning, Valentina manages their dental and doctor appointments. Aside from Daisy and my mom, Valentina's the first person other than me to take my kids to the doctor. Mostly because, as she pointed out, I over-parent.

The evenings, reunited with the kids and Valentina at Mom's, highlight my days. Then, usually, she returns with us to Meadowbrook. She's too kind to turn down the kids when they plead with those puppy-dog eyes, asking her to come with us and drive back in the morning. I don't plead, but I want her there too. Especially since our workouts together happen then.

Right now, I've been on the treadmill for twenty minutes. Since Valentina walked in, I've done nothing but stare at her through the mirror.

She's drawn her long dark hair up into a high wavy ponytail, and she's lifting dumbbells, bending up and down in a way that highlights her toned figure. When she catches me staring, I tumble and grip the handle. I'm about to make some joke, but words fail me. Heat courses along my skin as I drown in those deep-brown eyes, and the intensity of my feelings proves how deep this attraction runs.

I move to the bench where I can't see her through the mirror. I work through a series of bench presses, and my eyes betray me once more. She's now stretching on a mat nearby.

I lift the weight, refocusing for several minutes before her scent teases my senses. She's closer, leaning against the wall, watching me. "Don't... interrupt me." I croak, my focus on pushing the weights up. I wanted to go heavy this morning because I've got energy to burn—energy fueled by the need to distract myself from that kiss at the beach house. Valentina insists kissing isn't a good idea when we're unsure of our new friendship or what a serious relationship might mean.

"I was just saying hi." She waggles her fingers with that mischievous innocence.

"See? I lost count."

"You were at fourteen."

"How do you know?"

"I don't think you want me to admit."

I laugh, then holster the heavy weights before my distraction sends me to the hospital. I sit up and wipe my hands on a towel, taking my sweet time before I give in to the urge to look at her fully.

Her burgundy leggings and cream top cling to her, showcasing each curve. I haven't seen this outfit before, and I know that because I catalog everything she wears.

"I'll get coffee and breakfast ready." She nods to the clock, more aware of time on such mornings than I am.

"I'll be there shortly." I swallow, needing a moment to breathe.

We have a new routine now. Even when I try to work out before her, I'm never early enough. We're both early risers, and after workouts, we sip coffee and make breakfast together. Then I shower while she wakes the kids up, and she takes a turn showering as I ensure they get dressed before we eat together. We discuss our gratitude Bible verse and what might be going in our journals tonight. With a prayer, we head out. I've never before felt this close to God or excited to read the Bible. It's not as overwhelming as I make it sound to Ethan.

Daisy and I never did anything consistently together. Before Eden was born, we were spontaneous about doing fun things. Then kids happened, and it all came to a halt.

As spring flowers bloom in May, so does my heart. I run into Valentina at Eden's dance lessons when she's not watching the boys' soccer practice. I rarely go to soccer practices since I go to their games on Fridays. Tonight is the boys' final game of the season, and I'm trying to concentrate on them, not on Valentina. She's not making it easy as she springs to her feet, her hair shimmying over her shoulders and alight from the evening sun.

"Why's that a foul?" she shouts to the referee. "He barely touched him!"

She beckons me to verify, but I hang back, inhaling the fresh-cut grass scent and the musky popcorn odor. Whistles and cheers resound soon after she sits again. Then our team scores, and she leaps up again, high-fiving Eden, both cheering. They've become quite the team themselves. So why do the changes in my daughter terrify me? Must I be so pessimistic, focusing on when Valentina leaves? I've not asked her plans, fearing the answer. They always leave. No one stays with me, with my kids.

"Come on!" Carlos's voice booms. In a Jets jersey, he's appointed himself the twins' personal trainer, encouraging the boys now awaiting their turn. "We need to tie this game, then score another goal for a win." He claps. "Felix, remember what we worked on—the quick passes and staying open."

Coach calls a kid in to play.

Valentina's jaw drops. She shoves her popcorn bag toward Eden and strides over. "Coach, why isn't Felix taking a turn? He's barely played."

Coach disregards her. No doubt, he'd rather have the best players to help tie up the score.

Scooping up a handful of Valentina's popcorn, Eden chuckles. "He didn't count on Val when he picked Bobby. Bet he regrets it."

Valentina's already stomping back toward us, and I almost imagine Coach looks shorter than he was. She waves away the popcorn when Eden offers it back. Then the energetic crowd roars as Atticus scores the winning goal. Valentina shouts and scoops up Eden in an embrace before they entwine their hands and run to the field to high-five the boys, Carlos doing the same.

Their enthusiasm screams I've been failing my cheerleading duties these last years. After sprinting to catch up, I high-five the boys with our secret handshake reserved for victorious moments.

Aglow, Eden hugs me tight. "They won, Daddy! We have to go celebrate."

I tuck wispy hairs behind her ear and grin at her lips all puffy from the salty snacks. "What do you suggest? We've already gorged on popcorn from nearby vendors."

"Pancakes." Felix gives a fist pump.

Atticus smacks his lips. "Waffles."

"Smart boys." Carlos snorts. "Unless it's Mami's cooking, you can't beat syrup and whip cream."

"IHOP, it is." Valentina ushers us along.

Soon, we settle into a booth, our plates heaped with sugar and grease overload, and Valentina recounts the game, her fiery spirit igniting everyone's energy. She's the missing element in our family. If only I could expect her to stay forever.

As we leave, the boys pull her along through the parking lot, eager to see the soccer photos I insisted they waited until after dinner to go over. My cheeks hurt. I haven't stopped grinning this evening.

"I see the way you look at my sister." Carlos matches his slow steps to mine. "Don't worry. You and your kids are all she talks about these days."

I thrust my hands into my pockets, keeping it casual. But why pretend when Carlos already knows? "She's incredible."

"You'd better be serious. Mami's counting on her to change our family history."

We near the Pilot where Valentina and the kids are already seated. The overhead lights cast a warm glow on their faces tipped around her phone while it lights up the profession photos of the team season. Incredible scarcely covers it. "I hope I'm worthy of her."

"If you intend to hurt her like that jerk..." He grits his teeth, his muscles flexing. "Don't mislead her if you don't plan to see it through."

I jab his right biceps. "I wouldn't want to mess with you. Valentina brags about your kickboxing skills." Then I stop and lean against the SUV's taillights. "I'm not perfect, never will be. What Austin did..."

"She told you?" Carlos's eyes widen.

The back door swings open, and the boys leap out, followed by Valentina and Eden.

"Can Valentina come home with us?" Eden tilts her head.

"It's up to Valentina."

The boys extend an invitation to Carlos, who glances at his sister. Valentina exchanges a look with him.

He shrugs. "I'll let Tina go with you guys if she lets me take her car."

"You're sure it's not a bother if I go home with you?" Her mischievous eyes glint at me, and my heart quickens. Does she know how complete I feel in her presence? How thrilled that she used the word *home*? How right it sounds to think of her as part of our family?

"You can come home anytime." That word never sounded so good.

***

Jason

The bedtime routine takes longer with Valentina around since the boys insist we alternate telling a story. So, we've come up with two short stories that have scenes for each of us.

"Tonight, you get the dragon and the wizard, right, Val?" I drop onto Atticus's bed, and Eden scrambles in next to Val on Felix's.

"Not fair. *I* made the winning shot, so I should get to pick who sits with me," Atticus grumbles, still pouting over Felix getting his turn with Val tonight.

I can pretend I didn't hear that.

Then our voices animate the stories, and the kids laugh at our antics.

Afterward, Eden summons Valentina to tuck her in while I tuck in the boys. She doesn't seem to need me as much, but at least she has a female role model.

Morning comes too soon, waking me well before the real family ordeal of morning breakfast preparation. By the time I return with doughnuts, Valentina's in the kitchen with the kids, not caring when they break the eggs, spill the flour, and smear greasy fingerprints on the stainless steel fridge—stainless it might be, but it sure attracts fingerprints.

"Looks like you guys are having a blast." I brace against a counter and slide the doughnut box in front of Valentina.

The kids barely look my way before resuming mixing whatever it is. But her eyes widen when she glimpses the logo. "You went all the way to Brooklyn for that?"

"They don't deliver beyond seven miles." My chest expands when she mouths a thank you, then bites her lower lip, clearly holding in a smile. Discussing guilty pleasures, she told me about her favorite doughnut shop in Brooklyn.

Due to the kitchen mess, we spend more time cleaning than eating. But it's never been this fun. How does she manage that, anyway?

Afterward, the guys and I head to help an elderly couple from the church. The kids stay with Liam's and Russ's kids' nannies so Valentina can tag along. She doesn't complain when we pull weeds and then assemble a bookshelf, a sofa, and a bed.

Then she and the kids cheer as the guys and I play a pickup rugby game against some locals. I cherish every moment she's in our lives. From our regular Saturday games to picnicking under the pink cherry blossoms as the boys scale trees and Eden attempts to learn how this afternoon.

"Tree climbing isn't that bad, right?" Valentina asks.

"I guess you're right." I snatch a stray dandelion from the grass and tuck the flower behind her ear. My heart swells. Can it get better than this, just lying on our stomachs, talking about anything and everything? Spiritual things, jobs we've done before, and life's challenges...

"Daddy, Val, look!" Eden calls from her perch on a branch.

We cheer her on and her brothers too.

They announce a Bible summer camp at church the next day. After services, Valentina suggests the kids sign up, and they agree after she promises to volunteer—something I usually ignore since I have to work. But if she's volunteering for mid-June, then she's planning to stick around next month, right?

But is June enough? I want this to be more, to be a family again. I'm falling more and more in love with her. Her presence turns every ordinary moment into something extraordinary, and while I have no idea how to pray, I hope God can intervene and have this be our new forever.

CHAPTER 26

Jason

Anticipation thrums stronger than any jolt from the coffee brewing in the corner. I lean into a high-backed chair, my hands braced on the conference table. The lemon polish scent intrudes as we strategize an upcoming live stream at the Brooklyn food and music festival. Following Valentina's idea to branch into the city's life, we're transforming our network into a true family hub. My team has secured permission to live stream the event. This isn't my usual domain, but she believes the CEO's involvement will boost our profile and credibility. I also want to ensure the process aligns with our brand.

"Our setup and takedown should be easy." The event coordinator outlines the logistics, including security and emergency procedures.

"What about the equipment? Can we make it through without breaking anything?" I focus on our tech director. We had to buy new cameras last month after an event went wrong. "How many videographers do we have on Saturday?"

"Hunt's handling the videography team," Aila responds. The recessed lighting's soft glow accentuates her short hair. In her mid-forties, she's one of the best tech pros, and she's been with Family Sphere from the start. She now delves into the technical setup, detailing the camera placement, sound system, internet connectivity, and backup plans. All of which boosts my confidence.

I pat the table. "We've got this down, guys."

I pivot to our director of photography.

"You have nothing to worry about." Hunt nods. I can't quite remember his first name. Poised with an air of confidence, he's clean-cut with an imposing appearance. Probably older than me if those gray hairs give any indication. "I got our two best videographers for the event. The equipment will be safe."

The content producer outlines key segments, and the host discusses guiding the audience through the event, engaging with participants, and handling live interactions. The marketing director, creative director, finance manager, and head of public relations give updates.

I glance around the table, glad to be part of the planning process this time. "Bring family members along." My kids and Valentina might join us. "Let's make it a family-oriented project."

As we're wrapping up, my phone vibrates, and Valentina's name flashes. I excuse myself and step into the hallway to answer.

"School called." Valentina doesn't bother with a greeting. "Eden got in a fight."

"She never fights." I pinch the bridge of my nose, facing the Family Sphere tower painting on the wall. There must be a serious explanation.

"Matthew has a dental appointment." Or so Eden said when praying for him before we left this morning. "Take a taxi. Meet you there as soon as I can."

"You, um, want me to go?"

She's not just the kids' nanny now. "You'll get there sooner than me."

I hang up before it strikes me that she might not be at my mom's house and it might take her longer to reach the school. Back in the conference room, I can't focus on the remnants of the meeting, so I force a smile and gather my iPad. "Thank you, everyone, for your hard work. I need to leave you to wrap things up now."

Beatrix stops typing and eyes me, so I nod to assure her I'm fine. To everyone else, I add, "If you have any questions, please pass them to Beatrix."

The mild midmorning traffic moves smoothly. Otherwise, I might've run every yellow light or considered tagging along behind the police car wailing its sirens to some crisis ahead of me. I park and hurry inside the school. Soon, I'm ushered into the principal's office where Eden sits beside Valentina at the meeting table. Her hair falls in two loose braids she styled herself, courtesy of Valentina's lessons. I slide into a seat on her other side, then nod to the other parents across from us. Great, they're prominent school donors I recognize from parent leadership meetings. Their daughter nurses a beverage from a well-known coffee brand, her eyes blotchy and her nose bandaged—an unsettling sight.

The principal laces his hands on the table. "Thanks for coming." His bald head shines beneath the bright fluorescent light. He then outlines the school policy before turning his attention to Eden. "Would you now share why you hit Milan?"

I take Eden's hand, her palm moist against mine, but she remains stiff, eyes downcast. "It's okay, sweetheart. You can tell us."

"She"—Eden clears her throat and scuffles her oxfords as she resumes her whisper—"and her friends have been saying mean things to me."

My gaze slices to the other parents. I know she shouldn't have resorted to hitting, but several forms of bullying are going on here.

"Eden." Principal Caine cuts in. "You know we don't tolerate bullying or fighting of any kind at St. Martin's. Look at Milan now..."

Heat surges through my chest. "My daughter is not a bully."

"How come Milan didn't tell us why she got hit?" Valentina interjects. "In courts, we hear from both parties for a reason."

"Well, it's obvious. Milan's the one injured." The mom fans herself with her manicured fingers. She must need it with her brown hair pulled back so tight it's gotta be cutting off any air circulation.

Principal Caine gestures to their daughter to speak. "Milan, why don't you clarify this for us?"

"All I said was that she doesn't have a mom."

"That's not all you said!" Eden shrieks.

I squeeze her hand in assurance.

Valentina pats Eden's other shoulder, then draws out a breath. "Milan, how long have you and your friends been taunting Eden?"

"I just...we just—"

"Eden shouldn't have quit counseling," Mrs. Williams interferes while Mr. Williams remains silent, his gaze flicking to his vibrating phone as if he's expecting an urgent call.

"How do you know about my daughter's counseling?" I demand. "You're not the school psychiatrist, last I checked."

"There's been a breach of confidentiality." Valentina's protective tone bolsters my resolve.

"That's beside the point here." Principal Caine adjusts his tie. "Eden, you're going to be suspended for fighting."

"What?" I jolt.

Valentina speaks up. "Can we have an adult meeting first?"

He nods and dials for his assistant, who comes to escort the girls out. Eden's eyes are sparkly with tears, and I squeeze her hand. "It's going to be okay." I'm not sure how yet.

Valentina gives her a warm smile, squeezing her shoulder, and Eden looks at her, hopeful.

"I had to do what I had to do," Eden murmurs.

Valentina winks at her, a silent affirmation of some unspoken understanding.

As the door closes behind the students, I hold an open palm toward the principal. "This isn't just about a fight. It's about what led to it. My daughter never fights."

Valentina's silver earrings dance against her cheek when she nods. "If we're considering suspension, we need a comprehensive review. Assessing the environment to foster and support all the students involved in this is important."

"Bottom line"—Principal Caine wags a finger—"We have a no-bullying policy here."

"I understand." Valentina gives a saccharine smile. I thought I knew her before, but I didn't understand the extent of her fierceness. She sits up straight, taking charge. "Can you articulate the school's definition of bullying?"

"Well, Miss—"

"Valentina. Why don't I start with the usual standard of bullying and you can explain where—or if—the school's definition deviates." She then meticulously breaks down what constitutes verbal abuse. "It's clear someone else is involved. If Milan has been ganging up with her friends—"

"Our Milan is innocent," Mrs. Williams asserts, her husband nodding before he checks his phone.

"All parents consider their children innocent, unfortunately, even the real bullies." Valentina tsks. "Both Eden and Milan have violated St. Martin's strict and commendable antibullying policy. If Eden is suspended today, Milan must be suspended too, as must her friends who should've been summoned here already."

"I don't think so." Principal Caine scratches his salt-and-pepper beard.

Valentina chuckles and sinks into her chair, displaying that astounding and attractive confidence. Meanwhile, I'm a tumult of emotions, wanting nothing more than to pull my daughter out of this school and never face this battle again. I'm only still here because I'm now curious how this ends.

"Here's the thing—if you wrongly suspend Eden and let the real bullies roam free, how do you think she'll feel when she returns from suspension? Confident and bold, or cowed and victimized?"

Principal Caine shifts. "Do I have to answer that?"

She stands, her nostrils flaring. "Ever heard of Valentina Diaz? Look the name up and remember we have freedom of speech. You suspend Eden today and leave her bully unpunished, your school is my next reality show."

"You can't do that." He stands too, his eyes almost bulging out of their sockets.

She slings her bag over her shoulder and looks at me. "Ready to go?"

"Yes." My chest swells, still stunned by this incredible woman beside me. I stand and entwine Valentina's fingers in mine.

"Mr. Sterling, you need to talk to your girlfriend," he mutters.

No reason to correct him. She's listed under the kids' emergency contacts, after all, but girlfriend has a great ring to it.

"Let's have the kids back in. Wait here." At Principal Caine's request, we hover closer to the door as he dials his secretary. Soon, Eden enters and rushes to us, her brows knitted together. The principal stands, holding up a hand as if he's in command here. "Eden and Milan will both go back to class. But no more fighting."

"Or saying mean words," Valentina adds.

Mrs. Williams rolls her eyes. "You're being manipulative, and you know it."

"It takes a manipulator to know one," Valentina responds, radiating strength. Man, she's something. She's wearing a yellow dress with dainty print, and her wide elastic belt emphasizes her slender waist. Even on such short notice, she looks impeccable because she always dresses tastefully.

But today confirms what I've been pondering. I need to consider changes for the kids' school.

Before we leave, the principal offers us rooms to talk to our children privately. He lets the other family take his office while they send us to a room with a copier, the smell of paper heavy in the air, further proving they defer to the higher donors.

I draw in a deep breath of that air before facing my daughter. "I can't believe you beat somebody up. She must have really upset you." I touch the curls at the end of her braid. "Are you okay?"

Her nod swings the braid from my light grip. "Sometimes with bullies, you have to stand your ground and do what it takes."

"Look at you, speaking like a tough girl from Queens."

"Or from Brooklyn." Valentina smirks.

"Or Queens and Brooklyn." Eden links her left arm with mine, her right with Valentina's.

Valentina tips her head against Eden's. "Milan and her friend will have to find someone else to pick on."

"Wait a minute." I pull away enough to look between my two girls. Well, Valentina has no idea she's mine or vice versa. Her knowing smile catches me off guard. "Did you—"

"Val told me how she fought off a bully once."

"It's a long story." Valentina waves me off.

"If you want to be done with school today, you can come with us," I offer to Eden.

"Or you can stay and show those bullies you're not running away and you're ready to challenge the next one."

"I'll stay." She straightens her spine with a confidence I've never seen her portray.

As we say goodbye, she throws her arms around me. "I love you, Daddy."

I thought she was getting too old to initiate hugs. I squeeze her back. "I love you too, munchkin." I haven't called her that since Daisy left.

She then hugs Valentina and tells her the same thing. Valentina is quiet, hugging her back. When she responds, her voice is hoarse. "I love you too."

If it wasn't for Valentina, I might have lashed out and pulled all three kids out of school before the end of the school year. Then I'd be scrambling with what to do with them out of school sooner than necessary.

This connection between Valentina and me isn't just romantic—it's familial, it's protective, it's what Eden and I need.

After Eden leaves, I close the door for a moment alone with Valentina. I spin her around so her back is to the door, and I cage her in with my arms.

She wipes tears from her eyes. "She said she loves me." Her voice trembles, her breath warm, lips slightly parted, a subtle lipstick enhancing their roundness.

"She's not your only fan in my family." My voice dips low. "I'm your number one fan lately."

She adjusts the purse strap on her shoulder. "Is that so?"

I nod. "Thanks so much for coming with me." I dip my head until my forehead rests on hers, soft against mine. "I knew you were fierce, but today was on another level."

Her breath catches. "Does that mean my temper surpasses yours, Grumps?"

"That's still debatable."

She jabs me in the abs, and I chuckle. "You were like a mother hen in there."

"I'm sorry if—"

"I loved it. I love everything about you." My gaze travels from her eyes down to her lips. Like her yellow dress, she's sunshine on a rainy day. I thought she was the most beautiful woman I'd ever met. I revise that now—she's the only woman I've ever truly seen.

"I don't care about the rules and boundaries we made." Warmth floods me the way it does in her presence. "I think..." But I can't go on. My voice has grown too hoarse, and her rushed breathing intensifies my desire to kiss her.

"Me too." Her eyes, fanned with long eyelashes, search mine, and my lips twitch.

"I haven't felt like this with anyone in a long time. Maybe since I'm an adult, I see things differently."

"Same." Her lips brush mine.

Before I know it, I'm kissing her, my fingers caressing her neck, her hair like spun silk. She clenches my shirt, melting into me, and I'm floating. I savor the taste of her lipstick and breathe in her fresh scent. We're both gasping for air by the time we separate. I kiss her cheek again.

"I looked up your name, and it suits you. Strength."

She lets out a gasped breath and manages a shy smile. "I love that you call me Valentina." Her fingers trance my neck as she adjusts my collar.

"Have lunch with me." I run my hand through her hair, attempting to straighten it.

"Don't you have to go back to work?"

"I'm the boss." I wink, breaking the intensity. "I can afford to take the rest of the day off."

"As long as I take you to one of my favorite food trucks in Brooklyn."

"And I'll take you to mine."

"Deal." Her eyes gleam.

And I kiss her again, everything else fading until the whir of the printer tears us apart.

CHAPTER 27

Jason

It's been a long time since I meandered food trucks. I'd forgotten how scrumptious mozzarella sticks can be. "Tell me this is not the best cheese stick you've ever had."

Valentina shoves the last piece into her mouth, then snatches a napkin from her purse, and wipes her mouth. "The best."

"I love Queens, but I've always favored the food in Brooklyn." I wipe the greasy remnants of the breaded cheese stick from my hand.

"I'm glad we agree on something." She smirks. "Let's try this one." She gestures to a white food truck splayed with exotic art. The long line moves quickly though while scents of garlic and fried food make my mouth water. She orders our Korean barbeque beef and chicken with grilled broccoli, but I put her hand back from reaching for her handbag.

She wiggles free. "You bought the cheese sticks."

"We're on a date." I wink, and she scowls. Thanks to her jerk ex, she may never let me pay for anything. "You can buy ice cream."

We savor the food under a flimsy umbrella table. Our conversation flows into the vibrant atmosphere as others chatter just as cheerily while lounging in folding chairs, standing with food, or waiting in line. I dab a napkin on my mouth. "This is the best barbecue I've had in a long time."

"That's a huge compliment." She raises her water cup in toast, and I reach for my plastic cup to touch hers.

Next, I lead her to my favorite ice cream shop at Brooklyn Bridge Park. The sprawling park, with its stunning views of the Manhattan skyline and the iconic Brooklyn Bridge, is a hub for tourists and locals, but it's not crowded today. Her hair shines in the midafternoon sun, her smile gentle and inviting as we wander from stall to stall, hands entwined. She points out handmade crafts, and I inhale the aromas wafting from the food stands.

At the ice cream shop, she orders chocolate chip while I go for Hawaiian. When I swipe my tongue across the tropical ice cream, I almost close my eyes as it melts in my mouth.

"I can't believe you chose sherbet from all the options they had." She arches her delicately trimmed eyebrows.

"It's not sherbet." I hold it out for her. "Try it and see why it's my favorite." It seems so natural to share ice cream. Still, I shiver as our hands brush in the exchange.

"Hmm." She takes three long swipes with her tongue. "Sherbet has never been this good."

"It's ice cream." Well, technically they call it *guri guri*. She doesn't hand mine back, so I chuckle and lick hers. "You can keep mine. I'll finish yours. But next time, we'll get two Hawaiians."

"I'm glad there's a next time." She leans her head into me, and I savor her closeness, her aromatic shampoo that's become so familiar. This is unlike any first date I've ever had, yet it's the most real I've felt with a woman I'm attracted to.

When we polish off our desserts, it's not even one yet, so I guide her to a different pier. The air carries laughter, the distant hum of city traffic, and the gentle lapping of the river against the shore. One couple plays Frisbee. Others stroll past the families picnicking on the lawn.

"I've never been on this side before." She swings our hands as our shoes pad through the grass. "Is this where you and Daisy used to come?"

"Daisy was never a park person. She believes bugs have a battle against her." Which makes sense for a fashion and cosmetics model. I flinch at the thought of seeing her again at the upcoming partners' event.

As we approach the river, the boats bob near the dock while others hum in the distance. I untuck my shirt and lead Valentina closer to the water's edge.

"I thought you might want to skip some rocks after that lesson you gave me." I peer at the scattered stones along the shore. Finding flat ones might be a challenge with all of New York having combed the area already.

"I presume you're ready for a challenge?" Valentina bends to pick up a suitable stone.

"Always up for a challenge." We take turns skipping, and each flick of the wrist sends stones skimming the water. We count the skips and watch the ripples expand before they disappear. As we strive to outdo the other, our laughter mingles with the splashing. We share childhood memories. Mine involve mud football with friends. Hers center around biking adventures with her best friend, siblings, and other neighborhood kids.

She tells me about fighting off a bully, and I laugh when she mentions her mom put her up to it.

"Surprised she didn't send you with spray paint, but I guess I know not to mess with your mom."

"Let's sit." Valentina gestures to a nearby boulder. "All that food is making me lazy."

"I'll race you to that tree." I nod toward a secluded shaded spot that looks way more inviting. I don't intend to run, but she takes off, her flats slapping the ground.

I chase after her, laughing, pretending to be winded as she speeds ahead. When she glances back and giggles, slowing enough for me to catch up, we collide and collapse onto the grass. I cushion her fall, guiding her to land on top of me. We're both breathless, our grins wide. Then the world fades.

With her so close, our breaths mingling, I steal a kiss. She responds with fierceness, her handbag in the way. I nudge it aside until it slips off her shoulder. We roll on the grass, heat rising from our skin.

When we separate, we lie side by side, panting, our heads still tipped toward each other. The longing in her eyes mirrors my feelings. I grin, and she beams. Ethan's analogy of that single rose resurfaces. With Valentina, there's no comparison.

My fingers trace her soft hair curtaining the grass. I'm lost in the moment, a love-struck teenager.

We continue to share stories, her voice a soothing melody in our secluded retreat. The occasional passerby is a blur to our bubble. If the grass pokes at her arms, she gives no sign, fully immersed in our conversation.

"When do I meet Leah?" I twirl a strand of her hair around my finger, captivated by her every feature.

"You'll see her on graduation day."

"That's in two weeks." I've given high school and college commencement speeches before but not middle school. "I better prepare a speech."

"It shouldn't be hard."

Valentina sighs. "The principal today should've looked into things before such an unjust decision." She picks at one of my shirt buttons. "I know you work far from Meadowbrook, but have you ever considered switching the kids to a neighborhood school?"

"The thought crossed my mind earlier, but they probably don't have some of the sports."

She shrugs. "We could always start a team."

I don't miss the "we."

As she must catch it, her teeth sink into her lower lip. "I mean, I'm sure you and your friends could start something."

"We can figure something out when the time comes." I prefer to assume she's going to be a part of my family. "I was wondering... What if we gave ourselves a chance? Try the couples' route."

"Like what we're doing right now?" She kisses my cheek. "I like trying the couples' route... with you, Grumps."

I breathe out. That went easily enough.

Now I'm even more reluctant to end the perfect afternoon. "This Saturday, Family Sphere is attending the food fest you suggested in Brooklyn."

Her eyes light up. "That's great."

"I was hoping you and the kids could come along."

She nods, her smile warm. "I'll never turn down a gathering with food."

Matthew calls to remind Valentina about picking up the kids. I tell him to take the rest of the day off, and I'll drive her to get the kids. As we walk back, our hands find each other again. Joy unfurls inside me, content being with her in this ordinary moment.

Just like that, Valentina and the kids end up with me at the food fest. With Saturday warm, we're all decked out in yellow T-shirts sporting the Family Sphere logo. Over mine, I've added the taco-themed button-up overshirt she gave me.

She and the kids hand out T-shirts and merchandise at our booth alongside Beatrix. Other team members mingle through the event with their families, and those running the film crew keep a live stream going.

I reach to snatch another cookie from the tray, and Eden bats my hand away. "Dad, these are for people who stop at our booth."

"It's Valentina's fault for making snickerdoodles." I manage to snag a cookie. The cinnamon flavor melts in my mouth—pure bliss. I wink at Valentina, who rolls her eyes. I couldn't lay off the cookies when she was baking them with the kids last night either.

"You need one of your film crew to capture you eating your favorite cookies," Valentina says.

"Got it." Beatrix snaps a picture on her phone.

I wag a finger at her. "You share that on our platform's social page, and you're fired."

"Does Grumps usually talk to you like this?" Valentina says to my assistant.

Beatrix smirks. "Exactly like that."

I'll have to do some explaining later since my assistant was shocked to learn Valentina's nannying my kids, given our rough start. She has no idea yet about my newfound love for Valentina, but that secret won't last long after today.

People weave through the crowded park and booths, delicious aromas scent the air, and local bands add lively tunes. Children laugh, people chat, and the colorful decorations flutter in the breeze.

"Mr. Sterling?" The photography director approaches with a handheld camera, likely ready to capture some candid shots.

"What's up, Hunt?"

He blinks, his face pales, and I follow his line of vision to Valentina. Her mouth hangs open, and her gaze locks on Hunt. The air thickens as he fumbles with his camera.

"You two know each other?" I turn to Hunt.

He swallows hard, his face now crimson.

I'm met with silence.

"Do you need me for anything?" I ask to maintain a professional demeanor.

He nods, then mumbles the need for my presence before their shoot with an Indian family.

I wave him off. "I'll be there shortly."

Once he leaves, I turn to Valentina, and she draws out a breath, her shoulders relaxing.

Eden tugs at Valentina's hand. "Are you okay?"

"I'm okay, sweetheart." Valentina places a comforting hand over Eden's shoulder, but her smile doesn't quite reach her eyes. She's far from fine.

Then something suddenly snaps, and Hunt's first name becomes clear. No way he's the Austin she was talking about.

Beatrix is occupied, fingers typing away on her phone, doing whatever admins do at such events. Eden has the boys engaged in a game on our table, having them compete for a cookie—just the distraction I need. I lean closer to Valentina and whisper for her ears alone. "Austin Hunt?"

She nods, exhaling sharply. "He works for Family Sphere?"

My heart sinks. Austin has been with the company for less than two years, the reason I hadn't mastered his first name. "I never interview or hire the tech crew." If I had, maybe I could've prevented this painful coincidence. "You don't have to stay. I can meet you and the kids at your mom's."

"We'll stay until your next shift takes over."

"You're sure?"

With her shoulders squared and her chin high, she appears as confident as ever. "Yes."

"I'll be back." I take my assistant along in case she needs to remember something trivial. My mind isn't clear, my heart racing and chest on fire as we stride to the tent comprising our makeshift filming stage. I'll call Matthew to come get Valentina and the kids soon.

I locate Austin and the team hovering by the tent. "I didn't know Val is your—"

"Neither did I." I then address his partner. "What do you guys need from me?"

"The family wanted to meet you before we stream."

I gesture onwards. "Lead the way."

Several others, including the host, follow us. Austin keeps up with my stride as the videographer leads the way.

"What did Val tell you about me?" Austin demands.

You're a prick. The words are on the tip of my tongue as we weave through the crowd. I bite the inside of my cheek harder. It's burning from keeping my mouth shut. I can't shake off Valentina's pain when she described the guy who manipulated her, the reason she's guarded her heart.

Austin keeps glancing at me. If he isn't careful, his curiosity might cost him more than he bargains for today. If he knew me better, he'd realize I'm not one to stand on the sidelines when my loved ones are under attack. We step over a cord hooking up a generator to a smoothie stand, and we turn into an empty grassy spot dividing other vendors from the food vendor section.

"How long have you and Val known each other?" Austin makes the mistake of opening his mouth again.

"You know what, you're fired!" The words rip free before I consider the repercussions. The staff halts and remains silent.

"You can't fire me." Austin chuckles as if it's a joke.

"I just did."

Chatter and the event festivities continue, but my staff just gawks. Beatrix steps beside me, lifts on tiptoes, and whispers into my ear. "Maybe we should discuss this."

"You can't fire me for personal reasons," Austin huffs. As if that should change my mind.

"Unfortunately, some things go beyond personal." I then assign the videographer to take over Austin's responsibilities today. My priority is protecting my family—no matter the cost.

CHAPTER 28

Valentina

I flip the plantains in the hot oil, crisping them while Mami bustles about, opening and closing cupboards as she tends to the shredded beef stew.

"Where's the apple cider vinegar?" she calls out.

"It might be easier to use some of the distilled vinegar on the counter." I try to help without stepping away from my task.

"No, *Hija*, they serve different purposes." She resumes her search.

Through the kitchen window, I steal glances at Jason in the backyard teaching Eden how to throw a whiffle ball while Carlos and the boys swing bats nearby.

Gone is his taco shirt, and his T-shirt displays muscles flexing at each swing. My heart beats rapidly. He's officially my boyfriend. Jason is different from Austin—he's never told me he's better than me, yet he's better in so many ways.

Austin's image intrudes as he did earlier. I'm still surprised he's cut off the hair he used to spend hours preening. How did I ever fall for that man and, worse, let him make me believe I wasn't good enough?

My chest churns, and my fingers clench until the spoon's wooden handle presses almost to the bone. Why didn't I pretend I didn't recognize him? I thought I'd never let him make me feel small or intimidated again, but that was when we hadn't crossed paths in nearly a decade.

Why, of all places, did he end up working at Family Sphere? And why, of all positions, was he handling the camera instead of being an anchor or reporter, especially when he'd always prided himself as the best? Whatever happened to his lady friend?—

It doesn't matter. I shouldn't care whether he ended up in that relationship or not.

At least Jason hasn't brought up Austin. He arrived an hour ago, meeting the kids and me here. His silence, whether out of respect or uncertainty, provides respite from dealing with it all.

With a strainer spoon, I scoop out the now golden plantains and lay them on the prepared paper towels. The aroma of beef stew simmering and rice cooking makes my mouth water. Only Mami's food could compete with all the vendors at today's festival and have my mouth watering again so soon.

My gaze drifts back to the window, to *Jason*. My heart starts racing as our recent kisses flood back—kisses that have become increasingly frequent.

We've managed to sneak moments of intimacy in between our daily routines—in the gym during a morning workout, in the kitchen while I hand him his coffee, and in the quiet hallway after we tuck the kids into bed. Each stolen kiss, each thrilling burst of affection, deepens our connection.

"He's a family man. That's good."

I jump at Mami's words, and the spoon clatters to the hardwood floor. She doesn't miss a beat, stepping in to add more plantains to the oil as I retrieve the spoon.

"If you're falling in love again, Jason is a good choice."

My cheeks heat. Mami caught me gawking.

"The way he looked at you when he walked in... His face turned all red." Mami drops the last plantains into the oil, and they sizzle. She then hands me a clean spoon. "His children admire you too."

I place the fallen spoon in the sink, unable to deny my feelings if I'm unschooled.

"I'm not sure if I should keep looking for another job." I told Judy I'd stay as a nanny for three months, four at most.

"Pray, *Hija*. For now, you're where you're supposed to be. If God closes a door, you'll know whether you should climb in a window instead." Her certainty always comforts, and my chest swells now.

I lean against the counter. "I have no desire to look for TV jobs anymore. Not even therapist jobs. Where would I even start in that field?"

"You have enough things planned for May anyway." She cups her warm hand to my cheek. "One day at a time, *Hija*. That's all you need." She pats my cheek and resumes her search for vinegar. "We're all planning to come to Eden's dance recital, so make sure you buy extra tickets for Friday."

When I told her about Daisy's neglect and Eden's disappointment on spring break, Mami stood firm, insisting: "Then you will be the best family in her life while God has you there. And our job as your family is to show her that family doesn't have to be by blood only."

These words come to life again as I prepare Eden for her dance recital in Manhattan almost a week later. It's after three, and Eden holds her phone, Judy's image on the screen while I comb stray curls back into the bun for her big moment.

I glimpse Judy's face as she asks, "Are you still nervous about your lines?"

Eden exhales, a nervous flutter visible in her posture. "Val helped me practice, but I still feel nervous."

"We got seats on the front row," I promise. "Just focus on us, and you'll do great."

Her gaze meets mine in the bathroom mirror.

"Exactly what Val said," Judy chimes in, and Phil peeks his head into the camera's view, adding his well-wishes.

"You've got this, sweetheart."

After promising to take pictures and confirming they got the link for the live stream, I end the call.

Eden seems buoyed by the support.

"They'll be home in time for your birthday," I remind her as we finish up.

My family is already in front of the dance studio when we arrive. Mom clutches balloons. Carlos lugs a huge Jets stuffed bear. My sisters each hold bouquets. All of them greet Eden with enthusiastic well-wishes.

"Wow, your family really knows how to do things right," Jason murmurs into my ear.

It feels over-the-top, since most people are arriving with little more than a few flowers. I've brought chocolates and a bouquet to give Eden after the performance.

We enter the studio where she practices, and the air thrums. The stage curtains are drawn, hiding the dancers from view as we take our seats.

Ten minutes later, the instructor steps forward, microphone in hand, and the room quiets. "Thank you all for coming to our Spring Showcase."

At the mention of Eden's name, Jason takes my hand, his anxiety palpable through his cold fingers.

I squeeze back and scoot to the edge of my chair, my heart thudding.

"It's Eden, Dad!" Felix whisper-shouts from Jason's other side, and Atticus echoes the sentiment from my side, next to Carlos. The teddy bear almost blocks his view.

Eden scans the audience and smiles when she locates us. I grin broadly while Carlos lets out a sharp whistle. If it weren't for Atticus sitting between us, I'd be nudging Carlos to tone it down so he doesn't make Eden nervous.

"We would like to welcome you to our tenth annual dance recital." She performs exceptionally well, radiating the confidence we worked on during our rehearsals.

I fumble with my purse when I remember to take a picture, but by the time I pull out my phone, she's already finished her introduction.

The lights dim, and music plays as dancers glide onto the stage. Eden will be featured in all the dances. The kids sway to the music while Jason and I snap pictures.

Then "Rewrite the Stars" plays, and every word, every gesture, captures me until Jason's arm snakes around my waist. I steal a glance at him, and the intensity of his gaze warms me as if the song stirs something deep within him too.

He's no Austin, but can I change my family's history of fleeting relationships? Can he learn to trust again, to let me into his life without reservations?

When I tear my gaze away, I catch my mom's knowing look between those balloons. She doesn't miss a beat, nodding as if affirming the connection.

After the dance, we all rush through the crowd to surround Eden, showering her with hugs and congratulations. Everyone hands her their gifts, filling her arms until I enroll her brothers' help, though a couple of balloons pop in their care.

"We have an after-party at the house, *mi amor*," Mami announces, using the affectionate Spanish term for "my love."

"You do?" Eden's face lights up.

Before we leave, we gather for a group picture against the stage curtain. Then I take one with Jason and his kids, and he insists on one with just Eden and me and another with just him and me. I'm not sure if the kids read anything into that.

Daylight is vanishing when we get to the car. I hand Eden the flowers and chocolates I got for her while Jason surprises her with a camera.

Felix's brow scrunches, brown hair flopping into his eyes. "How come we never get gifts after our soccer games?"

"Never mind that." Atticus flops back against his seat, his arms crossed. "*I* didn't get anything after *my* volley *won the game*."

Jason rolls his eyes at me. "Next time, I'll get you something."

"I didn't even think about that." I peer at the back seat through the city lights. "We'll do something extra next time."

Mami has a mariachi band waiting in our backyard, and a giraffe piñata hangs from a tree. Loaded up with food from the spread she's put on, we chant as the kids take turns striking the piñata.

The kids giggle, scooping up candy, the inevitable sugar rush already taking hold, and Jason draws me to join the others on the grass dancing wildly to the music.

He twirls me, then catches my back flat against his chest. His hair tickles my cheek as he leans over my shoulder. His breath warms my ear. "Your family is amazing."

"Your family is incredible too." I spin free to face him, secure in his arms, and the lanterns illuminate his handsome face as I tip my head back to see him. "And you are amazing, Jason."

Is this it? Can an everlasting future be as bright and carefree as this moment?

CHAPTER 29

Valentina

My cheeks ache from the relentless smile as I stand among the crowd in the gym.

"Today marks a significant milestone in your journey, and I'm so proud to be a part of it." Jason's gaze sweeps over the students who fill the first five rows of folding chairs. "When I look at all of you, I see a room full of future leaders. You are at the beginning of a journey that will shape who you become, so the choices you make now set the foundation for your future."

He shares stories of triumph from his own life. "Each story is unique, just like each of you. Your journey will be full of ups and downs, doubts and joys. Embrace them all. They make life rich and meaningful." His gaze finds me in the back row. His voice falters as he adjusts the tie I picked out for him, paired perfectly with his blue button-down.

I pivot my head to the side. Clearly, he's distracted by me.

"Ahem..." He clears his throat. "I'd like to leave you with some advice I've learned along the way. Use your voice. Communication is a powerful tool to help you make a difference in the world."

His eyes meet mine again, locking in a moment of silent conversation. Butterflies flap in my stomach.

He then encourages the students to stay curious, embrace challenges, follow their dreams, and always be kind. "Build others up, and you, too, will rise."

The applause erupts, breaking through his last words. I join in as the urge to shout my admiration from the rooftops spirals. He could have been spending his day with his buddies or children, but he's sacrificing his time here, impacting young lives.

"Last but not least, remember success is not a destination but a journey. It's not about the awards or the titles, but the impact you make and the person you become along the way. Congratulations, class!"

Thunderous clapping erupts, and I stand with others. I don't stop clapping until I sit, blinking when he appears to sit next to me after the woman who had been there scoots over to an empty chair.

"Did you just swap chairs?" I whisper into his ears.

"What were you expecting when you left me on the front row with a bunch of strangers?" His hand slides around my waist, resting on my lower back, and awareness courses through me.

"Your speech was incredible."

"You were distracting."

The high-achieving student steps up for his speech. It's Hugo, one of my ESL students.

"Ladies and gentlemen, teachers, friends, and family"—his English is clearer than I've ever heard it—"coming as an immigrant from Nicaragua and learning a different culture and a new language has been challenging, yet rewarding."

As his words flow, I can't help but swell with pride.

He expresses gratitude toward his teachers for their patience and to his parents for their unwavering support through endless homework nights. "I wouldn't be giving this speech today if it weren't for my English tutor, Miss Valentina Diaz, seated toward the back."

My cheeks heat as heads turn. Jason pulls me close and kisses the top of my head while applause breaks out.

"There were moments of doubt, fear, and frustration. But these trials have taught me the importance of hard work. Like Ms. Diaz would say, 'Challenges are not obstacles, rather they are opportunities to grow.' Every time my family stumbled, we found a way to stand back up. Each failure was a lesson, pushing us to become better versions of ourselves. Ms. Diaz encouraged my family to, 'Begin each day with a grateful heart and thank God for the good things He has done, rather than focus on what you don't have.' Which is something to remember because God is the giver of every good and perfect gift."

Jason squeezes my shoulder, grounding me in this moment of shared triumph. I hadn't even known I'd passed that advice on to some of my students.

Hugo spreads his hands to encompass his fellow students. "As we move forward into high school and beyond, let us also remember what Mr. Sterling said in his speech. Success is a journey, and it's about the impact you make and the person you become along the way. Each curve on the road brings you closer to knowing who you are and where you're trying to go."

After the speeches comes a whirl of greetings and congratulations. I float among familiar faces—teachers and families of both past and present ESL students. With each introduction, I announce Jason as my boyfriend, delighting in their praise for his stirring speech. When I catch up with Hugo and his family, they reiterate their invitation for me to join their celebration next Saturday. Then I spot Leah's husband, Malcolm, and I introduce Jason.

Malcolm offers a hearty handshake. "Leah has told me a lot about you."

"I hope it's all good things." Jason's gaze flicks to me before the two discuss Jason's speech and their conversation flows to other topics.

I scan the crowd for Leah and find her smiling while pausing for a photo with a student. Once she's free, she waves, and I gesture her over despite students awaiting their turn with her.

"Sorry, we have to get to the kids." I apologize as I hug her. "Carlos and Anna took the kids to his buddy's print shop for a T-shirt-making session, but we're supposed to meet at Mami's for lunch." My brother and mother are getting their much-needed kid fix with Jason's kids lately.

"I need to thank Jason for coming and giving the speech." Leah's eyes light up beneath the gym lights. She pivots, acknowledging the students and parents signaling for a photo.

"You'll have time to thank him later." I nudge her toward her awaiting fans. But Leah leans in, her breath warm against my ear. "He couldn't keep his eyes off you during his speech. He even ditched his original seat at the front. Couldn't wait for another fifteen minutes to get to you?"

My insides warm, but I only laugh and nudge her again. "You'd better get back to your students."

She gives me a knowing look and rejoins the group. Leah knew about that initial kiss with my boss and our decision to stay professional afterward. I updated her on how things have changed.

Jason and I step out of the auditorium, hand in hand, and midafternoon light hits me with blue skies. He halts to face me. His blue eyes peer at me before he lifts our hands and his lips warm scant butterfly-like kisses on each of my fingers, making my knees weak.

"There's been a change in plans." His words kiss my fingertips. "Your family has agreed to watch the kids for the rest of the day. I'd love to spend the afternoon with you. I don't care what we do, but if it's okay—"

"Yes, Jason." My smile spreads as visions of a day together dance through my mind. It doesn't have to be anything fancy. I just want to stroll through the streets holding hands and lose ourselves in conversation. "I enjoy spending time with you too, so yes to anything or nothing as long as I'm with you."

He wraps his arms around me, and I slide my hands around his waist, savoring his warmth, his chest rising and falling against mine. Had he thought I might refuse? Him giving up an afternoon with his kids to spend time with me, speaks volumes of how he thinks of me.

Spontaneity has never been my strong suit, and Jason typically prefers everything planned due to the demands of his job. As we wander through Manhattan, we stumble upon an art exhibit and then enjoy a leisurely boat ride in Central Park. Each moment unfolds unplanned but perfectly aligned.

My stomach growls, a reminder of our missed meal as we step into a chic restaurant where Jason made reservations earlier. "Let's get you fed."

The hostess greets us, and he gives his name for the reservation. She scrolls through her tablet, pausing with a flustered expression. "I'm so sorry, Mr. Sterling. Your table isn't ready for another hour."

"What? Why?" we inquire in unison.

"Your reservation is for seven, and you're an hour early."

"I was sure I said six," he mutters.

"I'll see what I can do, but..." She gestures at the bustling dining room.

Jason's brows dip, but then he bolsters up a resilient smile. "How about we do something different? Does pizza sound good?"

I can't help but smile, relieved and charmed. "Pizza is perfect."

"And you love picnics," he adds as we step back onto the sidewalk, the daylight beginning to fade.

"A picnic this late?" I laugh. Talk about spontaneity!

"Who says it's ever too late to do anything in New York City?"

Almost forty minutes later, we find ourselves atop the Family Sphere building, enveloped in the evening breeze and seated on a thick blanket. The city lights cast a magical glow over the buildings. A box of classic New York-style pizza separates us, and the scene feels almost surreal. I'm cocooned in one of Jason's coats, which he grabbed along with the blanket from his office, and it's a physical extension of his warmth.

I pray for our food, and we pry slices free from the pie, cheesy strings still clinging to each other. We reminisce about the day's adventures, laugh at our quirks, and delve into our favorite books—mine, *The Chronicles of Narnia*, his, *The Lord of the Rings*.

"Can you believe I never read those books?" I admit as I take another bite of my pizza.

"Don't tell me you watched the movies instead of reading the books?" He chuckles, pointing his half-eaten slice at me as if waiting for my confession.

"Unfortunately, it's true." I loop an errant string of cheese from my slice.

His dramatic groan sends me into laughter. "The books and the movie are very, very different."

"Then I'll read them *if*—I hold up a greasy finger—"you'll join me for a movie binge afterward."

As our laughter fades, the conversation shifts to the graduation ceremony. "The kid was good." Jason swallows. "Something he said really resonated with me."

"How so?" I wipe my mouth.

"God is the giver of every good and perfect gift. Apparently, also something Ms. Diaz taught me and my kids, something about thanking God for the good things He's done rather than focusing on what we don't have."

Admitting my struggles, I share how my faith wavered during my time with Austin. "Until recently. Being with your family has helped realign my spiritual path." I'm grateful for the weight of my journey and the peace it's brought me.

Jason sets his slice down, his gaze through dim lights intensifying. "If I haven't thanked God for bringing you into our lives, then I'm saying it now with you as my witness..."

His words of gratitude and reflections on faith tighten my throat, and the bustling city blurs. The pizza in my hand feels heavy. I place it aside and reach for the water bottle we've been sharing. Perhaps a sip can clear my throat.

"Jason." His name escapes. With the pizza box a barrier between us, I push it aside and close the distance between us. "Everything... someday, I'll let you read my journal." My entries have been filled with reflections on him and his family. "You're so much to me, all that and more."

"Someday," he murmurs, his hand finding its way around my waist, pulling me closer. His lips brush my cheek. "I like the idea of being trusted with your secrets. I want to be better, not just as a father but also as a person, spiritually."

"Always striving to improve makes you the best version of yourself."

Our gazes lock. I'm stunned by how well we align.

He takes a deep breath, and I tilt my head to rest against his shoulder. "Would it be okay if I tell the kids about us? Before they figure it out on their own?"

"Are you sure?" Fear of the unknown almost clouds my thoughts.

"I like you—really like you." He kisses the top of my head and pulls me closer as if we aren't close enough. "Any reason I shouldn't?"

"Not one I can think of." My heart flutters, and warmth spreads through me as I peer up into his face. "I like you too. Eden will soon discover our secret if you don't tell her."

His hand moves up and down my back, sending a warm shiver down my spine. "I also have an event coming up. Financial donors at the company." His arm tightens around me, betraying a slight tremor. "Daisy will be there. Her new husband is a silent partner."

"You're asking me to come with you?"

"I know it's a lot to ask."

"Not from your girlfriend." I kiss his cheek.

His eyes search mine, relief flickering through them. "You'll come?"

"I know what it's like with exes in awkward—"

His lips press against mine, silencing my words.

I'm once again lost in the sensation of his touch, his taste mingling with the remnants of our pizza dinner. I respond with equal fervor, and the depth of my feelings consumes me. If I wasn't certain about Jason before, I'm now confident I want nothing more than to be kissed by him for the rest of my life. Am I capable of letting that happen? Why do I fear something will tear us apart?

CHAPTER 30

Jason

Excitement buzzes through me as I wipe down the counter, nailing every task I should let the kids do. I need somewhere to channel all this energy, besides hitting the gym. I tilt a yellow bottle, and lemon oil dollops the surface before I wipe it the way Valentina does it and the fresh aroma infuses the air.

I whistle "Rewrite the Stars" from the dance recital two weeks ago. Maybe that could be our song.

I glance at the stovetop. It's already past one.

In an hour, I should start getting ready for Brooklyn if I'm going to make a stop at the florist. Valentina stayed at her mom's last night so she could attend the party of one of her ESL students this morning.

She arranged for Willow, the owner of Sips and Scripts, to come watch the kids tonight. While I should be hesitant, the kids know Willow. Plus, they'll spend most of the evening with my friends and their kids.

Now, the evening's just about possibilities. Gone is the fear of running into my ex and her husband.

The boys' cheers ring through the kitchen window. Eden retreated to her room after a failed attempt to dictate which game her brothers should be playing with her.

I hang up the towel and reach for my phone to order pizza delivered to Liam's house since the kids and our friends will all be hanging out there. It's the least I can do for everyone watching my kids tonight.

"Daddy, you're whistling." Eden joins me, her eyes vibrant beneath the natural light streaming through the windows.

"I whistle sometimes."

"You smile a lot these days too." She slides up and sits on the counter, swinging her bare feet. "You're happy."

I put aside my phone and move to her, squeezing her cheek. "You're happy too, Edie." All thanks to Valentina.

"I wanted to tell you something."

"What's that?"

"Can I..." She breathes out, hesitating until my nod urges her to continue. "Can I not do dance anymore?"

That's shocking. I cross my arms. "I thought you liked dancing."

"I like to dance, but I'd like to try other things too."

"How long have you wanted to quit?"

"For some time. Are you disappointed?" Her face falls. "Val said you'd understand."

"Of course I understand." I tuck a stray hair behind her ear. It's pulled into a messy but organized ponytail that reminds me of how Valentina pulls her hair back sometimes.

"I want to try out volleyball."

"What would you think if you went to school in this town?" I might as well update her for the next school year. "I mean if you switched schools for sixth grade?"

"Really? I'd love that." She slides off the counter and wraps her arms around my waist. I have to savor these short-lived moments.

"Don't tell your brothers yet. I'll talk to them and see if they're okay with the switch. Otherwise, I'm not sure—"

"Maybe you can take the boys to their school, and Val can take me to the neighborhood school."

I'm not sure if Valentina will stick around that long. But I can't break Eden's heart with what I don't know.

"Is Valentina going to leave us?" She looks up at me, concern laced in her blue eyes. Apparently, my silence has her figuring out some things.

Valentina is only here temporarily, even if she and I have a different relationship, which I need to tell the kids about.

"If she leaves, I know she'll stay in our lives."

Her brows pull together. "But she said she won't leave."

I hug her. "If she told you that, then there's nothing to worry about."

I hope Eden is right and Valentina will always be around. But that's a matter I can't handle, so God will have to intervene. *God.* That, too, is new in my life. What started as a thirty-day gratitude journaling session turned into Bible reading and prayer time with my family. Yes, Valentina is a part of my family now.

The back door slides open in a rush, and the boys bustle in.

"Felix said I'm adopted, Daddy."

"He said it first." Felix points at his brother as I usher them toward the island.

"Good thing you're both in the same family."

"Take your muddy shoes back outside, ew!" Eden screeches, her face contorted. She can be bossy at times, but when I take a better look at the boys, I've got to agree.

They scamper back out and return in stockinged feet.

"Do you guys want some ice cream sandwiches?" I ask when they slide onto the stools.

"You gave us ice cream sandwiches two hours ago when we returned from lunch." Eden reminds me.

Right. With Valentina's absence, my mind must be in two places.

"Can I have another one, please?" Atticus requests.

Felix is already swinging open the freezer.

"Thanks, Daddy," they chorus.

Once I help them with their snacks and have them settled around the island, I present the boys with the news about switching schools. "They may not have good soccer teams, but I can guarantee they provide a good education." I'm taking Ethan's word on that, trusting my friends' judgment.

"Will I still fly airplanes if I go to school here?" Atticus's innocent question elicits a chuckle.

"Our friends go to the school here." Felix nods before biting into his frozen cookie sandwich.

I grin. This is the right decision.

Then my gaze flits between Eden at the counter and the boys at the island. "And..." My heart races. I need to utilize this moment while I have all three. I hadn't realized how hard this would be. "Valentina and I..."

"You're going to the party." Atticus lifts his half-eaten ice cream sandwich before licking a drip from it.

Eden looks curious, as if she already knows what I'm about to say.

I clear my throat. "You know how adults have girlfriends and boyfriends?"

"Ew, the kissing and stuff." A drip of cream falls from Felix's sandwich as he pauses.

Eden nods while Atticus looks puzzled.

"Valentina and I are thinking of—"

"She's your girlfriend?" Eden squeals, slides off the counter, and jumps up and down.

Felix scrunches his nose. "Does that mean you're going to kiss?"

Atticus jabs his brother's arm. "It means she might be our new mom."

Eden seconds that by asking if we're getting married. "Does that mean she'll stay with us forever?"

"We're going to take one step at a time, okay?" I try to steady the excited barrage.

Their faces light up as each processes the news. I'm still in disbelief. Can Valentina make our family complete?

***

Jason

With daylight ebbing, my anticipation mounts, but the bow tie almost stifles it. I resist tugging at it as a bead of sweat traces its way down my neck. I shift the rose to my less clammy hand and press the doorbell. Last time I rang that bell, my nerves were racked for different reasons. Three months ago, I could never have envisioned being here as her date.

Snippets of conversation bounce through the door. "I'm counting on you to rewrite our family history!"

"Mom! It's just a date." Valentina's voice floats with laughter, and I grin as the door swings open.

My mouth goes dry, and my heart kicks against my chest, nearly drowning out the city's din. Can she be more exquisite? Her hair falls in soft waves on her left, but she's pinned the other side back so it's easy to see her delicate jawline. The red dress graces her knees and accentuates her slender figure, and silver earrings dangle to her shoulders, catching the evening light.

Her affectionate gaze meets mine, and I'm dizzy with longing. No doubt, my gaze lingers too long on her full red lips before scanning the soft expanse of her partially exposed neck and shoulders, her skin aglow in the fading sunlight.

She sizes me up with a playful smirk. "You clean up pretty good, Jason Sterling." She adjusts her white clutch. "Ready?"

I step forward to meet her. "You look stunning." I finally remember to breathe, then lean in to kiss her cheek. Closing my eyes, I savor her scent, a new favorite.

I then offer my arm. "Wow." The velvet brushes against my wrist and reminds me of the flower I hold. I extend it toward her. "A single rose for the one and only."

Lifting the flower to her nose, she halts and sucks in a breath. "Thank you."

Her heels click against the concrete as we walk toward the sidewalk. I opted for a hired car tonight, so I can sit beside Valentina without the distractions of driving or the presence of Matthew.

The soft pop music I'd requested floats in the car. We have the same preference in music. Even though the back seat has enough room for three, we find ourselves close together, her delicate hand clasped in mine. I kiss the top of her hair again, inhaling a fragrance that seems a blend of roses and something uniquely hers. "How was the party?"

"It was busy. Ended up helping out in the kitchen." She shares details of the event—the music, the dancing, and the last-minute preparations.

"Did you dance with anyone?" I cringe.

"Not with anyone you'd worry about." She squishes her face playfully.

I try to suppress the jealous lover in me. She's here with me now, and there will be dances for us tonight and many more nights to come. Hopefully.

She shifts and laces our fingers together. "Were the kids okay with Willow babysitting them?"

I nod. "I, um, I told them about us."

Her fingers squeeze mine. "How did they react?"

"Eden... she wants to make sure you'll be in her life." I won't elaborate on Eden's real fear of Valentina's departure someday. "They like you a lot, maybe even more than they like me."

When I nudge her shoulder with my arm, her eyes sparkle. "That's not true."

I lift our entwined hands and kiss each of her fingertips painted a subtle white. They smell like fresh nail polish.

Once the car stops at the posh hotel, I'm out and around to her side in moments. I hand the driver a generous tip, then help Valentina out. With her hold careful on the rose now stashed in her grip, she quips, "I'll guard it with my life."

"And I'll guard you with my life." I wink.

"What time should I pick you up?" The driver is already angling for his next fare.

I hadn't thought that far. So I tell him I'm not sure what time the event ends. I can get a ride easily.

"Just text me when you're ready." He confirms I have his number in my call history.

Camera flashes ignite as we step into the hotel's grand entrance, photographers bustling around us. Under the bright lights, a buzz reminds me I'm here with the most beautiful woman in the world and I've been given a rare second chance at love.

We stride into the banquet room. Crystal chandeliers cast a sparkling light over a sea of faces and tables set with floral centerpieces and immaculate white linen. The rich scent of gourmet appetizers mingles with subtle perfumes, and with it, whispers of "that's Valentina Diaz" float toward us, followed by admiring glances from the well-dressed participants.

Pride surges through me. She's clearly known for a show that helped women navigate difficult life situations.

As we pass clusters of influencers and media figures, I exchange nods and brief greetings, my posture straightening under the scrutiny.

When I sight Daisy and Scott among the elite, a familiar unease coils in my stomach, and my confidence wavers.

Valentina must sense the shift. Her hand tightens around mine, and she leans in, speaking for my ears alone. "Everything okay?"

"Yeah." I offer a reassured smile. "Big night."

She squeezes my hand. Her smile sideways is as natural as if we've done this before. "You've got this."

And she's right. She's all I need to look at tonight, and my unease about Scott and Daisy vanishes. But I need her by my side forever.

CHAPTER 31

Jason

My business partner, Chris, approaches. His gray hair gleams under the chandelier lights before he slaps my shoulder. "Sterling."

I do the same, then introduce Valentina.

Chris shakes her hand, tilting his head. "A pleasure. Have we met before?"

"Yes, we have." Humor glints in her dark eyes. "I'll let Jason explain later."

His brows narrow as he attempts to figure out the scenario like the investigative journalist he once was. Then he flashes her a charming grin. "Can I steal your date for a sec, Miss Valentina?"

When she nods, we step aside, and Chris raises his voice over the MC testing his microphone. "That guy you fired?" He looks around as if to make sure no one's listening. "He's threatening HR with a lawsuit. Says it's wrongful termination."

Austin won't be the first grumbling employee. I sigh, my gaze drifting over to Valentina chatting with other guests. "That's why we have a legal team."

Chris rubs his jaw, his shoulders still taut. "Is that the same Valentina you cost us from hiring?"

I roll my eyes. "I like you better when you don't remember things."

He shakes his head. "Your assistant was right, thinking you had a romantic history involved."

I catch Valentina's eye this time. She smiles, unaware she's the subject. "Things change, but Beatrix will be fired next if she can't tame her tongue."

"Next time, keep me in the loop before firing major staff." His backslap this time knocks me forward a half step. "Not sure I can trust your abrupt judgment anymore."

We mingle as servers pass cocktails and appetizers. Then Valentina and I find our table with three other couples—media executives and their partners, all familiar faces in the industry. The light banter and polite laughter provide a perfect backdrop as the waitstaff serve dinner. Savory beef bourguignon with vegetables or a delicate vegetarian risotto. Valentina opts for the risotto, having eaten enough meat at the previous party. I choose the mouthwatering beef.

As we eat, our head of public relations, a charismatic woman with a sharp wit, takes the stage, warming up the crowd with her engaging presence. She then introduces me, and I head up as a hush falls over the room. The attention always feels heavy at these events.

I take a deep breath as I adjust the mic on my collar. "Good evening, everyone. Thank you for being here tonight. What an honor to see so many familiar faces and welcome new friends who share our vision."

My gaze flickers to Valentina, her smile a beacon in the sea of faces. "This year has been a landmark for Family Sphere TV station. We've reached milestones that seemed distant dreams not long ago." I weave through our accomplishments, our strategic expansions, and our vision for the coming years. Warmth spreads through me. We're not doing bad for a new network less than twelve years in the making. "This success is not mine alone but belongs to our dedicated team, our steadfast partners, and our loyal viewers."

The room buzzes as I nod toward the crowd, careful to avoid Daisy and Scott's table. "Your support is the foundation of our growth and success." I let the applause fade for a moment. "Tonight's charity is close to my heart. As a single dad, I understand the hurdles single parents face. With your support tonight, we aim to bolster those bravely navigating this path. Thank you for walking this journey with us. Let's enjoy the evening and forge new alliances. Cheers!"

Applause rings out as I descend from the podium, the weight on me lifting with each step.

Valentina's beaming smile guides me back to her, and she slides her arm around my waist, her whisper warm against my ear. "You did great!"

With her by my side, I'm ready to step into a future I hadn't dared to imagine these last few years. After dessert, the soft background music creates a relaxed atmosphere, perfect for easy conversation and networking as Valentina and I move from table to table.

Despite my intention to introduce her to key business contacts, she commands attention on her own, charming everyone she speaks with. I find myself separated from her, pulled aside by guests keen on discussing collaborations. But each time I glance back at Valentina, my chest swells. She handles every interaction with grace and warmth, her laughter mingling with the soft clinks of glasses and the subtle hum of conversations.

Caught up in an animated discussion about new media trends, I'm jarred by the sensation of being watched. I catch Daisy's gaze from across the room. She's engaged in conversation with two women, but her attention is fixed on me. I divert my eyes, focusing on the positive energy around me. I've ignored her recent attempts to reach out. I won't let her rend my daughter's heart again.

Garrett, a longtime friend and fellow business network member, claps me on the shoulder. "Ho ho, look who's here!"

"Good to see you." I shake his hand.

"Is she the catch you couldn't stop texting last time?" He nods toward Valentina engaged in a discussion nearby.

I smirk. "It was just a lunch meeting. I could get away with a text."

Garrett, a casting director with a keen eye for talent, remains one of the noblest people I know. He and I worked together as business journalists right after college, but he didn't want to work at my small network.

"We should plan a Jet Ski-day soon." I suggest our biannual summer water day when he usually joins me with my friends.

"I might only pull off one trip this summer." He winces. "We're starting a new health-and-wellness show this fall. Means going through hires. I dread things like that."

Another mutual friend joins, bringing news from another corner of the industry. Soon, the evening transitions into its music phase, and guests drift into the ballroom. There, the lights dim, and a well-known musician takes the stage, his melodic voice soothing the atmosphere. The dance floor beckons, and Valentina and I join the swirl of guests. The moment diffuses any earlier tensions.

"Your speech was wonderful." She leans close enough for her whisper to tickle my ear.

"And you're a star here. Known and still loved by everyone."

"So are you." She scans the other dancers. "Is Daisy here?"

I'd rather not talk about my ex right now. "Thank you for coming with me."

Valentina's smile broadens, her eyes sparkling. "I wouldn't have missed it for anything." Her arms encircle me in a gentle embrace. "You didn't tell me about your single-parent organization."

"It's not a big deal."

"You're a noble man, Grumps."

A warm glow radiates through me. But there's not enough support for the many single parents struggling to balance work and childcare.

"I wish I could do more."

"Any little bit helps."

The charity auction begins at around eleven p.m., and Valentina and I dive into the spirited bidding, laughing and competing with other guests. We only win tickets to a movie premiere, but she seems happy about it.

After Chris closes the event with words of gratitude, the ballroom empties. Valentina and I linger to thank every guest personally. With a handful of people left in the room, Daisy joins us, Scott in tow, her black dress swaying, her blonde hair styled in waves. She used to be the center of my life, and while she's beautiful, I see her in a different light now.

"Jason!" Scott offers a curt nod, which I return with equal stiffness. The man has a daughter in college. It makes sense Daisy settled with him since he's not planning to have more kids. Valentina extends a hand, her smile poised, and introduces herself.

"All successful men have a smart woman behind them." Scott's gaze skims over Valentina, his expression unreadable.

"You've got quite a catch," Daisy says, relaxed as usual. She introduces herself to Valentina, using her maiden name. "I'm a longtime fan of your show."

Valentina's smile tightens as she glances at me, perhaps piecing together the connection. "Jason mentioned you enjoyed my work."

Daisy nods, then refocuses on me. "You didn't return my calls."

"If you want to talk to your daughter, you'll have to show up." I squeeze my teeth to contain my calm. "I have no energy for your false promises."

"How am I supposed to know when you're home?" She adjusts her beaded clutch tucked by her elbow.

"You've lost the privilege of knowing when we're home." I'm done being silent while she does whatever. "She's out of school until mid-August."

I look toward the exit, eager to escape, but Scott engages Valentina. Thankfully, his questions seem professional. My gaze lingers on her as she handles the situation with composure, unlike the tension between Daisy and me.

Daisy pivots to face Valentina, clearly aware she and I aren't going to get anywhere in our conversation. "If anyone is going to be the mother of my kids," she says, and Scott stops talking, deferring to his wife, "I'd rather it's a woman who teaches them to handle things on their own." Daisy's history of indifference surfaces, a trait that makes her interactions complex. She never holds grudges, nor does she grasp the impact of her actions.

"I assume you've met my kids by now?" she asks Valentina.

"Your kids are wonderful, and they adore you."

Daisy winces. "I know it's hard to understand. I love the idea that I have kids, but I'm not meant to be a mom." You'd think she and Valentina were old friends.

"I was miserable when I became a parent. But I'm at peace. I know Jason takes good care of them—he's a kid person." Her voice cracks, her eyes soften, and her large earrings sway with each seemingly heartfelt word. Scott, sensing his place, drifts toward the entrance, giving them space. "Your show opened my eyes to go back and do what I love. Not that Jason was holding me back, but I was so reliant on him." Daisy shares her journey back to her modeling career, speaking of her newfound independence and how it feels right to pursue her passions.

Valentina listens, nodding from time to time. "You'll always be their mom, regardless." Valentina's response holds no judgment. "If you ever have a moment, come by and say hello. They don't expect you to do anything you don't want to do."

Their conversation ends with Daisy in tears. She wraps her arms around Valentina and then embraces me, which softens me a tad. "Jason, you've scored a gem. I'm so happy for you two."

I draw out a breath. The anger I'd held over the years melts with my newfound understanding. "The kids are doing great." My voice catches. "I'm happy you found your dream."

As Daisy prepares to leave, she exchanges numbers with Valentina, promising to stay in touch. The evening, which started with tension, concludes with reconciliation and hope. In the end, things have a way of working out just as they should.

With everything unfolding, I forgot to text the driver. I pull out my phone and call, relieved when he answers.

"I'm already in the parking lot. Wasn't busy anymore for the night."

What a generous tip can accomplish, indeed.

Peace envelops me as we settle into the car. I'm too overwhelmed to speak, and she must be as well. She rests her head on my shoulder, and we sit in contented silence, her presence a comforting weight against me. My hand finds hers, our fingers intertwining.

Outside, the city lights blur into a haze. Soon, a sigh escapes her, and I glance down. Her breathing is shallow. Her chest rises and falls. Her lips, slightly parted, still hold tonight's bright red lipstick. I love how her long lashes flutter, reminding me of the times she reads to the kids and the cute way she purses her lips when engrossed in a book. I love how sometimes she drops ice in her coffee or food to cool it down. I grin, loving everything about her, and my heart aches with longing.

Protective instincts swell as I bury my nose in her hair to inhale her fragrance in case I have to imprint her scent to memory. Valentina's impact tonight went beyond supporting me—she touched lives, like Daisy's, offering validation I couldn't provide when it was most needed.

Keeping her to myself as the kids' nanny is self-centered.

I'd do anything for her, not only to amend past mistakes but also because the world needs what she can offer—more people should benefit from her kindness and wisdom. She deserves a broader audience.

Garrett's health-and-wellness show. They're seeking a host. This would suit her, assuming the role involves providing support and relatable advice to viewers, maybe even conducting interviews with experts. I'll see him at a networking meeting on Monday. I still have her CV and résumé. I'll make sure she steps into a position where her talents can shine—even if it means losing her.

CHAPTER 32

Valentina

"Thanks again for inviting me." Daisy sets down her bubbly water on the patio table under the umbrella shading us. Her blonde hair, curly and whimsical, is pulled into a messy ponytail. Dressed in white bohemian pants and a sleeveless top, she radiates the effortless charm of the model she is. I'd be jealous, but I know how Jason feels about me and where his relationship stands with Daisy.

"You made Eden's day." I nod toward the splashes and shrieks emanating from the pool where Eden is the star among her chanting friends.

She winces. "I was worried she wouldn't speak to me again."

"Kids are forgiving."

"The twins don't even know me."

"They will." If she starts showing up more often.

I understand Daisy's fear of failing as a mother. While I don't support how she stepped back, her openness softens my judgment. She promised to come today—and she followed through—which means she's trying, even choosing to leave Scott behind to avoid stirring Jason's lingering resentment.

For now, I'll leave the Scott issue to Jason. He'll confront it when he's ready. As long as I'm part of his life, I'll ensure Daisy is included in these moments like the kids' birthdays where her presence counts most.

Laughter and chatter draw my gaze across Jason's bustling backyard to the pool a good distance from the house. He's in blue swim trunks with pink flamingos, his broad chest shimmering in the sun thanks to the lemongrass and peppermint sunscreen I sprayed all over him. He moves along the pool's edge snapping one photo after another.

At the shallow end, Liam keeps a watchful eye on the younger kids. Ethan and Russ stand outside the gazebo manning the grill behind a cloud of smoke.

We'd planned a small gathering, but Eden's ever-expanding circle of family and friends turned today into a festival of an affair. The crowd buzzes, most clustered around the cake and presents in the gazebo where my mom is rearranging the food table, while Leah and her husband and Judy and Phil hover around the gift table.

Laughter pulls my gaze back to the pool, and Eden beams with a group of girls before they splash into the pool.

Her friends are mostly new faces from the church camp she attended two weeks ago, though a couple came from her old school.

"Val! Mom!" Atticus calls out, poised for a dive at the deep end. Jason and I have ensured they know how to handle the deep end safely. "Watch this!" he yells before plunging headfirst and rising to our cheers and claps.

"I'll go take some photos." Daisy stands, and I do the same.

As we join the others, one of the girls' shoulders seems pinker than when she showed up. "Hey, sweetie." I crouch at the edge of the pool where her feet dangle in the water. "Let's add some sunscreen on your back." I guide her toward the makeshift first aid station where I stocked a utility bag with essentials.

Subtle essential oils scent the air as I spray her back before she darts off.

"Hey, girl." Leah saunters my way, a sarong over her swimsuit, a water bottle in hand. She hates swimming, but she'll venture into the water if I do.

"Caught up with Daisy a bit?" She sinks onto the bench beside me, fanning herself with a *Family Sphere* magazine she snagged from the table.

"She was thanking me for the invitation."

The sun is relentless today, even under the umbrella, and I can't feel any breeze. I'm wearing my swimsuit beneath the summer dress. As soon as I get a chance, I'll strip off the dress and dive into the pool.

"I'm glad she's at peace with you being the kids' stepmom. You've been a constant in their lives these last months."

I'm not sure I qualify as a stepmom yet. Though the way things are going, it might come to that. For now, I focus on today. "You should have seen Eden light up when she saw her mom."

Eden loves me too, but she has a special place for her mom. Maybe now, she can stop blaming herself for her mom's disappearance.

"You're a counselor at heart, seeing what's in their best interest." She shakes her head, her words soft. "Eden lights up around you too. God is using you here, and it could be where you're supposed to be."

"I think so too." My gaze lingers on all the kids but mostly on Jason. Their happy smiles make me want to join their pool volleyball game.

"Apparently, this is where we line up for sunscreen." Ethan approaches in a T-shirt and swim trunks. "Before I dive into the pool, I'd better map out where everything is."

"You're in the right place." I adjust the basket on the table.

"Leave it to Val. You have a ton of sunscreen to choose from." Leah pulls out a spray bottle with a yellow handwritten label for lemon and peppermint essential oil spray. "Thank goodness, I don't need any of these."

"What might you recommend?" Ethan examines a bottle.

"Depends whether you want to smell like lavender or peppermint—or both."

"I'll start with peppermint and lemon." He sprays it on his arms. "By the way, Val, I wanted to thank you."

"If you mean volunteering at the church camp, no need."

"That too." He sprays his other arm, dousing the air with a minty scent. "Rita said you gave her some great insights."

I smile, remembering the church's crafts session. When Rita and I volunteered, she shared her family's challenges. Her mother-in-law moving in with them had strained their marriage. "It was nothing, really."

Ethan replaces the spray in the basket. "It might be nothing to you, but it meant a lot to her family. You have a way of making people feel at ease."

I catch Jason's heated gaze from near the grills where Russ stands. Jason salutes, and I grin. He'd cautioned me about getting too close to his friends, so what's he thinking about Ethan chatting with me?

"I didn't know you're a counselor." Ethan chuckles. "Jason says you're good at it."

"Did he now?" I wink at Jason. Did he just mouth "I love you" before walking toward his mom and Phil outside the gazebo? They'd returned from their trip a week ago.

"He did. He also says you're a good Bible teacher."

My heart warms. "I'm not a Bible teacher though."

"Val is the best." Leah pats my arm. "With kids and adults."

"I've never worked with adults." Only on TV. Which is different.

"You have a chance to. Would you consider being our family counselor at church? There's no pressure, of course. Jason probably pays you more than the church will, but you don't have to quit your job with Jason's kids. We can work out a schedule for an afternoon or two. I haven't figured that out yet. All I know is the families at church could use your wisdom."

"You make me sound so intelligent." His trust is daunting. Plus, this opportunity could complicate my other new opportunity.

"I've seen it myself and heard a lot from you-know-who."

"I don't know." Jason submitted my credentials and résumé to NWAY Network without telling me, and the casting director contacted me. I can't guarantee I'll get the job I'm set to interview for next week, but what if I do?

"She'll pray about it." Leah speaks for me.

I blow out a breath. "It sounds like something I'd like to step into."

"Pray about it." His dimples deepen as he smiles. "We better eat soon so we can get to that cake before it melts."

I thank him again before he walks away.

"Look who's the busy one now!" Leah bats her eyes. "You have the dream option of moving to a big network—in your field, psychology, even. And then there's the church-counselor gig in a small town. Something you'd considered, right?"

"Not for a small town, though." I rest my chin on my hand, my gaze drifting to where Jason's kids splash around, then to Jason himself, who's laughing with his mom and Phil. His laughter almost decides for me.

"It's obvious what I should do, but I need to be sure before I dive into the wrong place." I glance back at Leah, finding her keen eyes alight with interest. "If I work for the network, it doesn't mean my relationship with him has to end, right?"

"Well, there will be a long commute every day to Manhattan if you choose to stay in this town for your boyfriend."

"I could see him in Manhattan when he comes to work."

"The kids are off for the summer—when will you see them?" Her eyebrows pull together.

That question hits closer to home. "On the weekends?"

"That's if the job gives you weekends off."

Doubt crowds in. Will Eden feel abandoned? Will she think I left them for a better job?

Leah's gaze softens. She grips my hand. "It's not just a job choice, is it? It's about where your heart lies and where you see your future."

This decision isn't about location or ambition. It's about where I belong.

She's so wise. "Aren't I supposed to be the one with the Psychology degree?"

At night, after the party buzz dimmed, the guests departed, and the kids curled up in bed, Jason and I settle onto the living room sofa. Dim light seeps through the big window from the porch, and the refrigerator emits a smooth hum.

"The party was wonderful." He drapes his arm over my shoulder, pulls me closer, and kisses the top of my head.

"You told Ethan I'm a counselor, huh." It's not a question, more an amused observation.

"What's wrong with a man bragging about his sexy and smart girlfriend?" The vibrations of his voice resonate against me.

"Nothing. As long as people don't expect too much of me." I smile into the semidarkness, content in his presence. "I'm still mad at you for submitting my résumé behind my back."

"Like I said." His warm lips touch my cheek, and I gasp in a breath. "Had to fix my mistakes. If you don't get hired, it will be their loss. I'll submit to another network."

"What are you going to do for two whole weeks?" My voice dips with the dread of possibly starting a new job and missing out on his upcoming time off.

"I'm hoping to take my girlfriend on a few dates." His thumb traces slow circles in my palm. "I expect it'll take me longer than two weeks to find a nanny. You set the bar too high."

His earnestness tightens my chest. "Are you trying to get rid of me, Grumps?"

"Never." He takes my face in his hand. I shift so our heads touch when he leans in and I close my eyes.

"This is one of the hardest things I've had to do." A tremor wobbles his voice. "I'd rather have you to myself."

At his sincerity, my words burst free, unguarded and true. "I love you, Jason Sterling."

"I was wondering when you'd fall in love with me."

I touch his chest, and his heart beats against my palm, similar to the thumping of mine. "I think I loved you way before we crossed that line."

"The line from?" His breath fogs my face, hovering on my lips, making it hard to hold up my eyelids.

"From dislike to something…"

I'm not sure if he or I initiate the kiss, but once again, we're sinking deep into the sofa, his hands in my hair and mine moving along his jaw, as our chocolate-cake breaths mingle. The intensity of his kiss heightens my longing and desire for him.

I love the way I feel small and protected beneath him, as if I've found where I fit, where I belong.

I'm not sure I can get enough of him. And that could be dangerous if we're living under the same roof. But I am sure of one thing: We belong together.

CHAPTER 33

Jason

Today is one of the rare days I get to be alone with Ethan, and it's the first time I sit across from him as my spiritual leader rather than a friend. The kids are at a sports camp for the afternoon, and Ethan set this time aside for us at my request. Birds chirp in the shrubs beyond his porch, and mature trees shade his deck from the midmorning sun.

Our conversation meanders through the mundanities of daily life and the challenges of parenting. Ethan talks about his kids' struggle to wake up for the sports camp. "Nap time should be easy this afternoon."

"Mine woke up easily, but they didn't want breakfast without Valentina." As excited as I am for her interview, the change for us leaves me uneasy.

"About Valentina." Ethan sets his water bottle on the table between us. "Now that you're dating, it would be smart not to sleep under the same roof. Until you're married, of course. Though I believe you said you'd never date again?"

As he reminds me of my words at the campfire when Valentina first watched all the kids, my cheeks heat, but I focus on the shared-space aspect. "If she gets the job, she's moving back to Manhattan or Brooklyn with her family anyway." She'll get hired, and it'll have nothing to do with my friendship with the producer but everything to do with Valentina's credentials. The jobs she interviewed for before didn't hire her because she was overqualified.

"And?"

I swallowed to mask the hollowness accompanying her departure. "That's one of the things I wanted to talk to you about. If you know a babysitter you trust, I'll be needing one soon."

"I see." Ethan nods. "Has Valentina said she wants to work for the big network, or is this what you thought she needed?"

"She has more to offer the world, and a big network will give her that platform." I clear my throat. Still, the fear of her moving on without us lurks beneath my words. "I robbed her of that chance once, yet she's given us so much."

Ethan has likely noticed the changes in my family, including Eden's newfound confidence.

"And finally, all the talk about faith, sin, and talking to God you've shared with us over the years is starting to resonate. Valentina helped bridge that understanding." I face the wildflowers in Ethan's backyard. Despite the grass to choke them out, they are vibrant. Firmly rooted. I need to remain rooted in God. "Which brings me to my next question. You talked about having a relationship with God. How do I know if I have that?"

Ethan's brown eyes catch the midmorning light, reflecting a thoughtful spark. "You know how your relationship with Valentina started on edge? Then you became friends, recognizing the good and bad in each other?" At my nod, he continues. "But the good outweighed the bad, and eventually, you told each other 'I love you.'" He pauses, ensuring I follow. "It's similar with God. It starts by talking to Him, inviting Him into your daily life, then a relationship unfolds."

Ethan elaborates on how God sent His son, Jesus, to die as a sacrifice so our sins could be forgiven. "We'll dig deeper into it later, but all you need to know now is to open your heart and let Him guide you through life, step-by-step."

Before I know it, he's holding my hands, and I'm pouring my heart out in prayer, asking for forgiveness and for God to be the center of my life. Happiness and peace like none before fill my heart almost to bursting, and my eyes itch, my throat closing up. By the time my eyes meet his again, Ethan is beaming.

"I agree. You've changed since you embraced Valentina into your family," he says. "I've been praying for this day, hoping it would come while I was still here to see it." He then delves into God's design for relationships. "He uses those connections to give us a taste of what it's like to have a relationship with Him. If we don't understand how to connect with those we see every day, how can we relate and connect to a God we've never seen?"

As he speaks, a breeze whips the trees and shrubs. The rustling fills the silence following his words, almost as if nature itself affirms his message.

"And to answer your question about a nanny, I'll keep my eyes open, but I have a feeling that, whether Valentina gets this job or not, you and the kids have become the center of her world too."

"I'm not sure what steps to take next with her. I don't want to interfere with her career path by pushing our relationship to the next level." Yet what's the purpose of dating if we don't plan to move things along?

"Do you see yourself spending the rest of your life with Valentina?"

"Without a doubt." My heart swells. "But with everything that went down with Daisy, rushing her into marriage—"

"I don't know Daisy, but I do know Valentina. They are different people." Ethan reaches for his bottle and waves it between us. "We know Valentina loves kids, her faith in God. Those are significant differences. Ask her what she wants out of this relationship."

"She wants marriage and all." Didn't Carlos advise me not to start anything I wasn't prepared to see through? He wouldn't have said so if she hadn't wanted a long-term commitment from Austin. His loss and my gain. I lean back, hands clasped between my knees. Ethan would be honest rather than tell me what I want to hear.

So here goes. "Do you think I have what it takes to be the husband she deserves?"

"Yes. You love her and she loves you. The rest will play out as it should."

"God is in the transforming business?"

Ethan nods, his smile knowing. "Just remember, faith isn't about having all the answers upfront. God will guide you through each step, even when the path isn't clear."

His words renew my hope and commitment as we depart. Anticipation rises, and my heart is loaded with possibilities as I pick up the kids from their sports camp.

Their excitement bubbles out on the drive home. Each speaks over the other as they share stories about more new friends, friends who will join them at school this fall.

"I'm so glad." My smile mirrors their enthusiasm.

As we pull into the driveway, the vibrant blooms in our garden catch my eye, their colors a vivid reminder of the season's joy. "It's a warm day." I suggest swimming to the kids. I'll see if the rest of the guys want to join us.

"Is Val swimming with us?" Eden asks.

The boys start chattering about swimming with Val. I missed working out with Valentina this morning too and our usual breakfast where we share what we were grateful for.

"I don't think she'll be here today." I step out of the car, the kids following.

Eden stops in front of me, and her nearly invisible blonde brows draw tight. "If she gets the job, will she still be with us?"

I place a comforting hand on her soft cheek. "She'll probably move to Brooklyn, but I'm going to make sure you have a new caretaker."

"She said she won't leave us!" Eden stomps on the concrete, her voice sending birds in flight from the tree hovering by the driveway. She then folds her arms and juts up her chin. "She promised!"

"She didn't break any promises." I assure her. Though maybe she made some she might find hard to keep?

"Did Val leave without saying goodbye?" Atticus steps forward. Felix looks equally worried.

"She wouldn't leave without saying goodbye." That's a promise I can keep.

"I told her not to throw a party for me." Eden's lower lip quivers. Oh no! The dear girl blames herself already.

"Hey." I pull her close to comfort her, but she wiggles out of my arms and rushes up the path to the door, slamming it behind her.

Glad I had a light, free morning while it lasted. Isn't life supposed to be perfect when you walk closer to God? Maybe day one is too early to expect changes.

To distract the boys, I suggest soccer tag and bring them to laughter as they team up to beat me. I'm breathless, unable to match their energy.

"I need a break." I slide my phone from my shorts pockets and urge them to keep playing, my mind already rushing to Valentina. She hasn't texted. Could she still be at her interview?

I've never used the location-sharing app she'd set up in case I couldn't reach her by phone and needed to know where she and the kids were. I scroll my thumb in search of the app. What was it again? I didn't realize how many inbuilt apps I have. Now, I click one unfamiliar app after another.

On the Axis. Finally. I click the pin location on the map just as my phone rings. It's Mom.

"How did Val's interview go?"

"She hasn't called yet." My shoes crunch in the grass as the boys scale a tree with ease. "I'll update you as soon as I hear anything."

"How did the kids' camp go?"

"They had fun." I press the phone to my ear, so I can hear over the boys' loud shrills. "Edie isn't taking Valentina's interview well." It's gotta be best to let her have a moment in her room where she must've vanished.

Mom sighs. "Sweet baby."

"She thinks Valentina is getting a job because she was burdened by putting on Eden's birthday party."

"Val is not like Daisy. I've seen the way she looks at you, the way she interacts with the kids."

"I know." Despite Mom extolling Valentina's qualities, doubt clouds my hope. Would she want to move to a small town with us? She says she loves the serenity here, but does she want to live here long term?

"I can talk to Eden if you want me to." Mom's voice through the phone pulls me back.

"She'll overcome the upset." Like Valentina said, we all need a moment to process our thoughts. "Let's give her some time."

"Keep me posted on the interview," Mom insists before we end our chat.

How long will it take all of us to adjust to Valentina's absence if it becomes long-term? And what about Ethan's advice to avoid the temptation of staying in rooms across from each other?

If everything changes, I'll need to revert to my old normal—doing things solo. Ugh. I've come too far to go back to now. I can't even remember what that looked like. If she gets the job and is willing to commute to Meadowbrook, she could move to the annex, and Mom and Phil could stay in her room when they visit. She'll be farther from me, but not too far for us to have family dinners together and the kids to see her often.

There's too much to navigate, and I don't want to coerce Valentina into anything that might backfire.

But how else will she know I'm serious about us and taking our relationship to the next level? Maybe this can be the exception. The time I do what I'd sworn never to do again. Ask her to marry me.

We're both past our twenties and against time if we want our forever to start now. But is it too soon to ask for marriage?

CHAPTER 34

Valentina

Anxiety typically clings to the edges of an interview, but it's not just about the job today. It's about where I need to be—should be. I shift in the plush chair, taking in the Manhattan skyscrapers beyond the window, then face the panel of men and women, some nodding, others jotting notes, and others still processing my last response.

I can't tell who'll be questioning me next, but this is far more inviting than Family Sphere's boardroom. I hosted a health-and-wellness show when someone was on leave, so if I get hired, this should be an easier transition.

"Valentina, could you tell us about a time you handled a particularly challenging situation on air?" A middle-aged woman with a kind smile and sharp eyes leans forward.

I clear my throat, sitting straight. "During a live segment, our guest became ill. I had to keep the audience engaged while signaling the crew for medical help without causing alarm."

Nods greet my response.

A man with brown skin folds his hand on the table. "What strategies do you use to convey complex health topics in a way understandable to the general public?"

"I believe in the power of stories and simplicity." I then break down information into relatable pieces, using personal experiences to make the content more digestible. I delve into mental health from what I've learned and seen, sharing scenarios that could happen to anyone. With each of their questions, I'm blessed to know the answers, which keeps our discussion engaging. I almost forget I'm in an interview as more people write notes on their notepads and others type on their tablets.

A tickle teases my nose, so I dig into my purse. But I fish out a crumpled piece of paper instead of the mini tissue pack. Memories rush in as I smooth out Felix's drawing from our family art night.

My heart aches. What would moving back to Brooklyn mean? Jason will find another nanny, but how will I explain to the kids, especially Eden, that things have to change? The bond we've formed, the trust... Can a weekly visit maintain that?

"Valentina."

I thrust back the paper, looking for whoever called my name. Had they called earlier and I didn't hear?

"Why should we choose you as the face of NWAY's new wellness initiative?"

I honestly didn't think this far. Do I want to be chosen?

To regain my confidence, it would be nice to get hired, but things are different now. Either way, they deserve my time, even though I'm sure they have better top candidates to consider than me.

"I'm passionate about promoting health and wellness because it changes lives." So far, no one asked about my show at Starwatch. Perhaps Jason just sent credentials that highlight my psychology expertise? Or perhaps NWAY didn't want to waste time asking about the gossip network. "My commitment extends beyond presenting information. I seek to form connections, understand the community's needs, and be present...." I'm not sure what I say next because Jason and his kids flash through my mind. I feel their warmth, love, and the difference they've made in my life. The challenges with Jason and Eden have brought me back to my knees, teaching me to rely on God. I've fallen so deeply in love with him and his kids. I'm fulfilled whenever I'm around them, and right now, I could be swimming, walking to the Sips and Scripts with them, or whatever he's doing with his kids while he's off work.

"I am excited about this opportunity, but I must consider where I can make the most impact, both professionally and personally." Did

I say my thoughts out loud? I might've because the producer nods and thanks me for coming.

"We'll be in touch."

For the first time as I leave an interview, I don't care about getting hired. I thank the kind receptionist, then head to the elevator. But I'm not supposed to be the next host here or anywhere on TV.

Jason's community needs me, his church, his family, and I need them just as much. Ethan's job offers little pay, not sure how much, but it doesn't matter because it's where I need to be.

As I wait for the elevator, a phone rings from behind the wall where I just left. Light streams through a window, the sky a clear blue above the Manhattan skyline. Then the elevator doors slide open, and three people step out. My feet remain planted, and my stomach churns when I recognize one of them.

"Val." Austin grins the devious smile of his that could fool any woman.

"Austin." The elevator doors close, stranding me in the hallway with a man who planted roots of hate in me. Sooner or later though, I must face him. I take a step back until my back hits the wall.

His once long and cherished hair now has a clean cut, no doubt infused with fancy products. The polished look suits him.

"Don't tell me you work here." His tone is light but edged with something I can't quite place. "I'm surprised you don't work at your boyfriend's network."

Why is he talking like we're old friends? "Not good to work with a love interest." I struggle to keep my voice gentle. "You taught me that."

Something crosses his face—remorse, perhaps? It's fleeting, replaced by his familiar guarded expression when he steps beside me, keeping a distance between us. His gaze rakes me from the head down, soft, familiar, but it doesn't make me melt the way it used to. "You look great. Always did."

I step further aside to widen the distance between us while staying close enough to hear him. He probably works here too. "I assume you're just here filling in for someone today?"

He lets out a humorless laugh. "What a small world. Of all the places, I end up working for your boyfriend. He fired me the day I ran into you. Apparently, you shouldn't have told him I was your ex."

"Jason fired you?"

The elevator opens again, people step out, and someone else rushes in before it closes.

"Sounds like he didn't tell you." He leans his head against the wall.

As I face him, sadness hits me, not just for Austin, but for the situation. Jason lost a videographer on my account?

If anyone hurts my family and those I love...

He loves me that fiercely?

His words from the night at the beach house flood me when he'd eagerly wanted to know about Austin.

"At least he recommended you for this job." Like he did with me, I guess?

Austin smirks. "Why would he do that when he made it clear he never wanted to see me again? This host job was listed for months. It pays off to have different fields covered. I don't intend to use Family Sphere as a reference—I doubt I'll get a good word there." He then rambles a plot for revenge. "If I get hired, my first paycheck goes to sue his company."

"I'm afraid God isn't going to help you get the job if you're planning to waste your money." My temperature kicks up. I want to bring up my show after we broke up. I strove to prove myself mostly because of him. "You need to work on how to treat people first."

I step back in front of the elevator.

Austin probably assumes I work here, and I don't volunteer that I just interviewed for the same job.

"Good luck," I add, despite all the questions I want to ask about why and how he left the network in L.A., how things ended with the woman who came between us. But the past is really behind me.

"You made a name for your show." His voice floats over my shoulder. "It was popular, and people loved you."

"It's not a big deal." I pull out my phone, needing a distraction, and I act like I'm checking the messages or the time. Why is the elevator taking so long? I need to escape this encounter. "Nice to see you again."

"I'm sorry I wasn't a worthy boyfriend."

I shift to look at him. His nod seems genuine, a brief acknowledgment of our past, before he salutes me as he leaves.

Finally, the doors open, and I step in.

At least he apologized. I don't like that he wants to sue Family Sphere, though I'm sure they have a lawyer for such things. Jason protected me, but he shouldn't have fired Austin. Yet he did because of what Austin did to me. Funny he never brought up Austin's name again. My heart swells with love. As the elevator descends, I check the location-sharing app on my phone. It's time to go home.

CHAPTER 35

Valentina

As I pull into the driveway, Jason and the kids amble back from the yard, all dressed in swimsuits. The boys spot me and burst into a sprint. The radiant smile transforming Jason's face penetrates straight into my heart. This is home. This feeling, this moment, is where I belong, in a family of my own.

When I push the car door open, I all but jump out with a tumble. I'm driven by the magnetic pull of my new family, and I don't even close the door since it would slow me down. My pace quickens, my heart pounding, as the distance between us closes. Then I'm enveloped in hugs as the twins collide with me. Their arms wrap around my waist. Their joyful assault would've knocked me off-balance, but Jason's steady hands are there, supporting me.

"You're here!" Atticus jolts back, clapping.

Felix grips my wrist, holding on tightly.

Bending to their level, I inhale the faint smell of chlorine, and I pepper the tops of their heads with kisses.

Atticus jumps up and down. "Can you swim with us?"

"Can you play the racing car game with me on TV?" Felix speaks over his brother.

Their requests tumble over each other, and Jason winks with a smile so sweet and tender my breath stalls. With the boys tugging at me, I can't hug him as I long to, but his understanding gaze tells me he feels the same.

Then Eden rushes into the house, her head low and arms crossed in stark contrast to her brothers' joy.

"Why is your sister so upset?"

Atticus's shoulders sag. "She's sad because you're leaving."

"She'll be okay." Jason attempts to gloss over the underlying issues.

Felix tugs at my hand, his somber face searching for reassurance. "Are we never going to see you again?"

"I'm not going anywhere," I reassure him, and that earns me another flurry of hugs, their small arms tighten around me and my heart overflows.

But then Jason touches my shoulder. His head tilts. "You knocked them dead at the interview?" His voice crackles. He's wearing a swim shirt today, probably to avoid sunburn, and my hands itch to ruffle through his rumpled hair.

"Let me first go and talk to Eden." Perhaps making things straight with his kids will allow us time to talk freely. "I'll tell you all about it later."

He nods, then ushers the boys toward the house. "Okay, boys, let's go play some video games."

Felix lets out a squeal and dashes ahead, Atticus at his heel. Then Jason volunteers to close my car door, and I request he bring my handbag.

In the hallway, daylight streams from the window at the end. I knock on Eden's door before entering her room.

She's seated on her bed, legs crossed, her giant stuffed pink giraffe with its hot-pink spots in her lap. She's still in her swimsuit. She glances at me, then at the candle and bottle of essential oils I gave her the first time I braided her hair. "You don't have to say goodbye to me."

I sit at the edge of her bed and touch her messy wet hair where it dampens her shoulders.

Her eyes meet mine again, frazzled and blotchy. My chest squeezes. Am I the reason for her tears? "You said you won't leave."

"I'm not leaving."

"You're not leaving?" She tosses the stuffed animal on the rug, then scoots closer. Scared blue eyes search my face.

"As long as I'm alive and things work out, I'll be here for you." I spread my arms wide, and she falls into my embrace, squeezing me tight. I laugh and shift to the center of the bed to prevent us from falling. I'm glad I wore flats today.

"You're going to stay here with us?" Her breath tickles my neck, and her hair smells like chlorine and the subtle scent of her lavender conditioner. "Will you marry Daddy?"

I tug a hunk of her hair, caught off guard. Did Jason say anything of the sort to his kids? "Who says I'm marrying your dad?"

She moves out of the embrace. "I thought you like him." She looks at me frazzled. "He likes you a lot."

"There's a *possibility* I'll marry your dad." I don't want to give her false hope if Jason still needs to build trust to love again. "I like him a lot." I tap the emerging freckles on her nose. "For now, how about you keep an eye on your brothers for a few minutes? I haven't even greeted your dad yet."

She nods and leaps off the bed. She literally skips ahead in the hallway and shouts before we make it to the living room. "Daddy, Val wants to greet you."

Jason stands and hands Eden the remote to take his place. His eyes meet mine, and he doesn't tear his gaze away when he reaches me. He takes my hand. Then, with long strides, he leads me past his and my bedroom until we enter his office. He closes the door behind us, clicks the lock, then turns me around, and edges me against the door.

My heart thuds. Before I can ask or say anything, his lips are on mine, kissing me tenderly, and he thrusts his hands in my hair. I automatically kiss him with all I can.

"That was quite a greeting," I say after we tear apart, still breathless.

He braces his arm above my head by the door. "That's how I wanted to greet you the moment you stepped out of your car." He taps my nose with his finger. "How'd the interview go?"

"I ran into Austin—interviewing for the same job."

His jaw tenses. "I'll call and tell them what a jerk he is."

I shake my head and rest my hand on his thudding chest. "You shouldn't have fired him."

"He hurt you." He looks at me like it was the obvious thing to do. "I didn't trust myself being around him without wanting to hurt him."

"I don't want your company to get in trouble."

The light streaming in the window highlights his calm expression. "He wouldn't be the first to claim a lawsuit, and he doesn't have the money to take it to court. Things got ugly with his past relationship. His lover's husband sued him over—" He shakes his head. "Can I not be reminded of having had a snake working under me?"

He kisses my cheek. "I'll see to it he doesn't get hired by the networks I trust."

He nuzzles my neck, my ear, and I giggle. "You are so vengeful."

"I'm a work in progress if you didn't already know." His fingers trace over my cheek ever so lightly. His proximity and intensity send my heart into hyperdrive. I can't think straight. "You told the kids you're not leaving, but if you're just planning to stay in town as my neighbor, it won't work out."

I let out a mock gasp. "You won't let me into your town?"

"I want you in my life, my house, and my family. You belong here." He cups a hand over his heart as he says it—and I know that's where I belong. "What do you want out of this relationship?"

"Marriage." My response is automatic. He must know it since I've said as much before. "A big family. Perhaps we can give Eden and the boys more siblings."

"Yes." His voice hoarse, he cups my face. "I'm still figuring out that perfect father role."

"Being you is all it takes. You're caring, loving, present, and protective."

"How could I not want to wake up each day with that kind of positivity and a stunning woman?" He catches my left hand and places a kiss where a groom would place a ring. "But about starting a family... How do you think we'll do that? We're both in our thirties."

"We better get started on that marriage soon, then?"

He beams, then kisses the top of my head. "Is tomorrow too soon to get married?"

"Perhaps this fall."

The look he gives me quickens my heartbeat. "You'd like to marry me?"

"If it involves waking up each morning next to the most handsome man in the world... We probably need to look into details about a marriage license and whatnot."

He's kissing me again with a tenderness that melts my insides.

When we separate again, I tell him about Ethan's job offer. "I'm considering taking that instead."

"You're going to work at the church?"

"And still watch the kids. The job's flexible. And it's probably best if I move out of the house since we can't keep our hands off each other."

He laughs, tossing his head back. "Ethan said the same thing." He then shares about his meeting with Ethan earlier. "I made a commitment today. To let God be in my life. I can't remember what Ethan called it."

"You gave your life to Christ?" My arms encircle his waist. I knew he wasn't against God, so it was only a matter of time. "I'm so happy."

"Not as happy as I am."

He tugs at my sleeve. "How about you move into the annex? Mom and Phil can stay in the house when they visit. Perhaps that could solve our temptation problem."

"You've thought through this already."

"I'm always thinking of you. Us." He then looks at me. "If you get hired at the network, we can commute together. Ethan will help me find a nanny."

"I belong here with you, and—"

"Oh, Valentina." His fingers trace along my jaw. His tenderness warms my whole soul. "You've changed my life in the best way possible."

"So have you."

"I love you."

"I love you too."

I'm glad for the life changes. I can live with knowing I'm married to a man with a heart of gold who loves God and will be the best father to our kids. The finality and completeness of the moment wraps around us, a perfect end to an episode and a beautiful beginning to the rest of our lives.

EPILOGUE

Valentina

Streetlamps provide a soft glow over the retreat center as Jason and I follow Ethan, our footsteps mingling with the splash of water from the pool. My diamond's sparkle catches my eye. I move my hand and lift my finger. A brilliant-cut diamond nestles in the center of the asymmetrical gold band, carrying me away to Jason's proposal a week after I declined NWAY's job offer. Now I'm marrying the love of my life in four days.

We pass a seating area where the guests' laughter and conversations blend with the ambient background music and the rhythmic splash of those in the pool.

For our final premarital counseling, we opted to meet Ethan here since he had a prior engagement. Only last week, did I discover Ethan started this retreat center to help people escape as they overcome their struggles.

He stops, his attention caught by something—or someone—near the pool. He squints against the low light, lifting the papers he's carrying toward the illuminated water. "Is that Ruby?"

"Should I know Ruby?" Jason asks.

I follow Ethan's gaze across the pool, intrigued by the connection Meadowbrook already has to our lives and the new memories we're about to create here. Clad in a black dress, a woman with tawny-brown skin strides with purpose. Beneath short well-styled hair, her silver earrings bounce against her cheeks.

"Who's Ruby?" Jason repeats.

But Ethan's steps quicken and he almost collides with another guest. He steadies the man with a hand and an apologetic nod, then resumes his pursuit. "Ruby!"

In his haste, his foot catches a table leg. Water bottles clatter to the tiles, and he plunges into the pool, sending a giant splash over a couple passing by. His papers scatter and float like water lilies on the surface.

"What's gotten into him?" Jason snatches a towel from a nearby stack. He takes my hand and leads me toward the spectacle.

"He's acting like a madman," I say. Over the three months we've worked closely together, I've witnessed countless single women from church test Ethan's calm with casseroles and baked goods. Yet, he's always unperturbed.

Now, he's the center of attention, all eyes fixed on his sopping-wet figure standing in the pool. "Sorry!" he shouts, waving a hand, then wiping his face.

The woman—Ruby—approaches, her heels clicking rapid-fire steps against the tile. Her hand flies to her mouth as if to hide the smile widening her lips. "Ethan?"

Ethan, still in the pool, chuckles and attempts to regain some dignity.

"We have a lot to ask our pastor," Jason quips beside me. "It's clear they've met before, and she's not just any woman."

"I can't believe it's you." Ruby shakes her head, then squishes her face. "It's unfortunate I have to be on stage in five minutes." Then, with a wave, she strides away, disappearing through one of the back doors, leaving gawking onlookers.

Snickering, Jason and I exchange a look before he offers his hand to help Ethan from the pool and hands him the towel. "Who is she?"

Ethan's face glows pink, his button-down shirt clinging to him, dripping water. "Someone from my past."

"Sounds interesting." I'll definitely pry for more details.

He wipes his hair. "It's a long story. For another time."

Jason chuckles and slides an arm around my waist. "Looks like our pastor has a few stories of his own."

"Perhaps he can fill us in on those details during tonight's counseling session."

"You two are going to be just fine." He swipes the towel over his arms and chest. "Just remember to keep open communication and support each other."

Jason kisses the top of my head. His chest rises as he inhales as if he can't get enough of my scent.

I love how he smells too, so I lean my head against his arm, feeling safe and cherished.

"You'd better not pull this stunt on Saturday." Jason wags a finger.

But his friend swings the damp towel in his direction, smirking back. "No promises if you have anything distracting in your backyard."

My joy bubbles free. "Distraction or not, I'm ready to be Mrs. Sterling in four days."

Even though hints of yellow and gold already tint the green leaves, Saturday arrives with just enough warmth for me to be comfortable in my flowy sleeveless gown.

As Mendelssohn's soft "Wedding March" begins, my heart swells with each note, guiding my steps down the aisle. Carlos's palm is clammy around mine. My poor brother must be nervous under the spotlight. Every head turns, gazes following us as we tread over the red-petal-sprinkled white runner.

My gaze stays fixed ahead on Jason. He looks every bit the man of my dreams, sharp in his dark suit and white shirt, and the red rose boutonnière adds a splash of color. Russ and Liam stand to his left, the twins, our ring bearers, adorable in their suits in front of the men. Ethan is to his right. If he hadn't been officiating, he'd be Jason's best man. Next to Ethan, Eden, Leah, and Willow all wear dresses as red as my bouquet.

Lanterns dangle from the tree branches in our backyard, and elegant string lights crisscross tree to tree. The arch boasts red and white flowers against the backdrop of golden and yellow leaves.

Halfway down the aisle, Carlos relinquishes me and Jason steps forward to meet me. Our hands join, and we walk toward Ethan, ready to seal our vows.

We stop before the altar, and Jason leans in. "You're breathtaking," he whispers.

Emotion clogs my throat. "And you're so handsome."

Ethan smiles at us before inviting the gathered friends and family to take their seats. "We are gathered here today to witness the union of Jason and Valentina...."

Jason and I clasp our hands, Ethan's words become a gentle hum, and I lose myself in Jason's gaze. We exchange vows, reaffirming promises we've made in quiet moments between us—promises of dedication, protection, and unwavering support.

Jason's vows are clear, his eyes shiny. "With your confidence in those you love—your love for me and my family—I could be gone for a month or a year and be assured you'd be home waiting for me...."

Each vow binds my heart tighter to his, the depth of our commitment girding every word spoken.

"I, Jason, take you, Valentina, to be my wife. To have and to hold from this day forward, for better, for worse, for richer, for poorer, in sickness and in health, to love and to cherish, until death do us part."

A single tear escapes as I echo the sentiment, my voice steady but lodged with emotion. "I, Valentina, take you, Jason, to be my husband. To have and to hold, from this day forward, for better, for worse, for richer, for poorer, in sickness and in health, to love and to cherish till death do us part."

Ethan declares us husband and wife. Cheers and claps fade into the background as Jason kisses me and I kiss him back.

Way after the reception, the food, and the dancing, and when everyone has gone, Jason's parents take the kids to Manhattan for the weekend. Now, it's finally Jason and me. We'll leave for our honeymoon to Venezuela next week, and our moms will stay here alternating taking the kids to school.

With our hands clasped, we approach the door beneath the porch light. Jason swings it open, then scoops me into his arms, and carries me across the threshold of our house. I'd been staying in the annex until last week when I moved back to Brooklyn with my family.

"I'm glad we had our wedding here." I kiss his ear as he closes the door with his foot.

"Whatever my bride wants"—his voice is soft and hoarse—"I'm happy to please."

"I hope it's okay with you that I wanted our first night to be here, in our home." My fingers trace the contours of his clean-shaven jaw.

"It couldn't be more perfect." His lips brush my cheek as he steps on the red petals creating a path to the hallway and his bedroom.

It's much bigger than my old room. He carries me to a bed sprinkled with roses, the air scented with fresh blooms. The bed dips beside me when he sits.

"Your bed is so big." I'd never peeked into his bedroom before.

"This is the new bed you helped choose."

My hands glide over the soft fabric. My smile widens as I take in the California king bed. Flowers adorn every flat surface of the room, and vases almost overshadow the essential oils and candles arranged on his dresser.

"I took the honor of getting some of your things." He winks.

He went shopping for essential oils and candles? I look at him, the love reflected in his eyes mirroring the emotions in my heart. "I love you so much, Jason."

He stands and draws me close. The steady beat of his heart merges with mine. "I love you, Valentina." Every word, every syllable, strings together like a thread connecting us tighter.

"Ready for a bath, Mrs. Sterling?"

"Yes, Mr. Sterling." I spin around, my back to him. "Could you help me out of this dress, please?"

"The pleasure is all mine." His breath warms my neck as the zipper slides down. His fingers trace the exposed skin of my back, sending a shiver through me. His lips follow, pressing soft reviving kisses that leave a trail of desire in their wake.

There are no reservations now, and under the weight of his love, I feel utterly cherished. If God decides to start expanding our family tonight, I'm more than ready to embrace every moment and every possibility with the man I love and in a place where I belong.

Find out what happens in 3 years with Jason and Valentina (Jaspon's POV) when you join my Insider Team. Here's your bonus[1]. I send out updates, and freebies from other authors weekly. I promise my emails are super short.

Ethan and Ruby's story is up next HERE[2]

Join My Facebook group[3] and connect with me and other readers.

Also, if you want the free 30 day Gratitude Journal, find it in my facebook reader group or on my website. https://rosefresquez.com/blog/

-THE END-

ENJOY THE 30 DAYS OF GRATITUDE BONUS

Day 1: People

Scripture: "I thank my God every time I remember you." - Philippians 1:3

---

1. https://dl.bookfunnel.com/qs7ewn5cen

2. https://www.amazon.com/dp/B0DH876VR7

3. https://www.facebook.com/groups/
243932449976110/?ref=pages_profile_groups_tab&source_id=435344610252020

Gratitude Prompt: Write about three people in your life who you are grateful for and why.

Day 2: Accomplishments

Scripture: "Commit to the Lord whatever you do, and he will establish your plans." - Proverbs 16:3

Gratitude Prompt: List three accomplishments you're proud of, no matter how big or small.

Day 3: Nature

Scripture: "The heavens declare the glory of God; the skies proclaim the work of his hands." - Psalm 19:1

Gratitude Prompt: Describe three elements of nature that bring you joy and why.

Day 4: Personal Traits

Scripture: "I praise you because I am fearfully and wonderfully made; your works are wonderful, I know that full well." - Psalm 139:14

Gratitude Prompt: Reflect on three personal qualities or traits you appreciate about yourself.

Day 5: Challenges

Scripture: "Consider it pure joy, my brothers and sisters, whenever you face trials of many kinds." - James 1:2

Gratitude Prompt: Think about a recent challenge you faced and how it helped you grow or learn.

Day 6: Health

Scripture: "Dear friend, I pray that you may enjoy good health and that all may go well with you, even as your soul is getting along well." - 3 John 1:2

Gratitude Prompt: List three things about your health or body that you are grateful for.

Day 7: Daily Comforts

Scripture: "Every good and perfect gift is from above, coming down from the Father of the heavenly lights." - James 1:17

Gratitude Prompt: Note three simple comforts you enjoyed today (e.g., a warm cup of tea, a cozy blanket).

Day 8: Friends

Scripture: "A friend loves at all times, and a brother is born for a time of adversity." - Proverbs 17:17

Gratitude Prompt: Write about three friends who have positively impacted your life and how they've done so.

Day 9: Family

Scripture: "Honor your father and your mother, so that you may live long in the land the Lord your God is giving you." - Exodus 20:12

Gratitude Prompt: Reflect on three family members and the positive roles they play in your life.

Day 10: Education

Scripture: "The heart of the discerning acquires knowledge, for the ears of the wise seek it out." - Proverbs 18:15

Gratitude Prompt: List three educational experiences or lessons that you are thankful for.

Day 11: Personal Growth

Scripture: "But grow in the grace and knowledge of our Lord and Savior Jesus Christ." - 2 Peter 3:18

Gratitude Prompt: Describe three ways you have grown personally or professionally in the past year.

Day 12: Creativity

Scripture: "In the beginning God created the heavens and the earth." - Genesis 1:1

Gratitude Prompt: Reflect on three creative activities or projects that you've enjoyed and why they're important to you.

Day 13: Community

Scripture: "And let us consider how we may spur one another on toward love and good deeds." - Hebrews 10:24

Gratitude Prompt: Think about three aspects of your community (local or global) that you appreciate.

Day 14: Technology

Scripture: "I can do all this through him who gives me strength." - Philippians 4:13

Gratitude Prompt: List three pieces of technology or apps that make your life easier or more enjoyable.

Day 15: Hobbies

Scripture: "So I saw that there is nothing better for a person than to enjoy their work, because that is their lot." - Ecclesiastes 3:22

Gratitude Prompt: Write about three hobbies or activities you love and why they bring you joy.

Day 16: Memories

Scripture: "I will remember the deeds of the Lord; yes, I will remember your miracles of long ago." - Psalm 77:11

Gratitude Prompt: Reflect on three happy memories from your past that make you smile.

Day 17: Opportunities

Scripture: "For I know the plans I have for you," declares the Lord, "plans to prosper you and not to harm you, plans to give you hope and a future." - Jeremiah 29:11

Gratitude Prompt: Note three opportunities you've had that have enriched your life.

Day 18: Acts of Kindness

Scripture: "Be kind and compassionate to one another, forgiving each other, just as in Christ God forgave you." - Ephesians 4:32

Gratitude Prompt: Think about three acts of kindness you've received recently and how they made you feel.

Day 19: Home

Scripture: "My people will live in peaceful dwelling places, in secure homes, in undisturbed places of rest." - Isaiah 32:18

Gratitude Prompt: Describe three things about your home (or living situation) that you are grateful for.

Day 20: Food

Scripture: "They broke bread in their homes and ate together with glad and sincere hearts." - Acts 2:46

Gratitude Prompt: Reflect on three meals or foods you've enjoyed recently and why you appreciate them.

Day 21: Future

Scripture: "Now faith is confidence in what we hope for and assurance about what we do not see." - Hebrews 11:1

Gratitude Prompt: Write about three things you're looking forward to in the future and why they excite you.

Day 22: Experiences

Scripture: "We know that in all things God works for the good of those who love him, who have been called according to his purpose." - Romans 8:28

Gratitude Prompt: Write about three experiences that have shaped who you are today and why they were significant.

Day 23: Books and Music

Scripture: "Let the word of Christ dwell in you richly as you teach and admonish one another with all wisdom, and as you sing psalms, hymns, and spiritual songs with gratitude in your hearts to God." - Colossians 3:16

Gratitude Prompt: List three books or songs that have had a positive impact on your life and why you're grateful for them.

Day 24: Mentors

Scripture: "The way of fools seems right to them, but the wise listen to advice." - Proverbs 12:15

Gratitude Prompt: Reflect on three mentors or people who have given you guidance in your life and why you are grateful for their wisdom.

Day 25: Laughter

Scripture: "A cheerful heart is good medicine, but a crushed spirit dries up the bones." - Proverbs 17:22

Gratitude Prompt: Think about three moments that made you laugh recently and why they were special.

Day 26: Kindness

Scripture: "Do to others as you would have them do to you." - Luke 6:31

Gratitude Prompt: Write about three ways you have been kind to others recently and how it made you feel.

Day 27: Skills

Scripture: "Each of you should use whatever gift you have received to serve others, as faithful stewards of God's grace in its various forms." - 1 Peter 4:10

Gratitude Prompt: List three skills you possess and why you are grateful for having them.

Day 28: Dreams

Scripture: "Take delight in the Lord, and he will give you the desires of your heart." - Psalm 37:4

Gratitude Prompt: Reflect on three dreams or goals you have for the future and why they are important to you.

Day 29: Support Systems

Scripture: "Carry each other's burdens, and in this way, you will fulfill the law of Christ." - Galatians 6:2

Gratitude Prompt: Describe three support systems (e.g., mentors, friends, groups) that have helped you and why you appreciate them.

Day 30: Gratitude Reflections

Scripture: "Give thanks in all circumstances; for this is God's will for you in Christ Jesus." - 1 Thessalonians 5:18

Gratitude Prompt: Look back over the past 29 days and write about three overall themes or insights you've gained from keeping this gratitude journal.

A NOTE FROM THE AUTHOR

Thank you so much for reading! It means the world to me that you chose my book out of the many other stories you could've been reading.

You can always Listen to some of my books for free onYOUTUBE[4]

Stay connected with Rose Fresquez

Bookbub[5]

Goodreads[6]

@rosefresquezauthor (Instagram)

Rose Fresquez

---

4.   https://www.youtube.com/c/RoseFresquezBooks

5.   https://www.bookbub.com/profile/rose-fresquez

6.   https://www.goodreads.com/author/show/13480223.Rose_Fresquez

Made in United States
Orlando, FL
01 October 2024